BELLES

BELLES

by Jen Calonita

poppy

LITTLE, BROWN AND COMPANY
New York   Boston

Poppy

Hachette Book Group
237 Park Avenue, New York, NY 10017
For more of your favorite series and novels, visit our website at www.pickapoppy.com

Poppy is an imprint of Little, Brown and Company.
The Poppy name and logo are trademarks of Hachette Book Group, Inc.

The publisher is not responsible for websites (or their content) that are not owned by the publisher.

First Paperback Edition: August 2012
Originally published in hardcover in April 2012 by Little, Brown and Company

Library of Congress Cataloging-in-Publication Data

Calonita, Jen.
Belles / by Jen Calonita.—1st ed.
p. cm.
Summary: Fifteen-year-old Isabelle loves her impoverished North Carolina beach community, but when her grandmother must enter a nursing home, Izzie is placed with distant relatives she never knew—a state senator and his preppy wife and children.
ISBN 978-0-316-09113-8 (hc) / ISBN 978-0-316-09112-1 (pb)
[1. Moving, Household—Fiction. 2. Social classes—Fiction. 3. Preparatory schools—Fiction. 4. Schools—Fiction. 5. Family life—North Carolina—Fiction. 6. Politics, Practical—Fiction. 7. North Carolina—Fiction.] I. Title.
PZ7.C1364Bel 2012
[Fic]—dc23
2011025416

10 9 8 7 6 5 4 3 2 1

RRD-C

Printed in the United States of America

Other novels by Jen Calonita:

The SECReTS OF MY HOLLYWOOD LIFE series:

Secrets of My Hollywood Life

On Location

Family Affairs

Paparazzi Princess

Broadway Lights

There's No Place Like Home

SLEEPAWAY GIRLS

RealityCheck

For my goddaughter Emma with much love

One

Isabelle Scott kicked her legs, propelling herself to the ocean surface with a final burst of adrenaline even as her lungs screamed for air. Breaking through the waves, she looked around, focusing on the tiny stretch of North Carolina coastline that she had called home for the last fifteen and a half years. Harborside Beach was still packed at 5 PM. She could see couples lounging on beach blankets while their kids dug in the sand or attempted to bodyboard, but beyond the roped-off swim area, Isabelle was flying solo. She had always preferred it that way. But that was before she'd met Brayden Townsend. As if on cue, he paddled his surfboard toward her.

"Go ahead and gloat, Iz," Brayden said, not sounding the least bit out of breath, even though he had just paddled over the breaking waves. He pushed a beat-up surfboard toward her. His favorite black wet suit, the one with the pirate skull on his chest, looked barely wet even though they'd both been in the water for almost half an hour.

Izzie, or Iz, as Brayden called her (only her grandmother called her Isabelle, when she called her anything at all), rested her arms on the bobbing board. She couldn't help but smirk at Brayden. "I didn't say anything."

"You didn't have to," Brayden grumbled even though his blue-green eyes were playful. Salt water dripped from his short, light brown hair and he wiped it off his face. "You win, Iz. I'm man enough to admit you can swim faster than I can paddle out here, *but*," he added before she could gloat, "let's not forget that I was carting *two* boards, and pelicans were nose-diving at my head."

Izzie tapped her chipped purple nails lightly on the board, the bathlike water lapping at her upper back, which was the only part of her torso not covered by the unflattering blue Speedo she wore for her job as a lifeguard. After four, she was off-duty, but unlike some of the other guards she worked with, she didn't change into her own suit before going for a dip. Why waste time? When she wasn't working, there was no place she'd rather be than in the ocean. Brayden was the first guy she'd met who seemed to feel the same way. They'd only been friends since mid-July, but they had been meeting up practically every day since, and this was the best time of day to do it. By 5 PM, the soupy North Carolina heat had started to subside and there was even a light breeze. The sun was still bright, but low enough that they didn't need sunscreen, and the water wasn't overly crowded with kids goofing around or adults twice her size who could barely swim. Five PM was "me" time, and when me time included Brayden, it was that much better.

"It only took you half of July and all of August to realize I pretty much know everything there is to know about being in the water," Izzie teased, staring at his woven rope necklace that had a pirate coin dangling from it. "*You* surfers are all alike. Cocky."

"Hey," Brayden argued even as he smiled an extra-adorable grin. "It's not cocky; it's called confident. There is a difference. *You* lifeguards seem to forget that."

Izzie coyly pushed her wavy, shoulder-skimming brown bob out of her hazel eyes. "It's kind of hard not to when we're pulling you guys out of a rip current at least once a day."

Brayden gave her a sharp look. "I told you a million times, I was fine."

"You didn't look fine," Izzie reminded him, wrinkling her freckled nose at the memory. "You were going — "

"Against the current instead of with it," Brayden interrupted, and shook his head. The dimple in his left cheek began to form. "I'm never going to live that down, am I?"

"Nope," Izzie said, feeling at ease, like she always did

around him. They were just friends — friends in a teasing, sort of flirty way — but for some reason it didn't matter. Well, it mattered a little, but they had such a good time together that she almost forgot he wasn't her boyfriend. She knew practically everything there was to know about him, from how much he loved to surf to his favorite iPod playlist. They liked the same bands, preferred water over dry land, and would take a slice of pizza over a hot dog any day. Maybe that was why she was beginning to dread the thought of school starting in two weeks. When would she see Brayden then? They hung out only at the beach. She wasn't even sure where he lived. Whenever she asked, his cryptic answer was always "Nearby."

Brayden looked at the shore as he bobbed up and down on his board, and Izzie tried not to ogle his toned arms. "So, ready to try surfing again? Maybe you can actually stay on the board today."

Izzie pulled herself up on her board and floated next to him, their tan knees touching. Brayden's, she noticed, were beaten up and bruised from some crash landings. "Do we have to keep doing this?" she groaned. "Why do I need to know how to surf?"

"I told you — so you can do it with me. Let's try this again, okay?" Brayden instructed, his square jawline set. "I'll make you a deal. If you can manage to get up this time, I'll buy at Scoops."

Izzie grinned. "You're on, surfer boy."

She reached down and attached her board's leg strap to her ankle. She'd learned her lesson about being untethered last week when she had to swim after a runaway board. Then she paddled after Brayden, trying to remember his instructions — when to stand up, how to lean left or right into the wave for balance, how to hold her legs. Brayden had given her this board after he bought one that had a pirate ship on it. The gift had come with one condition — that Izzie keep both boards in the lifeguard hut for him. Brayden said his board didn't fit in the back of his Jeep. He had just turned sixteen and his parents had bought him the truck for his birthday, which led Izzie to assume that Brayden didn't live *that* close to Harborside, because she lived there and no kid she knew owned a car, let alone a new one.

Izzie looked for the balance point Brayden had marked with wax and tried not to "cork" the board, as he'd called it. Something about too much weight in the back. She watched Brayden almost fifteen feet ahead of her — the proper safety distance — and saw him effortlessly stand up on the board as a wave began to crest. She tried to remember what he'd said as she got closer to the waves and pushed up on the board, keeping her legs on the stringer and gripping the board with her feet. She was supposed to look like a sumo wrestler, and it was working. She was up! Was Brayden seeing this? Even her feet were in the right positions! Then two seconds later, she fell and cursed herself for looking down, which is what Brayden had told her *not* to do. The surf was swirling around her, and as she swam to the surface, her board whacked her in the head. She dragged the board behind her as she hit the beach a few minutes later with a scowl on her face.

Brayden watched her as he stood next to two kids playing in the sand with plastic army men. His board was staked next to him, giving him the appearance of a guy who had just won a Teen Choice Award surfboard. Brayden probably could win, for looks alone, if he lived twenty-five hundred miles away in California and was discovered by a film agent. Robert Pattinson's mug had nothing on Brayden Townsend's.

"I can't believe you looked down, Iz! It was going so well!" Brayden said, as if she needed reminding.

Izzie rubbed her head. "I know, I know, and I'm going to pay for it with a big, fat headache."

Brayden put his arm around her, smelling like a mix of coconut and salt water. His black wet suit hugged his taut stomach and Izzie felt her breath get stuck in her throat. "You'll get it eventually, lifeguard. Or maybe not." He rubbed her head like she were a kid brother. "Tell you what: I'll buy even though you screwed up." She started to protest. "You save that paltry salary of yours."

Fifteen minutes later, after they had both toweled off and Izzie had pulled on frayed jean shorts and a tank top over her suit, they flip-flopped across the crowded boardwalk toward Scoops, where her friend Kylie Brooks worked. Izzie knew it sounded silly to have such deep affection for a place, but almost everything she loved about Harborside was on these planks. She'd learned how to play *Dance Dance Revolution* at the arcade, scored her first hole in one with her mom at the Mermaid Putt-Putt, made pizza with Grams at Harbor's Finest, held her first job at Scoops, and had her first kiss on the amusement park roller coaster. But what she still loved best about Harborside Pier was the community center. Sandwiched between the boardwalk and the main drag, the community center had been her family ever since her mom died. And Izzie had very little family to speak of.

"Look who's here! The beach bum and the lifeguard!" Kylie yelled as a tiny bell on the door announced Brayden's and Izzie's arrival at the homemade-ice-cream parlor. Kylie's loud voice startled some of the customers eating at the tiny tables. Izzie and Brayden walked up to the long counter, where Kylie was making an ice-cream sundae. "So what are you guys having?" Kylie asked. She slid the sundae over to the startled customer and leaned toward Izzie, her long blond hair falling in front of her face.

"Um, hello?" said a cool voice. "I believe we were next."

Izzie noticed a well-dressed couple in their twenties at the other end of the counter. The guy nudged the girl, who gave him a sour face. "What? You wanted homemade ice cream, right?" she whispered. "And I want to leave this boardwalk before some pickpocket dips into my Tory Burch bag."

The guy rolled his eyes. "Hannah, you're overreacting."

"You heard what the taxi driver said," she said in hushed tones. "I know you like to 'keep it real,' but I'm not hanging out all night on some dodgy boardwalk when our hotel has a private beach."

Harborside Pier may have been as popular as it ever was, but it was dogged that summer with stories about teen gangs and how shady the area had become. One of the pier shops had been broken into and robbed, and a knife fight earlier this summer between locals and gang members had turned ugly. No one Izzie knew had been involved. Her friends hung out under the boardwalk at night, but they weren't thieves or hoodlums. There just weren't a lot of places for them to hang. Izzie knew she didn't live in Beverly Hills, but she also knew Harborside wasn't unsafe if you knew how to navigate it. She wished she had the nerve to tell the customer that.

"Kylie, you should help them first," Izzie said instead. "They were waiting."

Kylie rolled her eyes and pulled at her stained white Scoops tee. "Whatever." Like most of Izzie's friends, Kylie didn't mask her feelings, even if they stung. "What do you want?"

Brayden glanced at his diver's watch. "I've got to check in

at home. Order for me?" he asked Izzie, then winked. "She'll give you extra toppings." He pulled his phone out of his orange backpack and walked outside as Izzie scanned the day's ice-cream flavor chart.

When Kylie was done serving Miss Uptight her kid-size fat-free vanilla cone, she planted herself in front of Izzie and grinned slyly. "So?" she said meaningfully.

"So what?" Izzie repeated slowly.

"So have you told Mr. Hot Surfer Dude that you want to be the topping on his soft-serve cone yet?" Kylie asked.

Izzie felt her face flush. What if Brayden had heard Kylie say that? She turned around slowly and to her relief saw Brayden's butt leaning against the glass window as he talked on the phone outside. "Kylie, geez!" Izzie said, her color returning to normal. "I told you a million times. We're just friends."

Kylie gave her a knowing look. "You don't act like just friends."

Izzie looked down at the ice cream under the glass counter and stared at the Cookies-and-Cream tub. If she looked at Kylie, her face might give something away. "Well, we are, so would you lay off? Besides, I don't have time for a boyfriend."

"That's true," Kylie said, walking away to wash the ice-cream scoopers in the small sink. "I don't even know how you have time to sleep between work, swim practice, taking care of Grams, food shopping…"

Izzie shrugged and pushed her still-damp hair behind her ears. "It's no big deal."

"It's a huge deal," Kylie disagreed, and then smiled slowly. "Which is why I think you need a little fun." She looked at Brayden's butt and sighed. "And Mr. Hot Surfer Dude definitely looks like fun."

"*Kylie*," Izzie said, starting to feel both annoyed and uncomfortable. "Drop it."

Kylie rolled her eyes again. "Fine. You should snap that boy up, though. If you don't, believe me, someone else will."

The bell hanging from the door jingled, and Brayden walked back in, his flip-flops making a scuffing sound against the sandy floor. "Did you decide what you want yet?"

"Oh, she knows what she wants," Kylie said, staring at Izzie intently. "She just hasn't figured out how to order it."

"A scoop of Oreo, a scoop of Marshmallow Supreme, and one of Butter Toffee," Izzie said quickly, "with gummy bears." Brayden looked amused. "I'm a growing girl."

"No complaints here," he said. "I like a girl who eats."

Izzie tried to think of the appropriate comeback, but before she could, she felt her cell phone vibrate in her pocket. She didn't recognize the number, but she picked up anyway. "Hello?" She instantly regretted her decision. "No. I'm at the beach." Pause. "Nope. I have to stop at the community center first. I forgot my swim meet registration forms." Her smile slowly faded, and the room began to spin around her.

"Yeah, I can be there at six thirty. Bye." She snapped the phone shut, her eyes blinking rapidly, and grabbed the counter to steady herself. This couldn't be happening. "I'm going to have to take you up on that free ice cream offer tomorrow," she said quietly, not looking at Brayden.

"Everything okay?" he asked, his brow wrinkling with worry.

"Did Grams lock herself out of the house again?" Kylie asked as she finished Izzie's order and slid it toward her.

Izzie pushed it back. "No, I just have to get home." She avoided their stares.

"Let me drive you," Brayden suggested.

Great. For the first time, Brayden was offering her a ride, and she had to say no. "I've got to go to the center first," Izzie explained, looking up at him. He had to be at least six foot two. "Besides, I'm only a few blocks from there. You stay and hang out. I'll see you tomorrow."

Brayden grinned. "Okay, because you, my friend, seriously need some more surf lessons."

Izzie forced herself to groan playfully. "Don't I know it? See you, Kylie," she managed with a smile even though she felt like the floor was going to fall out from under her.

Leaving Scoops, Izzie unlocked her dirt bike from the rack and raced down the boardwalk bike path, feeling the wind whip her hair around her face as if she were at the top of the Ferris wheel. Then she slowed down her pedaling and reminded herself of the truth: She wasn't on the Ferris wheel. She would soon be on her way home, where her social worker, Barbara Sanchez, was waiting.

The questions ran through Izzie's head almost too fast for her to keep up. Was Barbara there to push foster care again? Barbara and Grams had been discussing the idea ever since Grams's health started going downhill last year, but Izzie was still vehemently against it. When Grams remembered things (which felt like ages ago now), she had said another option was to find a distant relative to take care of Izzie, but Izzie hated that idea, too. She had lived with her grandmother ever since her mom brought her home from the hospital as a baby. Izzie had never met her dad. Her mom hadn't even told anyone who the guy was. So it was Grams who became Izzie's legal guardian when her mom died in a car crash a few years ago. Now that Grams was sick, it was Izzie's turn to return the favor. Grams was the only family she had left, and she wasn't going to let the state of North Carolina take that away from her.

Izzie pressed hard on her dirt bike brakes, the tires squeaking loudly to a halt in front of Chicken, Ribs and More. She let the familiar smell of barbecue sauce and crisp sweet-potato fries wash over her as the reasons behind Barbara's house call began to overwhelm her. Izzie's thoughts were darker than she would have liked, and she shut her eyes to block out the scenarios. Without thinking, her feet went back onto the bike pedals, and within minutes she was in front of the Harborside Community Center.

HCC wasn't much to look at. Weeds poked up around the cracked, aging stucco, and the windows had a permanent film from years of neglect. As rundown and forgotten as it looked from the outside, though, once Izzie walked through the glass doors, the building had a different story to tell. The community center was bustling, loud, and as cheerful as the cinder-block walls that had been painted in vibrant yellow-and-blue beach scenes. Hanging from corkboard strips were bright flyers and banners screaming things in large print like upcoming samba lessons, teen bake sales, Xbox Kinect tournaments, and directions to the next swim meet. Summer camp was winding down for the day just as some of the adult evening classes were starting, and the halls were a mix of young and old voices. Izzie knew most of them and said hello or waved as she walked down the hallway toward the pool.

Mimi Grayson wrapped her tiny wet arms around Izzie's waist as Izzie passed her. "Are you done saving lives, Izzie?" Mimi wanted to know.

Izzie patted the top of her curly hair. "For today." She gave her a mock stern look. "What about you? Have you been practicing your lifeguard training today, too?"

Mimi nodded. "Just like you showed me at swim class this morning." She mimicked a frog, showing Izzie her breaststroke. It seemed to be the easiest stroke for Mimi to master, so they'd concentrated on that one first.

"Perfect," Izzie said with a smile, and then began swinging her arms in a circular motion forward. "Tomorrow we'll work on this one, okay?"

"I can't do that one." Mimi's face scrunched up in frustration. "My arms don't go fast enough."

"What do I always tell you?" Izzie asked, and then the two of them said it together: "No guts, no glory." She nudged Mimi with her elbow, and the girl smiled. "I'll see you at nine AM."

"Thanks!" Mimi pulled her falling towel around her tighter as she ran down the hall.

"No running in flip-flops!" Izzie called after her with a smile, then turned and paused as she always did outside the pool doorway and looked at the glass case of swim team trophies and pictures. Her fingers grazed the glass in front of the swim team picture from 1988. Her mom's young face smiled back at her. She was taller and skinnier than Izzie was at the same age, but Coach Bing said they had the same spark and determination.

"I can't do it," Izzie remembered saying to her mom like it was yesterday. *She was five. They were in the center's pool, and she was clinging to her mom's torso like it was a life preserver. "I won't be able to breathe!"*

"Isabelle, relax," her mother said calmly. She set Izzie on the side of the pool. "No one can breathe underwater unless they

have an oxygen tank or a snorkel tube. Well"—she scratched her chin—"except for the fish and the baby belugas."

Belugas were Izzie's favorite sea creature. She and her mom loved the Raffi song about the little whale. It was Izzie's goal in life to swim with one, and that would never happen if she never learned how to swim.

"But you go underwater," Izzie reminded her. "And you do, like, a zillion laps!"

Her mom nodded. "Yep, but I still can't breathe underwater."

"How do you do it?" Izzie folded her wet arms across her chest to keep from shivering. The water was warm, but the air felt cold. She watched other kids happily jumping in around her. They looked like they were having so much fun.

Her mother looked at her seriously. "I do what I've been telling you to do, Isabelle. I breathe out." She demonstrated. "I take deep breaths. We start by blowing bubbles, remember?"

Something inside Izzie clicked. In her hysteria of having her face underwater, she always seemed to forget that bubbles part.

Her mom rubbed her back. "No guts, no glory, kiddo. Want to give it another shot?"

Izzie noticed the swim team sign-up sheet for older girls on the far wall. She had always wanted to be on the team, like her mom had been. There was only one way that was going to happen. She slipped out of her mom's grasp and back into the pool. "No guts, no glory," she repeated, and then submerged herself fully, bubbles escaping from her nose.

"Izzie! You missed me that much already?" Coach Bing pulled Izzie back from her memories. She saw he had on his usual attire: swim shorts and a Harborside Community Center tee. Coach always said you know you have a good job when you get to wear shorts and swimwear to work every day. He opened the heavy pool doors and let Izzie enter first. "Are you doing another workout? You were already here this morning!" Kids' voices bounced off the cavernous ceiling as Izzie followed Coach into the pool area, which smelled overwhelmingly of chlorine. She watched the senior citizens glide slowly by in the lap lanes, stopping every once in a while to give an annoyed glare to the kids splashing alongside them.

"I forgot to get my permission slip for the next meet," Izzie spoke loudly to be heard over the kids. "I wanted Grams to sign it tonight." *Liar!* a little voice in her head yelled. Grams hadn't been able to hold a pen for months. Izzie had become a pro at forging her signature on everything from permission slips and report cards to Grams's Social Security checks (how else would they buy groceries?).

Coach Bing looked at her kindly. "Izzie, I know you sign them yourself."

So she hadn't been fooling him at all. How many other people knew about her forgeries?

He patted her shoulder. "It's fine. I signed it. Your social worker said it was okay. You can still go to meets."

Izzie nodded, trying not to show her embarrassment. "Thanks, Coach."

"No problem," he said, and they both felt water pelt their legs. "Hey! Let's keep the water *in* the pool, not *out*," Coach turned around and barked to the increasingly rowdy kids in the pool. They stopped splashing immediately. Coach Bing's bark was much worse than his bite. He turned back to Izzie. "So how is Grams doing, anyway?"

"Great," Izzie lied again. It was easier this way. Otherwise she got those pitying, worried glances, and worried glances led to calls to Barbara Sanchez. Izzie knew everyone meant well — Harborside Community Center and her neighbors had been looking out for her for years. They knew her family, they knew her mom, and one thing they'd never do is let Izzie feel alone.

Coach Bing didn't look convinced, but he didn't say otherwise. "I was going to give you this tomorrow," he said, and led the way to his office. She stood in the doorway and watched as he opened a small refrigerator and took out an aluminum tray. "Tara made lasagna for you and Grams. Oh, and Ricky from Harbor's Finest said to tell you he's delivering spaghetti, meatballs, and pizza on Friday."

"Thanks," Izzie said gratefully, and grinned. "Although, you know if you keep carb-loading me and Grams like this, I'll sink to the bottom of the pool at the next meet."

He chuckled. "I'm not worried. You move and swim too

much to ever become an anchor." There was a knock at the door, and they both looked up.

An older woman, dripping wet, glared at them. "Could you get those children to stop swinging from the ropes of the lap lane?" The coach and Izzie looked at each other.

"I'll let you go," Izzie said, suppressing a grin.

As Izzie left the pool, her eyes darted to the clock on the wall and she frowned. It was 6:30 PM. She should have been home by now, which was her first problem. Her second was still Barbara Sanchez. Her social worker didn't make social calls, which meant if she was coming by the house to see Izzie, the news couldn't be good.

Two

When Grams had a good memory day—as opposed to a "Who are you? I don't have a granddaughter!" day—she liked to talk about Harborside, the early years. Grams's version of Harborside in the year Izzie was born sounded like it was plucked from a Hallmark movie (considering Grams's memory these days, she might have confused the two): neighbors bringing neighbors homemade apple pie, block parties, softball teams for grown men, and streets so safe that no one locked their doors. Harborside today was very different. The cereal factory shut down ten years ago, tanking the real estate market and causing foreclosure signs to pop up like weeds, and Harborside suffered a quick but brutal downward spiral.

This was the Harborside Izzie knew well, and while she

was used to it, she was still smart about how she navigated her hometown. Take her bike ride home, for example. Leaving the community center, Izzie knew that if she cut through sketchy Shore Park, she'd be home in seven minutes. But she also knew that biking through the park was asking for trouble. Besides, the town padlocked it shut at six thirty. Option B was to take Second Avenue. The route was longer and safer, even with the guys hanging out in front of the convenience stores, check-cashing shops, bars, and small fruit stands who leered at her when she rode past. *Option B it is,* Izzie thought. She put her right foot back on the pedal and pushed forward, making sure she pedaled as slowly as she could without falling off.

Before long, Izzie was heading toward Hancock Street and then making a right turn onto her block. She wove around a few broken beer bottles and waved to the five-year-old McGraw twins, who were playing in their overgrown front yard. She avoided eye contact when she passed a group of boys who looked like they had nothing to do.

Izzie could see Barbara's red Taurus parked in front of her house. She pushed open the broken front gate and wheeled her bike around back to lock it in the shed, trying to see 22 Hancock the way Barbara probably did. The lawn needed a good — okay, major — mow. There was graffiti on the fence and there was a crack in the bathroom window on the second floor, most likely made by a BB gun. (A group of kids

20

had been targeting windows and parked cars all summer like they were hunting deer.) Izzie took the porch steps two at a time, making sure to miss the one that was broken in half, and walked slowly to the front door. Taking a deep breath, she put her key in the lock and walked inside.

"I'm home!" she announced with as much fake enthusiasm as she could muster. Izzie had learned long ago how to play things with her social worker: Think of Barbara like a friend, even if she wasn't one. The more upbeat Izzie made life sound, the quicker Barbara got off her case.

Barbara was sitting at the cherry wood dining table, which had been in the Scott family for more than a hundred years. From the looks of it, the floral wallpaper had been around just as long. The only thing that didn't need replacing was the hardwood floor. Whenever Grams had people over — or, at least, when she used to have people over — someone would inevitably comment on how beautiful the floor was. Grams would smile proudly and say something like "Us oldies hold up nicely. No one is trading me or this floor in anytime soon." It was hard to believe that the frail woman staring out the dining room window was the same one who'd raised her only grandchild by herself when her own daughter and husband died within a year of each other. Izzie was around ten at the time.

Izzie planted a kiss on her grandmother's head. "Hey, Grams, how was your day?" Her thinning hair was combed back so far it made her forehead look huge, and her blue eyes were like cloudy marbles. Her grandmother didn't respond. She stared out the window like she hadn't heard her.

Izzie looked at Barbara and smiled forcefully. "Hi, Barbara," she said with added enthusiasm. Barbara had been her social worker for the last year. Of all the social workers she'd had since they'd started coming about three years ago, when Grams's decline started, Barbara was Izzie's favorite. *If* you could call any social worker who came to check out your living conditions a favorite.

Barbara glanced at her wrist, sliding back the sleeve of her navy button-down shirt to look at her Timex. Her sleek black hair had gotten so long it hung over the blue leather notebook she carried for appointments. "I was starting to get worried, Izzie," Barbara said by way of greeting. "We agreed to meet at six thirty."

Izzie made an apologetic face. "I'm sorry. I lost track of time talking to Coach Bing." She looked at her grandmother, who had barely moved her fingers since Izzie walked in. "He says hi, Grams. He sent a lasagna for dinner. His wife made it." Izzie nodded to Barbara and placed the tray on the dining room table. "People send us meals at least three times a week. Our friends are so generous."

Barbara's brown eyes bore into Izzie's skull. "That they are." She tapped her pen.

Izzie noticed the move right away. Barbara was nervous. Izzie could read people well, and she had spent enough time with Barbara to know what kind of mood she was in. Tonight, she was uncomfortable, and that made Izzie uncomfortable, so she just kept talking. "Yeah, it is nice, isn't it? That's what I love about Harborside. We take care of each other. Coach Bing gives Grams and me these incredible meals, and I'm teaching swim lessons for free at the community center." Izzie pointed to a gold medal hanging on the mirror in the dining room. "First place in the last meet. Grams was cheering me on, right, Grams?" *Cheering* was a stretch, but Grams was there. Their neighbor brought her. His daughter was on the swim team, too.

Barbara's face was unreadable as she said, "You told me, Izzie. I'm proud of you."

"Thanks!" Izzie squeaked. *Ugh.* She wasn't sure how much longer she could keep up the sickeningly sweet cheerleader act. It was giving her a headache. "It's been a great season for us this summer. So has work. Lifeguarding is amazing, and I'm making almost eight dollars an hour. I'm one of the youngest lifeguards they've ever had, but Brian says he hired me because I'm so determined and focused." God, did she really just pat herself on the back?

"Izzie," Barbara interrupted, "you can drop the cheerleader routine. It's not you."

Izzie fiddled with the tiny silver band she wore on her

middle finger. "I know." She sighed. "I thought it might lighten the mood."

Barbara smiled. "Thanks for trying." She pulled out a heavy dining room chair next to her. "Why don't you sit down so we can talk?"

Izzie grabbed the back of Grams's chair and hung on. "I think I'd rather stand."

"You might want to sit," Barbara said gently.

"Listen, if this is about Grams's care, she's doing amazing on this new medicine Dr. Finniman gave her. He said her hip looks stronger than ever and she might not need a second replacement. She may even be able to lose the cane."

"That's great, but—" Barbara looked at the cuckoo clock ticking on the wall.

The silence in the room was so complete, the pendulum sounded like a marching band. Izzie quickly moved to the doorway between the dining room and kitchen. She pointed desperately to the fridge, where a dry-erase board was marked with different colors. "I charted all her pills, and they're labeled in containers on the counter. Most days her nurse is here and helps her take them, but sometimes her friend Ida stops by. We put the paperwork in to Medicare to get her a full-time aide and—"

"She's not getting a full-time aide, Izzie," Barbara said, cutting her off. "I spoke to Medicare, and they denied the claim. They feel she'd be better suited for a nursing home that has physical therapy on-site." She kept talking to keep Izzie from interrupting. "We knew this day was coming. Your grandmother and I have been preparing for this. You've been doing a great job taking care of things, but that's not your job. Your job is to be a kid."

"I'm not a kid," Izzie said sharply. The time to act sweet was over. "I'm fifteen."

"You're still a minor, and someone should be taking care of you, not the other way around." Barbara stared sadly at Izzie. "Your grandmother and I have had a solution to this problem in place for months, but we've been waiting for the details to be finalized. I think once you've had time to process what I'm going to tell you, you'll be very happy, Izzie."

"What do you mean, you and my grandmother?" Izzie glanced in Grams's direction. "She doesn't know what day it is. How can she make a decision about her care or mine?"

"Last winter, she called me and said she had found some papers about your family history," Barbara explained. "She was very lucid. She said she'd found an uncle of yours on her side who has a wife and three kids and lives only twenty minutes away. She was very excited."

Izzie shifted back and forth. Her flip-flops suddenly felt very heavy. "Grams called you?" Why would Grams tell Barbara about an uncle Grams never knew before she told her own granddaughter? Grams and Izzie confided in each other about everything. At least, they used to.

"She was insistent that I call your uncle," Barbara explained. "She had already spoken to him herself and they met, and" — Barbara's pen started tapping crazily — "he wants you to live with them." Izzie's jaw dropped. "Your grandmother wanted you to go. She drew up papers for the transfer of guardianship so that when this day came, we'd be ready."

The cuckoo bird popped out of the clock with a loud chirp, startling them both as the clock chimed seven. The bird made seven chirps while Barbara and Izzie stared intently at each other.

Izzie shook her head, feeling a lot like that bird — trapped. "No," she said, wondering if she'd heard Barbara wrong and hoping that she had. "Grams wouldn't do that."

"She wanted you well taken care of, Izzie." Barbara stood up. "She knew she wasn't up to the task anymore, and she wanted to put things in order."

"*No,*" Izzie said more urgently, and took two steps back, stumbling slightly. Barbara reached out to steady her, but Izzie pushed her away and glanced at Grams. Her grandmother barely flinched. "We're a team. She always said that. I'm not leaving her just because she's having a little setback."

"This isn't a setback, Izzie," Barbara said bluntly. "The woman you know is gone. She saw that coming, and she found a way for you to avoid foster care. This is what she wanted."

Izzie felt her breathing become rapid. She looked around

wildly, wondering what she should do. She wanted to run —
far. But where was she going to go?

"Your uncle's name is Bill Monroe," Barbara told her, as if
the name should have had some sort of meaning. It didn't.
"He's a state senator, and they live in Emerald Cove. You're
going to attend private school and get opportunities you've
never had. Most people would kill for a chance like this."

Izzie looked at the floor. It felt like it was moving. "I'm
happy here."

"You'll still be able to see Grams," Barbara continued like
she didn't hear her. "Your uncle made sure Grams will have
the best care at the nursing home, and on Fridays they
even..."

Izzie felt a ringing in her ears, and Barbara's voice began
drifting away. The room felt like it was closing in on her. She
ran to her grandmother and shook her shoulders. "Grams!
Say something! Tell Barbara not to do this."

Her grandmother's blue eyes lit up with recognition, and
Izzie felt a sense of relief. Grams could fix things before they
spun out of control. She'd kept them together this long. But
Izzie's momentary relief vanished when her grandmother
started talking.

"Chloe, when did you get here?" Grams asked. "I was hoping you'd stop by before you went to New York." She wagged
a finger at Izzie. "I still don't think you should be going. That
town is trouble, I'm telling you."

Izzie froze. She could feel Barbara's eyes on her. Chloe was Izzie's mom. "Grams, it's me," she said quietly. "Your granddaughter, Isabelle."

Grams obviously didn't hear her. "Chloe, it's drafty in here. Can you go get my shawl?"

Grams's shawl was already around her shoulders. "Okay, Grams," Izzie said, and pretended to put the shawl on her. She blinked rapidly to hold back tears. She was not going to let Barbara see her cry.

"Izzie, she knew what was happening to her," Barbara said softly. "She was so happy when she found family for you. She wanted to make sure you had what you needed in life."

"I need her," Izzie said desperately, pleading with Barbara now. "If you just give us some time, I'm sure this new medicine will kick in and Grams will be back to her old self and…"

The doorbell rang. Barbara didn't flinch, but Izzie did. She looked out the dining room window and saw a white van that had *Coastal Assisted Living Center* on it. A man and a woman with ID tags around their necks walked up the path. Izzie's heart started to beat rapidly again.

"The nursing home is here to help gather some of your grandmother's things for her move," Barbara said quietly. "The rest you can sort through before the house is sold, and the lawyer your grandmother hired will help with the house and the furnishings and…"

"Wait, this is happening tonight?" Izzie felt as if a boa

constrictor had wrapped itself around her heart. The tears started to come even though she willed them not to.

"They'll take Grams and settle her in, and I'll go with you to your uncle's," Barbara explained. "You can have half an hour to pack, and anything else you need, I'll send later."

Izzie had lived here for her whole life and she had half an hour to put her world in a duffel bag and say good-bye? *No. This was wrong!* The room felt like it was spinning. Her thoughts came fast and furious. Mimi was expecting her to teach her freestyle tomorrow morning....She had a lifeguard shift from one to five....Brayden had promised to give her another surfing lesson....Then there was the swim meet on Saturday. How could she just disappear without saying good-bye?

"I can't go tonight," Izzie insisted. "I made plans for tomorrow already."

"We'll let everyone know," Barbara said kindly, and handed her a large black duffel bag that had been hanging in the hallway closet. Izzie had no clue how Barbara knew it was there. "It's going to be okay, Izzie. I promise."

Izzie wasn't so sure of that. In fact, she wasn't sure anything in her life would be okay again.

Three

The air at the Emerald Cove Country Club pool was so oppressively hot and sticky that Mirabelle Monroe started to worry she was going to wind up looking like a broiled lobster. "I'm caving!" she announced as a sweat bead rolled down her forehead and landed on the tip of her nose. "I don't want skin cancer! I'm putting on SPF 50!" Mira reached under her lounge chair for the canvas tote that held her sunblock, but a slim, tanned hand swatted hers away.

"Mirabelle!" Savannah Ingram surprised Mira by using her full name. She stared at Mira stonily, looking like one of those überserious cops on those police shows Mira's dad was obsessed with. "We swore we'd have a deep bronze by the time school starts, and sunblock will ruin everything." Savannah snatched Mira's tote away and placed it safely on the other side of her lounge chair. "If you put any more sunblock on those pale legs of yours, people are going to mistake you for an alpaca."

Mira sat up carefully, covering her chest to keep her favorite green bikini top from sliding off and giving the entire Emerald Cove Country Club a peep show. "An alpaca?" she deadpanned, then started to giggle.

Savannah's long pale blond hair was scattered over the top of the lounge chair like a crown. She sat back up and started to laugh, too. "So maybe I was up late last night and caught a teensy bit of an alpaca farm infomercial." She stopped laughing and looked at Mira. "Tell anyone and die."

Mira pretended to zip her lips. She threw her long, definitely not pasty legs over the side of the chair, leaned over Savannah, and snatched her bag. Savannah scowled at her. "There's more to proving you had a good summer than just looking tan," Mira said, and squirted a huge glob of white cream on her right thigh. Savannah made a skeptical grunt as Mira continued talking. "Okay, so I didn't spend my summer in Paris like you, but we did vacation in Costa Rica for two weeks, and I saw ninety percent of North Carolina doing campaign stuff with Dad. Most important, Taylor and I are better than ever." That was the truth. With half the football team at their summer homes in Maine or the Florida Keys, Mira had had her boyfriend all to herself, and it had been bliss. The football team as

31

a whole could be suffocating. They practically shared jockstraps.

Savannah examined one of her pale pink nails. "I guess you didn't *totally* waste eight weeks off." She smiled at Mira. "Now next summer, that will be pure frosting. Once your dad goes from state senator to a U.S. Senate seat, we'll be jetting to Washington for private movie screenings with the president's daughters." She stared dreamily at the sun at the thought of it.

"*If* my dad wins a seat in the U.S. Senate," Mira corrected her. Her attention turned to a puddle of water near their lounge chairs. The sun dipped behind a welcome cloud, and the shadow in a puddle near their lounge chairs caught Mira's eye. It reminded her of a galloping horse. "He hasn't even run yet," she said absentmindedly.

"He'll win," Savannah said, and sipped her iced tea. "My dad will make sure of that. He's going to throw lots of green at your dad's campaign once it becomes official." She raised one eyebrow thoughtfully. "Even if you do look like an alpaca." Mira threw her towel at Savannah, who ducked. Her eyes locked on someone across the pool.

Mira didn't have to look hard to see who Savannah was staring at. Her best friend's mouth curved into a small smile as she watched a pudgy girl at the snack bar. The girl was wearing an unforgiving tankini that bulged around her middle. She stood awkwardly with a friend and drank a milk shake. Mira's mouth watered at the sight of it.

"Kristen Thompson should not be allowed near dairy." Savannah's Southern twang dripped with disdain. "Look at what it's done to her thighs this summer!" Almost as if Kristen could hear her, she looked up and stared at Savannah and Mira. She gave an awkward wave. "Hi, Kristen!" Savannah yelled across the crowded pool. "Cute suit!" Then through a forced smile, she added quietly, "That girl should have to wear a muumuu at the club. She's a total eyesore."

Kristen wasn't a fool. "Thanks!" she yelled back, even as she pulled helplessly at the bottom of her tankini, hoping that would give her more coverage. It didn't.

Even after being friends with Savannah for three years, Mira still felt uncomfortable when she went on a bashing bender. If you were one of the lucky few to be part of Savannah's inner circle, she treated you like royalty. But if you were on Savannah's "not" list, Emerald Prep's unofficial Queen Bee could be more cutting than a switchblade. Kristen's downfall had been questioning Savannah's world history oral presentation in front of the entire class. Savannah hadn't forgotten. Ninety percent of Emerald Prep worshipped Savannah and yet 87 percent of them never got a second glance unless they were being made fun of.

Before Mira could comment, a huge pair of arms wrapped around her waist, practically lifting her off the lounge chair. "Taylor!" Mira's voice was high. "You're soaked!"

Taylor Covington clung tighter as he kissed her neck. "Of

course I am. I just swam twenty-five laps. Did you see my impressive arm strokes?" He showed his bulging biceps to all within range.

It was hard to miss Taylor even when his arms were covered. He was almost six foot four and had that California boy look that said he should be catching a wave rather than taking an English lit exam. He had layered blond hair and pale blue eyes the color of Mira's screensaver on her Mac, and he looked good in both a swimsuit and a tux. Mira's brother Hayden called Taylor "Ken." He really was Barbie's perfect boyfriend come to life. And to the envy of most of the girls in their school, he was all hers.

Mira grabbed Taylor's bicep and squeezed. "Nice. You looked great out there, babe." She hadn't seen him doing laps, but he didn't have to know that. Taylor's shadow had changed the reflection in the puddle again. Mira thought it looked like a small dog. Or maybe it was more like a cat.

Taylor's blue eyes brightened. "Thanks, babe." He leaned down and kissed her softly.

"Get a room." Savannah rolled her eyes and lay back down on her lounge chair, spreading her hair carefully all around her.

Taylor smirked. "If your man were here, you'd be all about the PDA. When is he going to be done with that boathouse, anyway?"

"Who knows? Why he has to help build it is beyond me.

That's what contractors are for." She looked at the Movado on her wrist. "I've texted him four times to find out when he's getting up here. It's three PM and he hasn't replied once."

"It's three?" Taylor jumped up. "I have to hit the showers and be at practice at four." He grabbed a towel from a passing pool worker carrying a large stack. "You're stopping by, right?" he asked Mira. "We're going to run some drills. Then the team is going to Corky's for dinner." He rubbed her bare shoulders. "Maybe you and I can get ice cream alone after."

It's football season again. Mira sighed. She adored her boyfriend, but he tended to be needy during football season — and by needy, she meant needing to see his teammates twenty-four-seven, with Mira glued to his side. They did what Taylor wanted, when he wanted, and sometimes Mira felt more like a glorified cheerleader than a girlfriend. Maybe it would be different this fall. Taylor did just suggest they do something alone, didn't he? Mira stared at the puddle again. This time the reflection reminded her of a gorgeous peony. She really wished she could sketch this.

Then Taylor's shadow blocked the reflection and just like that, the picture was gone. "So I'll see you later?" he asked again, still waiting for an answer.

Mira nodded. "Yes. Sorry. I wouldn't miss it."

"You would if you had plans with me," Savannah said once Taylor had walked away. "You don't really want to sit on the bleachers and watch them practice, do you? Wouldn't you rather be in the cool, air-conditioned mall, school-clothes shopping with me?"

Mira thought for a moment. "That does sound more appealing, but Taylor would kill me. He already thinks I hate the entire football team."

"Please. Just because you don't want to date them along with your boyfriend doesn't mean you hate them." Savannah finished her iced tea. "Where is a waiter when you need one? We have to get to the mall!"

"I didn't say yes yet," Mira said with mock indignation.

Savannah shook her empty glass, the ice clinking loudly, and smiled. "As if you were really going to say no to me."

Savannah may have been the most popular girl at Emerald Prep, but when it came to fashion, she was still a bit lacking. That's where Mira came in. The two clicked during seventh grade right around the time Mira's dad won his state senate seat and Savannah's personal shopper moved to New York. Mira became Savannah's new stylist, and Savannah gave Mira the runner-up spot in her clique. Sometimes Mira still couldn't believe she was now one of the most popular girls at school.

Savannah waved madly at a waiter across the pool. "I thought we'd start at Nordstrom, and then if we don't like anything, we can move on to Anthropologie and…"

Mira's phone went off in her bag. Cell phones weren't

allowed on club grounds, not that anyone she knew actually abided by the rule.

LUCAS'S CELL: Clear your schedules ASAP. Your dad has called an emergency family meeting at Buona Terra restaurant at 5:30 PM sharp. Everyone must attend. Call if you need me to send a ride.

Mira pushed her hair behind her ears. "Scratch the mall plans and football practice," she said mournfully, and gathered her things. When Lucas Hale sent a text, Mira moved quickly. Her dad had his campaign manager get in touch only if something major was going on. Otherwise, Mira's mom was the one who broke bad news — like Dad missing a field hockey game, or having to skip Harborfest because the whole family was needed in Washington, D.C., for a UNICEF event. "My dad is calling some emergency powwow." She frowned, pursing her lips. "I wonder what's going on this time. Do you think Hurricane Harold is actually going to make landfall? I thought they said it was going out to sea."

"I'm going to become a category five gale if I don't get to the mall today!" Savannah griped. Her hot-pink bikini straps fell off her shoulders when she shot up. "Geez, what is with your dad and family meetings? Can't he just call or text when he needs to tell you something, like a normal dad? I haven't actually laid eyes on my father since last week."

"Sorry, Vanna, I have to go." Mira tossed the latest *Us Weekly*, her phone, and her sunblock in her bag. "You know how he gets if we're late. He'll send his goon to find me."

"I think Lucas is kind of sexy," Savannah said, momentarily forgetting what she was annoyed about. "In a buttoned-up, anal kind of way."

Mira gave her a look. "He's almost thirty. And you have a boyfriend."

Savannah shrugged. "I'm allowed to look."

"Gross." Mira stifled a laugh. "I promise we'll hit the mall tomorrow, okay? I'll even get my mom to give me her platinum card. We can eat lunch at that sushi place you like."

Savannah grinned. "Now you're talking." She put her iPod buds in, closed her eyes, and lay back down, which was exactly what Mira wished she could do. She could think of a zillion things she'd rather be doing than spending one of her last days of freedom in the company of Lucas Hale.

⁓

An hour later, Mira waited in the club's circular driveway. Her long, curly brown hair was damp and she'd only had time to apply lip gloss and eyeliner. At least she got a chance to shower and put on a cute pink strapless dress. She kept a few sundresses in her family's club locker for just this sort of emergency. Lucas was all about the family image, and he would have freaked if Mira showed up at a restaurant in a beach cover-up.

"Sorry to pull you away from your tanning time," her older brother, Hayden, teased as he pulled up in a red Audi convertible. Just seeing Hayden behind the wheel of the car made Mira envious. She was fifteen, but her parents wouldn't let her get a learner's permit till she turned sixteen. Hopefully, by that time, her dad would let her have the Audi and buy Hayden something new. "I'm sure Savannah was kicking and screaming about you having to leave," Hayden added.

"You stalk my Facebook page, don't you?" Mira joked as she slid into the front seat.

"Yes," he said solemnly, and adjusted the collar of his white polo shirt, which showed off his tan. "I get a printout of your conversations and your day's activities every morning at the office."

She hit him in the arm. Her brother was so charming and good-looking, she couldn't believe he hadn't been scooped up yet. Every girl she knew had a crush on him (or Taylor), but Hayden was too focused on cross-country and working with their dad to notice. While Mira looked like their dad, Hayden and their younger brother, Connor, who was six, had their mom to thank for their good looks. Hayden in-herited her pale blond hair, chiseled heart-shaped face, and her green eyes. With looks like that, it would be easy for

Hayden to be vain, but he was the most down-to-earth guy Mira knew.

"Sorry you had to leave work early — and I mean that, since you probably hated to leave," Mira said wryly. "I thought Mom would give me a ride. She usually is here on Tuesdays." Tuesday was her mom's tennis day. It said so on the family's huge calendar in the kitchen. "But then I texted her and she said to catch a ride with you because she had an 'appointment.'" Mira made air quotes after the word and smirked. "Maybe she finally went with the trend and got Botox?" she asked with a head tilt.

Hayden gave her a sharp look. "Nice. You're just lucky cross-country practice was this morning. Otherwise I wouldn't have been able to pick you up, either. And Mom, by the way, is already with Dad. They were together all morning, actually. Lucas said they had to attend to some personal matters." His eyebrows rose slightly. "Of course, he wouldn't say what those were."

"Of course not." Mira sighed. Getting an answer out of Lucas was like trying to break into Fort Knox. "You haven't heard anything?" He shook his head. Mira put on her oversize black sunglasses and leaned her head against the seat. "I guess we'll find out soon enough."

"Top up or down?" Hayden asked before he put the car into drive. He didn't give Mira time to answer. "I'm guessing top up. You probably don't want to mess up your hair."

She grinned mischievously as she felt her still-wet hair. "I'm going to shock you and say — top down!"

"*Whoa!* New school year, new Mira Monroe." Hayden smiled. "What's next? Sneakers outside the gym?"

Mira shook her head. "Never." What was the point of wearing sneakers if you weren't a jogger? Mira didn't get it. She did, however, understand what her dad's tightly wound campaign manager would say if she showed up at dinner, in a public setting, with a wet head. She shook out her curls and prayed a ten-minute drive with the top down would do the trick.

Four

As they pulled up to the restaurant, Mira's hair was still damp, and a less-than-appealing frizz had taken over. That's what Lucas Hale got for giving her no time to get ready for a family powwow.

Mira had no clue what could be so urgent — a state budget crisis? Another oil spill? Hurricane Harold making landfall? Lucas could find a way to turn any disaster into a Bill Monroe campaign opportunity, and usually the family was dragged along for the ride. Lucas was their dad's unofficial campaign manager for his unannounced senatorial run, and he totally gave Mira the creeps. He kept their dad on such a tight leash that she rarely saw him unless she was scheduled in on his iCalendar or an emergency came up (like today) that usually required their dad to leave town ASAP for both crisis meetings and TV opportunities ("Good morning, America! Bill Monroe has something to say about North Carolina's dwindling peach crop this year...."). The guy was like her dad's own personal BlackBerry, whispering talking points in his ear, calling him at all times of day and night to talk about the campaign and to give advice. That advice extended to Mira's and her brothers' after-school activities and wardrobe as well. Lucas made sure every decision the family made gave the Monroe name more bang for its buck come election time. Mira hated all of it.

Hayden, on the other hand, liked being in the thick of the political machine. He was interning for their dad this summer and was more gung ho about politics than ever. Mira didn't know how he could stand seeing Lucas that much, but Hayden said the internship was too good an opportunity to pass up. The Monroe name would get him far, even if Hayden was determined not to trade on it.

"I'll bet you ten dollars tonight's dinner has nothing to do with a natural disaster and everything to do with Emerald Cove's centennial," Hayden said as the two walked out to Buona Terra's private patio overlooking the bay. Their family usually came to this Italian restaurant once a week; that's how much their dad liked its lobster. "Lucas wouldn't shut up today about ribbon-cutting ceremonies and two-hundred-dollars-a-plate state dinners, even though the centennial is over two years away."

"I'd rather this dinner be about the centennial than Dad coming to tell us he has to go away for six weeks," Mira said as they reached their regular table. "Lucas can talk about the centennial all he wants as long as he doesn't try to stick me on some high school planning committee. I have enough going on, and school hasn't even started yet."

Between her honors classes, field hockey sessions, and her Emerald Prep charity club, the Social Butterflies, Mira's schedule was overbooked. Sometimes she wished her commitments were things she actually looked forward to doing, rather than things she did just to look good. The Butterflies would give her brownie points on a college application, but Mira longed to find something she could claim as her own. She took the water goblet on the table and twirled it around, watching how the condensation pooled on the sides of the glass and wondering what it was that she was constantly searching for.

Hayden's eyebrows rose playfully as he removed his tie. "I think you and Savannah would be perfect for a centennial high school committee. No one knows how to bend people to their will better than you two."

Mira hit him in the arm with her linen napkin as their younger brother, Connor, walked in flanked by two of their dad's drivers. The six-year-old looked like a pint-size version of their senator dad in his dress shirt and khakis — the standard uniform at his private elementary school, which started a few days earlier than Emerald Prep. Connor's normally playful grin was replaced with a scowl.

"I can't believe I have to miss soccer. Again." He slumped down in a seat at the table. "Where's Dad got to go now?" His eyes lit up for a moment. "Is it Africa? Do you think Mom would let me go, too?" Conner was obsessed with going on a real safari. The safari ride at Disney World's Animal Kingdom, which he had ridden a dozen times, just wasn't cutting it.

"Sorry, squirt," said Hayden as he roughed up Connor's mop of blond hair. "I don't think it's Africa. We have no clue what's up with Dad." Hayden looked at his watch in surprise. "Or where he is. Dad is officially late. This is a first." He winked at Mira. "You and Dad are never even thirty seconds behind schedule."

"Nope," Mira agreed smugly. She was punctual to a fault and hated when others weren't. She leaned back in her seat and stared at the choppy bay beyond the patio. From the terrace, it was easy to feel like you were on an ocean liner in the Mediterranean. Mira liked being surrounded by water. She just didn't like being *in* the water. "If Dad's late, blame Lucas," she added. "He's probably got Dad delivering puppies at an animal shelter."

"That's not a bad idea, Mirabelle."

Mira heard Lucas's even-keeled voice and froze as he appeared at their table. "The animal-compassion angle would work great at campaign time," he added, revealing a mouth full of perfect veneers. "But as for today, the reason your father is *detained*," he enunciated, "is because he had to sign some paperwork with your mother."

"What kind of paperwork would that be?" Hayden pried.

Lucas answered Hayden's question with one of his own, a habit that drove Mira nuts. "They don't make you wear ties at school anymore?" He touched Connor's shirt, and Connor stuck his tongue out at him when Lucas turned around. "Hayden, at least, had one on earlier, I believe." Hayden fumbled for the crumpled tie in his pocket as Lucas looked Mira up and down with disdain. "No time to dry your hair at the country club? You three better step up your act before this campaign gets in full swing."

"It's a family dinner, Lucas," Mira said, keeping her tone light. She was polite with adults, but at twenty-nine, Lucas didn't really feel like her elder.

Lucas nodded approvingly as Hayden knotted his tie again. "That's a little better," he said, and placed his hands in the pockets of his expensive suit. "So, now that we're presentable, let's catch up. How was the rest of your summer?"

Connor rolled his eyes at Mira. None of them liked talking to Lucas. They didn't get why their dad liked the guy so much. Okay, so maybe he had led two other state senators to victory in their U.S. Senate bids and he'd only been on the job for three years, but Lucas was still a complete snake. Their dad, however, loved the guy's ambition.

"Summer was fun once we actually got to do stuff," Connor muttered. Lucas laughed.

"Touché. I did keep you guys busy. But it's all for your dad, right?" Lucas patted Hayden on the back. "We want to get him to Washington, don't we?"

The patio doors opened before Mira could really think about her answer to that question. Mira's parents walked in looking like they were ready for a meeting with the governor. Her mom wore a fitted navy dress with pleats, and her long pale blond hair was pulled back to show off the simple trinity diamond pendant she wore almost every day. Their dad was in a suit (shocker) and his slightly graying brown hair had its usual Kennedy-style pouf. The only thing that looked off about her parents was their strained smiles.

"Cute dress, Mirabelle," her mom said, sounding unusually tired. "Sorry I couldn't give you a ride here. I had to cancel everything on my calendar today, including the EC Greeters meeting and tennis." Mira's mom pushed her hair behind her ears. Mira knew her mom did that only when she was getting ready to relay bad news. But then her mom's green eyes lit up. "But I ran into the school headmaster this morning, and guess what? They are changing your uniforms next year! I told him it's about time. They really need something more flattering for the girls." Her mom's BlackBerry vibrated, and she quickly started typing something as she walked over to greet Connor and Hayden.

"Hi, sweetheart." Mira's dad kissed her on the cheek. "How was the club?" He folded his large arms across his chest. "Did Mr. Connick like my gift?"

The joke in Emerald Cove was that Bill Monroe was more in demand today than he had been fifteen years ago when he played for the Atlanta Braves. He was known for telling great sports stories, and he had so many trophies, World Series rings, and Hall of Fame photos in the house that every guy Mira knew wanted to meet him. That he had gone from having a successful sports career to running a multimillion-dollar business group that led him to become a North Carolina senator only made his appeal greater.

"Mr. Connick flipped for the autographed Chipper Jones baseball," Mira told him. "But he still said he misses seeing you at your weekly tee times."

"That makes two of us." Her dad made a face. "But there's a lot going on...." He looked at Lucas.

"Yes, maybe we should get started." Lucas motioned for everyone to sit as a waiter appeared with menus. "They'll be at your house around nine o'clock, Bill."

"Who will?" Connor asked.

"Let's order," Mira's mom said. "Should we order first, Bill? I think we should, don't you?" Mira glanced at Hayden.

Since when did their mom get all worked up over a menu? She barely ever ordered more than fish and salad.

"We'll have our regular, please," Mira's dad said, and handed the waiter back his menu. Once the waiter disappeared, he turned to the group. "Your mom and I have some big news. Huge, actually." He exhaled slowly. "We're hoping you'll be understanding."

The sound of the water hitting the pier under the patio magnified as Mira waited for the bomb to drop. She was sure she was about to hear about how she was getting a private tutor and would have to sleep on an uncomfortable tour bus for the next three months. Lucas had mentioned taking the family around the state that fall once the campaign was announced. Mira and Hayden would have to drop their sports; Connor would have to quit soccer. And what would Taylor say? He would freak if she missed any of his games.

"You guys are having a baby!" Connor blurted out. Mira's stomach lurched.

"No!" Mira's mom laughed. "That would be…wow. What with my charity work and you three, how would I find the time for diapers? That's not it, but…" She trailed off.

"I know you probably thought I called this meeting to say I was going away again, or that we were all going on a campaign tour," Mira's dad held her mom's gaze. "But a family road trip has been put on hold."

Thank God, Mira thought, resisting the urge to cheer.

"There is something more important going on," he added, looking around the table seriously. "I know this is going to sound unexpected. It was unexpected for us, too."

Mira grabbed Hayden's hand and squeezed. Now she was getting nervous. What was going on?

"I'm not sure how to explain this, but you see, I didn't know…" Her dad never rambled. Her parents weren't getting divorced, were they? They seemed so happy. "We're going to be…"

"It's okay. I know we're not getting a golden retriever," Hayden said, trying to break the ice. "I'm over it now. It's been six years." Their father barely smiled. "Dad, just spill it."

Mira's dad sighed deeply. This was the first time Mira had ever seen him look anxious, and she'd seen him in some pretty stressful situations, like the time he met Angelina Jolie at a benefit, or when he was inducted into the Baseball Hall of Fame.

"I'm sorry, it's just this is big news. Our family is expanding, Connor, but no, it's not a baby — or a golden retriever," he added as an afterthought, and Hayden shook his head sadly. "Several months ago, your mom and I got a phone call. It was a distant relative of mine who was raising a girl about your age, Mirabelle. The woman had recently found out she had Alzheimer's and was worried about whom her granddaughter would live with when her mind started to fail," he explained. "We looked into the situation extensively, and we really are their only living relatives. Things went downhill pretty quickly for this woman, and, well, tonight, your cousin is coming to live with us. Permanently."

Her dad looked relieved, but Mira wasn't. Her hands went numb. They had a cousin who was coming to live with them? Permanently? Who? The news was too big to comprehend. She stared at her water glass again. She could almost hear the ice cracking.

"We've never met her before?" Hayden asked as if he'd heard Mira's thoughts.

"No," Mira's mom said softly. "None of us have, actually." She looked at her husband pensively. "This is a huge commitment. We know that. I wish this was happening differently, but this is the way it is. We knew about your cousin's situation last winter, but her home life was more stable then, so there seemed to be no need to rush things or upset anyone." Her mother played with her necklace as she stared out at the water. "We thought there would be time to meet her, introduce all of you, and then discuss her moving in with us. But her social worker feels the home situation is deteriorating quickly, and last week it became apparent that the situation needed to change right away. Thank God Lucas has connections." Mira's mom smiled at him.

This was getting weirder by the second. Something didn't add up. "I don't understand," Mira said, trying to piece the story together. "Doesn't this girl have any other family? You'd think she'd want to live with people she knew."

"We're not doing a very good job of this, are we?" Mira's dad said nervously, looking at Lucas, then at her. Her dad cleared his throat. "It's complicated, but the girl's mom died when she was ten, there is no dad in the picture, and the grandmother is in her eighties. Her health has steadily worsened since the diagnosis a few years ago. She'll be moving into a nursing home immediately."

"It's us or foster care," Mira's mom said grimly. "There is no one else. Her social worker says she's a good kid. She's on the swim team and she lifeguards, but her life hasn't been easy. She takes care of her grandmother, works, and goes to school. We could really change the course of her life," she added, getting that glint in her eye she got when she found a new pet project.

"Why does she have a social worker?" Hayden asked.

"The situation she's in, mainly," Mira's dad said, and tapped his fingers on the table. "It's...not good. She was raised in Harborside."

"Harborside?" Mira repeated, surprised. The Butterflies sometimes did holiday toy drives for kids in Harborside. They had the largest trailer park in the state, and there were always stories on the news about break-ins and occasional gunfights. The area was less than savory. She knew people who visited the Harborside boardwalk, but Mira's parents never let her go there. Was her cousin as rough as the town she was from? Oh my God, was she going to have to hide her wallet under her bed at night? Mira's face reddened. She couldn't believe she'd just thought that. "How is she related to us again?"

"She's a distant cousin." Lucas surprised her by answering for her dad. "On your dad's side."

"Which cousin?" Mira pressed, wanting to picture people in her head.

"She's my third cousin's daughter," her dad told her.

"And who is that?" Hayden was apparently confused, too.

"It's Tracy's girl, right, Bill?" Mira's mom said.

"Is that the one with the lazy eye?" Connor asked, and Mira's mom gave him a stern look.

"Tracy's the one with the thirteen cats," Mira reminded them. "She's the one who lives in Oklahoma City, and her house smells like mothballs, remember?"

Hayden laughed. "Oh yeah. We had to stay there for the family reunion because there were no hotels for twenty miles. You kept sneezing because you were allergic to the cats."

Mira laughed, then stopped abruptly. "Tracy didn't have kids." She looked at her parents. "We were the youngest ones at the reunion."

"Sorry, I meant my cousin Chloe," her dad said, and took a sip of water. "You haven't met her. We weren't close growing

53

up, but the point is, she's my cousin's daughter, and your mother and I feel the need to step in and help her."

Mira stared at the ocean, feeling like at any second the waves would become a whirlpool that got bigger and bigger until it engulfed the restaurant. Her parents didn't even make a dinner reservation without consulting Zagat's. Now they were legal guardians to a complete stranger? And a girl from Harborside, no less? Weren't they worried about how her cousin would mesh with the family? She saw stories on TV like this all the time, and things never ended well. And what were her friends going to say? She didn't get it. But before she could voice her opinion, Lucas spoke up again.

"I know this is hard on you three, but can you imagine how this girl feels?" Lucas asked. "She's losing the only home she's ever known." Lucas's face was solemn. "She'll need counseling, Bill. We should talk about how you want to position this story in the press." Mira resented his weighing in.

"We can discuss that later," her dad said. He looked at his children again. "The timing is rough, I know that. But your mom and I have discussed this a lot, and in the end we knew we had to do the right thing. We hope you'll understand someday." Mira noticed he sounded choked up. Suddenly she felt bad for grilling him.

Two waiters arrived with trays of food. Lobster for Hayden, her parents, and herself, and filet mignon for Lucas. Connor had his standard mac and cheese with applesauce.

Mira couldn't even think of eating the lobster that was staring up at her mournfully. An hour ago, she had been worried about her hair and getting out of dinner early enough to make it to Taylor's practice, and now she was getting a semisister? The idea was too much for her to comprehend. She didn't do well with change. She'd had the same laptop for the past three years because she loved the keyboard. She refused to change her field hockey stick because she thought it brought her luck, and she slept with a Mexican worry doll under her pillow because a waiter had told her it would ease her fears. She might need to invest in a case of worry dolls after this news.

"Does she know about us?" Hayden used his fork to expertly pull a piece of lobster from a claw.

"I believe she only found out about us today, too," their dad said, sounding like he was choosing his words carefully. "The social worker is bringing her tonight at nine."

Mira's jaw dropped, and it took all her energy not to let her fork clang onto the plate.

"The guest room is made up," her mom told them. "I had Paula put fresh linens and flowers in there, and we registered her for school. We need her size for uniforms...." Her mom listed the items like she would for one of her to-do lists. But this was much bigger than needing to buy a new comforter at Bed Bath & Beyond.

"We'll introduce her next week or the following at a dinner,

I think," Lucas said, having a one-track mind. "And I'm readying a press release. I think the reaction will be positive. This is an incredible thing your family is doing." Mira resisted the urge to gag. Of course Lucas was working an angle already. She was still trying to figure out how she and this girl were related.

Her dad looked at her. "What are you thinking, Pea?" That's what he always called Mira as a baby — Sweet Pea. Later it was shortened to just Pea. At the moment, that's how small she felt.

"It's a lot to digest." She thumbed her glass again and looked at the melting ice.

Her dad hardly asked her opinion anymore. He used to all the time, but now he was too busy reforming the North Carolina school lunch program to ask Mira what she thought of his necktie. Today he wanted her approval, and Mira couldn't let him down. She never had before. She sighed. "I think what you're doing is amazing."

"We're all doing it," he said, and squeezed Mira's hand. "We'll make her feel welcome, and before you know it, it will feel like she's always been a Monroe."

"You never told us her name," Mira realized.

"It's Isabelle," her dad said, and smiled softly. "Isabelle Scott. She spells her name the same way we spell yours," her dad added.

Her mother nodded approvingly. "So pretty that way."

"It sounds like your name!" Connor exclaimed to Mira.

"It does, doesn't it?" Mira said thoughtfully, unsure of how she felt about the similarity. She wasn't sure what she thought about any of this, really, and she didn't have a lot of time to sort her feelings out. Whether Mira liked it or not, Isabelle Scott was on her way.

Five

Barbara's car pulled away from 22 Hancock Street at the same time the Coastal Assisted Living van pulled out of the driveway with Grams tucked inside. Izzie watched the house disappear into the distance. She had a feeling this would be the last time she'd ever see it.

Barbara didn't push her to make conversation in the car. She'd worked overtime trying to do that while Izzie had packed. Didn't Barbara know how upset Izzie was? The last thing she wanted to do was make light conversation with her social worker while she tried to pack up her life in half an hour. She grabbed her first swim team medal and the framed picture of her and her mom at the shore the summer before she died. She tucked the frame between her Michael Jackson tee and her *Harborside Beach Lifeguard* jacket to keep it from breaking. The lavender paisley comforter Grams had bought her but Izzie never really liked would "accidentally" be left behind, along with the collection of dusty Beanie Babies Grams never wanted her to throw away ("You spent your allowance on those!").

Izzie knew Barbara was just trying to do her job by loitering nearby while Izzie filled the large duffel bag to the brim, but her job didn't give her the big picture. Izzie may have hated the lily wallpaper (which was why she'd covered it in black-and-white beach photos), and she wouldn't miss the green garage-sale desk where she did her homework, but this was still her room, and had been her whole life. She couldn't imagine loving anywhere as much as she did 22 Hancock Street. She liked how smooth the worn wooden banister felt on her hand as she hurried down the stairs (late for school—again) and how the sunlight hit the antique glass window in the foyer. She'd even miss the crooked front porch with its leaning porch swing.

She'd never again bike over to the Associate to buy a Powerade. She wouldn't ride up to the boardwalk and feel the wind on her face. She didn't know the next time she'd see her friends, the community center, or the swim team. Maybe there was a way she could still come back and compete. And she could probably take the bus to the boardwalk, right? Izzie didn't know the Monroes, but they'd probably appreciate her earning her keep. If she kept lifeguarding, she could still see Brayden, and picturing Brayden's face was the only thing giving her a calm exterior. Inside, she was freaking out. She quickly sent a text to him and Kylie so they'd know where she was.

IZZIE'S CELL: Don't freak out. IM OK, but had 2 leave town & won't B back anytime soon. Grams going into nursing home. Social taking me 2 new digs. Not sure what will happen, but will explain all when I resurface. Miss U guys already. xoxo Iz

Was the "miss you" part too much to write to Brayden? Izzie didn't have time to debate it. She hit Send as Barbara turned onto Harborside's main drag. She pressed her face against the window and watched the storefronts she knew so well scroll by. When they passed the community center, Izzie felt a pang in her stomach so sharp that she had to grip the door handle. Izzie felt like Barbara was torturing her by moving so slowly, but the truth was, Barbara drove like a snail all the time.

Barbara's voice suddenly filled the dead air. "Do you want me to put on some music?"

"No." Izzie kept her hand pressed to the window and watched as the center disappeared from sight. She slumped back in her seat. There was nothing left to see as far as she was concerned. They'd pass the school next, and she couldn't actually say she would miss the metal detectors and

60

bag checks. She closed her eyes and thought about going to sleep, but the hum of the Taurus's engine kept her from drifting off. Finally she opened her eyes again and looked outside, hoping for a distraction.

They were cruising down a forest-lined highway Izzie had never been on. She hadn't traveled anywhere outside Harborside, except on field trips. After a while the highway turned into a local road, and they passed coastal towns with boatyards and tackle supply stores. The GPS alerted Barbara to make a right, and she slowed down. That's when Izzie saw the large wooden sign.

EMERALD COVE
HOME OF THE FIGHTING CARDINALS
ESTABLISHED 1888

Harborside didn't even have a sign. Emerald Cove's was carved with gold Gothic lettering that seemed to hint at the town's status. But fighting cardinals? Seriously? Izzie didn't have time to debate it. She was too busy staring out the window. Forget sweet Victorians. Here, the houses all had a football field for a lawn. They sat on hilltops and were so big they could fit Izzie's entire block inside (okay, *slight* exaggeration). Then the car passed more ornate signs that announced things like the Emerald Cove Yacht Club, Emerald Prep, Emerald Landing, and the Emerald Cove

Elementary School Administration Building. Finally they crossed a bridge that led onto a main street that looked like it had been plucked from a movie. Small, one-story shops with pretty, identical storefronts passed by. There was an ice-cream shop, a Gap, two different bookstores, a swimwear boutique, Italian restaurants, something called the Library that actually looked like it served food, an Apple Store, bakeries, and a crazy cosmetic store with white plastic models in the window. The only thing that seemed out of place was a fifties-style diner called Corky's that had neon lights. Barbara passed a park where a band was playing and then slowed to a stop in front of a guard booth.

"Hi. We're going to the Monroes on Cliffside Drive," Barbara told a guy in a uniform that had the words *Emerald Cove Estates* embroidered on his lapel.

"Name please?"

"Barbara Sanchez and Isabelle Scott."

You need permission to actually drive down their street, Izzie thought in awe. *Who exactly are these people?*

The guard picked up a telephone and said their names to someone, and the next thing she knew the gate was lifting and Barbara had permission to drive past the most stunning homes Izzie had ever seen.

"This is it," Barbara said, pulling up to a gorgeous moss-green Colonial with a wraparound porch. Izzie's jaw practically hit the floor. This was not a house; it was a mansion!

What looked like three brand-new cars sat in the driveway and a dirt bike she'd drooled over at the bike shop blocked the long brick path to the door. Every light in the house was on, and the front door was wide open. She was still upset, obviously, but she couldn't help being impressed. This was where she was going to live now?

Her duffel bag was thrust into her arms. "Ready?" Barbara asked, startling her.

No? Izzie felt slightly dizzy and too shocked to move, but she managed to get out of the car and follow Barbara to the front door. Barbara rang the doorbell and a blond woman in a navy dress came trotting out.

"You're here!" she said, sounding both overwhelmed and excited. Izzie felt the same way. "She's here!" she yelled to the empty hallway. Her smile was bright as her eyes darted from Barbara to Izzie. She slid the bag off Izzie's shoulder before she could protest. "You're beautiful!" she said, staring at Izzie intently before realizing what she was doing. "Sorry. Where are my manners?" She extended a slender hand. "It's so nice to meet you, Isabelle. I'm your aunt, Maureen."

"Hi," Izzie said, unsure of what to say after that. What did you say to someone who was taking you in without even meeting you first? *Thanks for having me* just didn't cut it.

Her new aunt looked at Barbara. "Did you find the house okay? I hope the ride wasn't too long. I meant to have Bill's assistant send you directions for a shortcut, but…"

"Isabelle," a tall, graying man in a dark suit said her name so seriously, Izzie felt like he was doing roll call at school. Barbara and her aunt stopped talking as the man took Izzie's hand. "I'm your uncle, Bill." He squeezed her hand. "It's a pleasure to meet you," he said hoarsely, and let go of her hand. "I—we're—so glad you could join us."

The sentence sounded funny, as if Izzie were being invited to a party. "Thanks," she said, and stared at her flip-flops.

"The drive here okay?" he asked, looking from Barbara to Izzie and back.

"Yes, Senator, no traffic at all. We made good time," Barbara told him, and her voice petered out.

Senator, Izzie reminded herself. Her uncle was a senator. No wonder they had a place like this.

A grandfather clock in a nearby room ticked loudly as everyone stood there awkwardly. No one seemed to know how to make conversation with a girl who'd landed on their doorstep with a few hours' notice. It didn't help that Izzie could feel her uncle staring at her. She finally looked up, and he blushed.

"Sorry. I didn't mean to... You just... you look a lot like Chloe."

Izzie's breath caught in her throat. She was always this way. Even though it had been a few years since her mom passed, it hadn't started hurting any less. She couldn't talk about her mom. Not tonight. Losing Grams, her home,

64

coming here…Her mouth felt too dry to find words that made sense.

"But of course, I haven't seen your mom in a long time.…" Izzie's uncle trailed off. "Are you hungry?" he asked quickly, his voice changing gears. "You must be hungry. We can make something for you. Or maybe you're tired? Do you want to see your room?"

"Yes, your room," Izzie's aunt said exuberantly. "Mirabelle is going to show it to you. She'll be in the same grade as Isabelle this year," she told Barbara, "which should ease Isabelle's transition to Emerald Prep immensely."

Izzie's eyes glanced around the spacious foyer. A living room with a huge fireplace was to her left and a formal dining room to her right. The chandelier that hung over the table was so big it looked like it would crack the table if it ever came crashing down. That's all she could think about as two boys in dress pants and pressed shirts approached her. The younger one was carrying a soccer ball. Both had white-blond hair and green eyes and looked like their mom.

"Isabelle, right?" the one who appeared to be close to her own age asked. She nodded. "I'm Hayden," he said. "And this is Connor." The younger boy smiled and shook her hand gruffly. "It's nice to meet you."

Izzie's aunt frowned. "Where's Mirabelle?"

"I'm here!" A beautiful girl with wavy brown hair ran down the stairs. Izzie noticed the girl quickly give her a once-over, her hazel eyes lingering on Izzie's beat-up flip-flops. Mirabelle was dressed like she was on her way out to a party. "Sorry! I was on the phone. Friend drama!" She rolled her eyes and laughed. "Hi," she said to Izzie, shaking her hand. "I'm Mirabelle, but everyone calls me Mira."

"Your friends are always fighting," Connor moaned.

"Here's your first piece of Monroe advice," Hayden told Izzie. "If Mira is on the phone with someone named Taylor or Savannah, you might want to use your cell to make a call."

Mira swatted him. "Don't give her the wrong idea!" She smiled brightly at Izzie. "It's not like I'm on the phone twenty-four-seven. And I'm never late."

"That's true," Izzie's uncle agreed. "Punctuality is a family motto to a fault."

Izzie wasn't about to mention that the Scott tradition was the opposite — never on time.

"Do you need help with your stuff?" Hayden asked, and the whole family peered out the door at Barbara's old Taurus.

"Good idea," Izzie's aunt said. "Do you have boxes in the car, dear? Or did you need us to send a moving van? I'm sorry we weren't there to help you move. This all happened so quickly," she said, and pushed her hair behind her ears. She had on diamond studs the size of golf balls. "Or we can go pick your stuff up in the morning before we get you fitted for your school uniform."

66

"I brought everything with me," Izzie said, coloring slightly at the fuss. "Unless you need to send for my bed and dresser." Barbara had carried two large boxes in with her, and there were a few left in the car, but she had taken everything that was important. At least she thought she had. Her head was still spinning from packing.

"That's her bike strapped to the top of my car," Barbara said, motioning to the Taurus.

"I can't believe that's all you brought," Mira said. "I would have needed a U-Haul." Her mother gave her a look and Mira instantly stopped talking, but it was too late. Izzie could tell already that her cousin was nothing like her, and she had a feeling Mira was thinking the exact same thing.

Izzie's aunt wove her arm around Izzie's awkwardly. "I guess we have some shopping to do this weekend. You're in good hands, Isabelle. I'm an expert shopper."

"She is American Express's best customer," Izzie's uncle said, and Hayden and Mira laughed.

"We'll have time to get you everything you need before school starts," Izzie's aunt said confidently, and Izzie tried not to feel weird that her aunt still had her arm. "I've already called ahead to make sure they have various sizes of the school uniform for you to try on at the town shop. We might even be able to get you a few dresses this weekend if we have time." She winked and peered at Izzie's duffel bag. "And I guess you'll need a laptop, too, and — do you have a cell phone? No matter. We'll have to switch you to our family plan anyway. I wonder if we have time to get to the Apple Store before brunch at the club. Hmm…" She waved her hand before Izzie could answer her. "Never mind. There will be time to go over all this. Things will be well in order by Monday. I promise." She smiled. "This is a whole new start for you, Isabelle, and we want you to have everything you need to succeed."

Uniforms? Laptops? Dresses? Izzie didn't think she'd worn a dress since her sixth-grade graduation. She felt like she had just entered the twilight zone. How could people who barely knew her be so willing to give her everything she needed and more? The idea would have been exciting if she wasn't still so upset.

"Why don't you three give Isabelle a tour of the house while we go over a few things with Ms. Sanchez?" Izzie's aunt suggested. "We can meet up for dessert in, say, half an hour?" She looked at her watch, and Izzie wondered if she was about to set a timer. "If you think of anything you might need for tonight, Isabelle, just let Mirabelle know. Pajamas, a toothbrush — she'll get it for you." Izzie watched her aunt, her uncle, and Barbara turn and walk down the hallway. They were talking in hushed tones.

"They are probably headed to Dad's office. We'll just go this way," Mira told her, smiling as she led the group in the opposite direction. "So this is the living room," she said, gesturing to the cobblestone fireplace and massive built-in bookshelves that covered one wall. Lights shone on several trophies and photographs, one of which looked like Izzie's uncle with the president. *Yowza.*

"What grade are you in?" Hayden asked as they headed back through the foyer, past the dining room, into the first of what appeared to be two dens.

She was so busy trying to count the fireplaces she'd seen so far that she almost missed the question. "Tenth," she said.

"Me, too!" Mira squealed. "So fun! Hayden's in eleventh and Connor's in first, but he won't be in Emerald Prep till sixth grade. Do you play any sports? I play field hockey."

Izzie ran her hand along a mahogany table. "I swim."

"My best friend is on the swim team!" Mira gushed. "You're going to love Savannah."

Hayden coughed. "You're so not." Izzie bit her lip. She had a feeling she would like Hayden.

"Tryouts are the second week of school," Mira continued. "What team were you on? Have you been swimming long? Because"—Mira thumbed the gold necklace around her neck and looked solemn—"our school is supercompetitive. It's the most prestigious high school in the state. It's tough to get into, but don't worry, you're already in. They didn't name the new sports complex after my dad for nothing! Wait till you see the swim center." Mira was talking so quickly, Izzie could barely keep up. "Our swim team has won our division the past two years. Not that you're not good, I'm sure, but just so you know what you're up against." Izzie's stomach started to churn with nervousness. Her new school sounded both incredible and horrifying.

"Don't worry," Hayden assured her. "You can practice here before tryouts. We have a pool in the backyard and a lap pool, too. No one uses it. Dad thought he'd take up swimming, but I guess he forgot you need *time* to exercise."

"It is so cool!" Connor added. "It counts the laps and times you and everything. Sometimes I go in with a tube just to get bounced around."

"What is your best time?" Mira pressed. "Best stroke? When did you learn how to…"

Izzie stared at the den. It was her favorite room so far. A fireplace roared underneath a flat-screen TV, and the brown leather sectional looked so inviting, Izzie wanted to go lie on it and sleep for a week. On one wall were framed photos of each of the Monroe kids. Hayden running, Connor on rocks at the beach — Mira's garden shot could have been ripped out of *Vogue*. Maybe it had. Her cousin looked like she could model.

Izzie couldn't concentrate. How did she get here? Three hours ago she'd been biking home from the boardwalk, worrying about what Barbara wanted, and now she was in a mansion that she was supposed to call home and was talking about private schools and personal lap pools. She knew she should be excited. Connor was right—a lap pool *was* awesome. So were mall trips for new clothes and a laptop, which she'd always wanted. But as soon as she started to get excited, she thought of Grams and Harborside and felt guilty. She was so confused. Was it okay to be amazed by this new life being dangled in front of her? Or should she feel bad?

Hayden watched Izzie carefully. "You've probably had a long night, huh?"

Long *doesn't begin to describe it*, Izzie thought, grateful Hayden noticed. "Yeah, I'm sorry. Do you think we could cut the tour short and I could see my room? I have to crash."

"But we still have a few rooms left to see." Mira sounded disappointed. "And we have dessert downstairs. Paula made an apple strudel that is to die for."

"When is the last time you tried her strudel?" Hayden asked coyly.

"It smells good," Mira said defensively, crossing her bare arms. Several silver bracelets dangled from them.

"I'll take a rain check," Izzie said, looking across the great room at the equally big kitchen that was attached to it. A strudel, plates, silverware, and glasses, including champagne, lay on the island waiting.

"It will taste better cold at breakfast," Hayden agreed. "Let's show you your room."

The second floor was just as dazzling as the first. The tour stopped briefly so that Connor could show off his room, which was baseball-themed and had several large decals on the walls, one of Connor at bat. Izzie's and Mira's rooms, Hayden explained, were in their own wing.

"We'll have to work out a bathroom schedule," Mira said. "Just so neither of us gets a late start. Unless, of course, you want to use one of the other four bathrooms we have up here." Hayden cleared his throat. "What else can we tell you?" She rubbed her hands together and her bracelets clinked. "Our housekeeper handles all the day-to-day stuff, like making school lunches — not that any of us actually take them. And you can leave her a list of food you like so the kitchen is stocked. Now, about laundry…"

"Connor, why don't you show Isabelle those pictures on the wall?" Hayden suggested.

It didn't take a genius to figure out what he was doing. He probably thought she couldn't hear him over Connor's chatter, but Izzie still could.

"Could you stop laying it on so thick?" Hayden whispered. "You sound fake."

"I'm trying to be friendly!" Mira protested. "This whole situation is weird, okay? I'm trying, which is more than she's doing."

Izzie's cheeks flamed. Is that what Mira thought? It wasn't that she was unhappy — she didn't know what she was at the moment. She only knew she was tired. She wished Mira realized how strange this all was for her, too. She needed time to wrap her head around what had happened tonight and what was going to happen from here on out. She wanted to be grateful — she *was* grateful — but she had no clue how to express it. Instead she'd ticked off Mira. Izzie felt bad, but she was too exhausted to rally with conversation as cheerful as Mira could pull off.

"She's tired, remember?" Hayden pointed out. "This has got to be hard on her."

"And us," Mira hissed. "This is as tough for us as it is for her."

"You sound like Savannah." Hayden's voice rose slightly. "What's wrong with you? Ever since you started hanging out with her, you've been —"

"Savannah has nothing to do with this," Mira said through gritted teeth. "This is hard on everyone. She could at least try...."

"Isabelle, come see your room," Hayden interrupted, calling to Izzie. "Mira, want to tell her about it?"

"Sure," Mira said unsurely before purposefully strutting forward and flashing a grin.

Did she really think Izzie hadn't heard what she'd just said? Mira let Izzie walk inside ahead of her.

"Mom said you can have it repainted, and she wants to get you new linens," Mira explained, still talking. But all Izzie could do was gape. "It's so cute and cozy, isn't it?"

Cozy wasn't the right word. The room was four times the size of Izzie's old one. The walls were a creamy yellow and the queen-size bed had a muted floral comforter on it with lots of throw pillows. There were two bedside tables, a desk, and a framed Renoir poster. Or maybe that one was a Monet. Izzie's boxes were already stacked in the corner along with her duffel bag.

"My mom loves redecorating," Mira told her.

The sound of static kept Izzie from having to reply. Her aunt's voice beamed down from somewhere in the ceiling. "We're ready for dessert!"

"Intercom," Connor explained to Izzie. "You know, because the house is so big?"

Mira walked to a small box near the room door and pressed a button. "She's tired, Mom. She doesn't want to come down."

"But it's apple strudel! Just one small piece?" There was mumbling in the background. "And Barbara wants to say good night." The others looked at her.

Izzie took a deep breath. How could she not go downstairs when they were rearranging their whole lives for her? "Okay."

"She's coming down," Mira reported back.

Everyone was waiting for them around the kitchen island, where Izzie's aunt was cutting small pieces of the strudel. Barbara was talking to a man Izzie didn't know, but as soon as she approached the table, he smiled at her. He was youngish — *early thirties, maybe?* — with blond hair and brown eyes. He had on a navy suit and he smelled like a mix of cigars and musk.

"Isabelle, hi! I apologize for interrupting the evening," he said, and shook her hand. "I just wanted to introduce myself. I'm Lucas Hale. I'm your uncle's campaign manager for his upcoming bid for the U.S. Senate. I've heard so much about you." He continued to pump her hand. She wasn't sure how to pull away without looking odd. For some reason, she happened to glance at Mira. Her cousin was glaring at Lucas. "I hope we can help you settle in as quickly as possible. Over the weekend, we can introduce you to the press and—"

"Actually, we were talking before you arrived, Lucas, and we think it would be good to give Izzie a few weeks," Barbara interrupted. "Maureen and I think it would be best to explain the situation to Izzie before she's put in the spotlight, and now is not the right time."

"I thought we agreed to put out a release right away so there is no confusion," Lucas said slowly, but even Izzie could detect the annoyance in his voice. "Bill, I really think I should keep this story under control, and the best way to do that is to be the one who actually puts the story out there."

"I agree," Izzie's uncle said even as he stared at his wife's stony expression. "Sweetheart, Lucas knows what he's doing. This is the best way for us to stay on top of things."

Izzie's aunt handed him a piece of strudel without looking

at him. "Isabelle is starting a new school next week. Would it really hurt to sit on this story for a week or two? She needs time to settle in before the world forms an opinion about her new situation."

Izzie looked around the table, confused, but her cousins didn't seem surprised. She was being introduced to the press? Why did they need to put out a press release about her, Isabelle Scott? She looked away, feeling uncomfortable, and caught Connor sneaking a cookie from the dessert tray.

"I'm with Maureen," Barbara told the group. "As you know, I will be checking in from time to time, and I really do hope you'll make Izzie's well-being your top priority."

"We will," Izzie's uncle said, and looked at Lucas. "This story can wait a week or two, I think. But we can finish this discussion later, either way." Lucas nodded stiffly and waved off the piece of strudel Izzie's aunt had offered him.

"I think that would be best," Barbara agreed. She grabbed her bag and keys and looked at Izzie somewhat guiltily. "I should be going. I'll check in with you tomorrow, okay?"

Izzie was still annoyed with Barbara, but the thought of the only person in this room she knew leaving made her chest hurt.

"Any questions before I go?" Barbara asked gently.

Izzie did have one. "Could someone tell me how we're related?"

"Well, we're...you tell her, Bill," Izzie's aunt said.

He looked down at his strudel before scooping a bite. "Your mom, Chloe, and I were third cousins."

Izzie tried to piece the news together. "I thought Grams and Pops were only children."

"Grams had cousins," he said, and looked at Barbara. "Right?"

"If that was what was in the report," Barbara said after a long pause, "then yes."

This wasn't clearing anything up. Even the Monroes and Barbara didn't seem to know the family bloodline, and yet she was now in their care. Suddenly Izzie felt too tired to keep her head up. "I have work tomorrow, so I should probably get to bed."

"About lifeguarding," Lucas spoke up, "this is one thing we all agree on. While we admire your tenacity, we feel it would be best for you to find a job more local. If you even want a job. The boardwalk is sort of far from here and, well, shall we say, unsavory?"

"You work at the boardwalk?" Connor asked in awe. "Mom and Dad never take me there! Matthew in my class said they have knife fights all the time and you can watch."

Izzie felt like the room was spinning. She was dizzy again. "I've never seen a knife fight, and I've lived by the boardwalk my whole life," she told Connor, but she said it more for the family's sake. "The boardwalk is totally safe and a lot of fun."

"That may be, but we still don't think it's the best place for you to work now that you're living with us," Izzie's uncle said gently.

She wished they would just be honest with her: The problem wasn't the boardwalk; it was Harborside. She'd seen outsiders react this way before.

"What about my swim team?" Izzie asked, even though she already knew the answer. "I have a meet this Saturday."

The adults looked at each other. Izzie's aunt spoke. "I'm sorry. It's just too far to take you to practice every day. You can try out for Emerald Prep's swim team, though. They have an excellent team."

"You're going to love it," Mira chimed in. Izzie noticed she was drinking water. A slice of strudel was nowhere near her. Suddenly Izzie wasn't hungry, either. She pushed her strudel away.

Izzie felt like her heart would break. No lifeguarding, no community center, no surf lessons. Her mind kept going back to Brayden. When would she see him again? He hadn't texted her back yet. Kylie had practically blown up Izzie's phone with calls after receiving Izzie's text, but she hadn't had a minute to herself yet to call her back.

"We have a lifeguard job lined up for you at our country club," her aunt said with enthusiasm. "People hardly even go in the water. I'd be surprised if you ever had to do a rescue."

"That sounds real exciting, Mom," Hayden joked.

But Izzie wasn't laughing. She liked making rescues. The

adrenaline was enough to keep her pumped up for days. Suddenly she felt so overwhelmed with heartache she thought she might burst into tears. She would not let herself do that in front of a group of strangers. Or Barbara. "Could I be excused?" she asked quietly.

"Of course," her aunt said, and glanced at her husband worriedly. "This has been a long day for everyone. We'll talk more about all this tomorrow."

"We're just so glad you're here," her uncle added.

"Thanks for having me," Izzie said as if on autopilot. She could feel Mira watching her as she brought her untouched plate to the sink.

"Izzie, is there anything else you want the Monroes to know about you before I go?" Barbara asked.

Izzie turned around and looked at the faces staring at her. "Izzie," she said quietly. "I prefer to be called Izzie."

"Izzie," Lucas repeated as if he were learning a foreign language. He held up his coffee mug in a toast. "Welcome to the Monroe family."

Six

Every high school has a rumor mill. Emerald Prep's just tended to be on a more extravagant scale. Three years later, people were still talking about Perry Stanton's dad supposedly buying the headmaster a Range Rover to keep Perry on the football team. And there wasn't a week that went by that someone didn't bring up the rumor about an ancient pirate treasure being buried somewhere on school grounds. Mira's favorite gossip was the one about the Underground Railroad. Supposedly, passageways under the main schoolhouse were a part of history. Mira would have given anything for that rumor to be true. It was the first day of her sophomore year and yet all she wanted to do was find a tunnel and wait for the whispers about her family to die off.

In classic style, Lucas had pressed Mira's dad to go ahead

with a press release about Izzie straightaway—even though it was obvious at dessert the other night that Barbara and her mom were flat-out against it. Lucas's real-life fairy-tale spin had the newspapers and morning shows in a tizzy. Who wouldn't eat up a story about a poor girl from Harborside getting taken in by a wealthy ballplayer-turned-senator and his family? Lucas looked like a kid who'd *bought* a candy store as he whisked Mira's dad out of the house Saturday morning to give interviews all weekend about helping out those "less fortunate than yourself." Everyone wanted to meet the insta-princess, but Mira's mom—who stopped speaking to her dad when the story hit—whisked Izzie to Atlanta hoping the barrage of camera crews would disappear by the time they got back. From what Hayden told Mira, Izzie didn't have a clue that the world now knew everything there was to know about Isabelle Scott. Her old cell phone had been shut off, and Mira heard Izzie say she was having trouble with her new phone, so she couldn't retrieve messages.

Not that Izzie said any of this to Mira. Oh, no, even after Mira had done her best to be the sweetest hostess this side of the North Carolina state line, Izzie still barely said two words to her. She pretty much kept to herself. The whole situation was driving Mira crazy. They were turning their lives upside down for her, and Izzie could barely spend two minutes with them! Hayden told Mira she was expecting too much. ("You don't lose your life overnight and just jump headfirst into a new one," he said, sounding wise beyond his years.) But Mira wanted Izzie to seem grateful. Was that too much to ask?

Maybe who Mira was really mad at was her parents. It wasn't like them to do something this rash. Dad usually talked every situation to death, whether it was switching cable providers or how he wanted his family to stand at a ribbon-cutting ceremony. But he added a new family member to the house and said zip? It was bizarre. As Mira eyed her EP classmates walking to homeroom, she wondered what they were thinking about the Monroes. Being a senator's daughter — and Savannah's BF — put her on everyone's radar, and sometimes Mira still couldn't get used to the glare. She wasn't supposed to care what anyone thought of her, but she did, and she was dying to know what they were thinking as they walked past her at that moment. She hadn't spoken to anyone but Taylor since the story broke and Taylor hadn't brought it up. He was more concerned about the new football jerseys the team was getting. She had never been more worried about her friends' reactions than she was at the moment.

"Over there is the Monica Holbrook Arts Center," Hayden said to Izzie as they walked across the main quad. He had taken over the role of tour guide that morning when Mira claimed she had a headache. "You and Mira have homeroom in there this morning and second and third period." He took Izzie's schedule and scanned her list of classes. "Then you have to go to the Neil Hancock Science Center. You should have more than enough time. We have six minutes between classes since everything is so spread out, but the science center is right over there." He pointed across the lush lawn, where students were catching up after a long summer.

"Six minutes," Izzie repeated, fidgeting in her navy blazer with the yellow EP emblem. Mira's mom had shown her how to layer her white shirt and tie, and which kneesocks to wear for school and which to save for assemblies. Thankfully, she had persuaded Izzie to remove her blue nail polish and lose her clunky, silver rings for the first day. "I really appreciate your help, Hayden," Izzie said shyly.

"I know this place can be intense, but you'll get the hang of it," Hayden told her. Izzie didn't look convinced. She had her eye on the school drop-off zone a few yards away. Several teachers and aides monitored the parade of BMWs, town cars, and Range Rovers that were dropping off uniformed students as young as sixth graders and as old as twelfth. As students passed them, Mira could hear them blabbing about their summers in Key West or about the new Gucci bag their mom had bought them as a back-to-school gift.

Mira knew Emerald Prep was intimidating. Even she had been petrified of the place when she started there in sixth grade. It was much bigger than the Catholic elementary school that Hayden and she had gone to. The buildings were huge and stately, the landscaping looked like the White House grounds, flowerbeds dotted every walkway, and gardens with fountains and quiet study areas were around every turn. EP had every sports team imaginable, and if you could think of one they didn't have, all a parent had to do was raise a stink at a meeting and pony up some seed money, and there would be a team by nightfall. EP athletes took stretch Hummer limos instead of buses to away games. There was a zip line outside the gym, and the cafeteria served gourmet eats prepared by a former celebrity chef. When she'd started, Mira couldn't find her way to the lunch line, let alone the bathroom. She didn't know anyone other than Hayden, either. She must have looked like a tool. Thank God she and Savannah became friends in eighth grade, when they bonded over their shared recognition of the lower school headmistress's tacky fake Tory Burch purse. Mira would tell Izzie all of this if she would actually turn and look at her for a moment. But she wouldn't. Mira had the distinct impression that her cousin didn't like her.

"I should run," Hayden said as a bell chimed to give the ten-minute warning till homeroom. "Play nice, ladies," he said as he straightened his navy vest and winked at Mira. "That one is more for you." Mira stuck her tongue out at him as he jogged across the lawn. The image of Hayden's navy-clad back against a sea of plaid would make an awesome picture. Mira sighed. She wished Hayden didn't have homeroom in another building. Izzie didn't seem as stiff around him.

The girls stared at each other awkwardly. "We should get going, too," Mira said, and examined her plaid skirt for wrinkles. She adjusted her headband, pulled her paisley backpack higher on her shoulders, and scanned the crowd for Savannah or Taylor. No such luck. Emerald Prep students were from over twenty-five zip codes, and of every size, shape, and color, yet they all looked the same in their navy uniforms. Mira always liked that part of school. As much as she valued her *Vogue* subscription, there was nothing easier than slipping on the same outfit five days a week.

The two walked the rest of the way in silence and Mira felt as heavy as the art center's double doors as she swung them open and led Izzie into the atrium. She noticed Izzie's jaw drop slightly. The massive octagon-shaped ceiling had a Civil War battle painted on it. Mira looked down at her pricey ballet flats, avoiding eye contact with everyone on her way to class. She didn't want to be late, and explaining who Izzie was would take a longer conversation. But she had to say *something* to Izzie, didn't she? How come Izzie and Hayden seemed so comfortable, but when Izzie was with her, it was like pulling teeth?

"So what do you think about Emerald Prep?" Mira asked. "Incredible, huh?"

Izzie looked like a deer caught in headlights. "It's huge."

"Yeah, but once you know the layout, it's easy," Mira said as she led the way upstairs to class. "We have the first few periods together, but then you're on your own. You can call me if you need anything, though. We're not really supposed to use cell phones, but you can in the halls if it's an emergency."

"I'm sure I can find my way around," Izzie told her, and Mira couldn't tell if Izzie was being honest or rude. She tended to think it was the latter, which made Mira want to ditch her there and then.

"Great! Well, here we are." Mira pushed open the homeroom door and instantly the volume was louder. Savannah was nestled in a corner with Lea Price and some of their other friends. When Savannah saw Mira, she looked up and gave a little wave. Her beautiful blond hair covered the right side of her face, but her brown eyes immediately locked on Izzie. So did everyone else's.

Time for introductions, Mira thought with a pit in her stomach. Mira adopted her cheerleader voice again. "Hey, guys! I want you to meet my cousin, Izzie."

"Dizzie?" Lea repeated. Lea was desperate to be in Savannah's back pocket and was always vying for Savannah's attention.

"No, Izzie, as in Isabelle," Mira said patiently. "She just moved to Emerald Cove."

"Yes, from Harborside, right?" Savannah asked, smiling sweetly as she took in Izzie from head to toe. "It's so nice to meet you, Izzie. I'm Savannah, Mira's best friend."

"Hey," Izzie said, and shifted the strap on her messenger bag closer to her chest.

"Do you like Emerald Cove so far?" Savannah asked, and twisted a ring on her middle finger around and around. "I couldn't imagine living anywhere else."

"How much do you like that house?" chimed in their friend Lauren Salbrook as she straightened the headband holding back her long brown hair. "I want Mira's bathroom so bad. It has a Jacuzzi tub!"

Mira started to relax a little. Her friends were being really nice! This wasn't going as bad as she thought it would. They probably felt sorry for Izzie after reading all the articles, Mira realized guiltily. That was the one thing she'd forgotten to be so far herself.

"And Mira's dad is such a teddy bear," Lea added.

"You are so lucky to be living with the Monroes," Savannah said, and looked at Izzie's feet. Mira's mom had bought her the same pair of ballet flats as Mira. "Cute shoes! I have the same ones."

"Thanks," Izzie said, continuing her tradition of one-word answers. Mira slid into the seat next to Savannah, feeling relief wash over her, and opened her book bag to retrieve a notebook.

Izzie went to take the seat next to Mira, but Lea quickly slid her notebook over to block her. "I'm *so* sorry, but this seat is saved for Jill," she said apologetically. "She should be here any minute."

"Oh, okay." Izzie grabbed her bag and turned to the desk in front of Mira.

"This seat is taken, too," Lauren said, sticking her hand out like she was blocking traffic. "Bernadette texted me that she should be here any second." She wrinkled her face like a prune.

Is Bernadette even in this class? Mira wondered.

"God, you must think we're so rude!" Savannah said to Izzie with a condescending smile. "We've sat in a clump like this since we started at EP. But there are still some seats nearby." Savannah looked around, then pointed to a row near the front that the geek quotient dominated. "There's a free one."

Izzie's expression changed slightly. "Thanks," she said to Savannah. "I'll catch up with you guys later."

"Absolutely!" Savannah nodded. "We'll see you after class."

Mira's face flushed pink as Izzie walked away. She knew what was happening. They were freezing Izzie out in the only way EP's elite could — politely, sweetly, and by being as cunning as a fox.

"She's cute," Savannah said, studying Izzie closely as her

brown bob swished back and forth on her walk to the front row. Mira could see Izzie making an effort to introduce herself to the gawky girl next to her. Why was Izzie so willing to do that with a stranger, but not with her?

"She is pretty," Mira agreed.

Savannah's head tilted as she examined Izzie further. "Highlights would do wonders for her dull brown hair, don't you think?" she added. Mira hadn't noticed, but she nodded. "I think it's incredible what your parents are doing, Mira."

"So generous," Lea agreed, and took a sip from the water bottle on her desk.

"Especially considering where she's from," Savannah added, and twirled a piece of blond hair around her finger. "My mom says Harborside is the ghetto of N.C. I hope your mom locked up her jewelry. She has a gorgeous collection."

Lauren gasped. "I didn't even think of that. Do you think she would steal it?"

"Well" — Savannah pushed her hair behind her ears — "I'm not accusing her of anything, of course, but it's practically a given considering where she grew up. She was raised differently than we were. Not that there is anything wrong with that," Savannah added, looking at Mira.

"I don't think she's like that," Mira said awkwardly. Mira had initially had the same fear herself. Izzie was a little standoffish, but Mira quickly realized she didn't seem like a common criminal. Did coming from a place like Harborside automatically stamp her as one?

~

By the time third period ended, Mira was mentally exhausted. All morning, her friends kept Izzie at arm's length — not that any of them would admit the banishment had to do with her being from Harborside. "I don't want Mr. Issacs to partner us on the *Illiad* project," one of Mira's friends had said when she switched seats to get away from Izzie during English. "What if she thinks Homer is Homer Simpson?"

Once Izzie set off for fourth period on her own, with barely a thanks to Mira for escorting her around all morning, Mira knew she couldn't make it another second if she didn't get rid of the killer headache that had started when she'd arrived in homeroom. Coke might be the only thing that could get rid of it, and there was a Coke vending machine on the ground floor of the arts building. Mira decided to head straight there, whether it made her late for study hall or not. It was practically a nonissue anyway. Ms. Page had been her monitor last year, too, and she barely showed up long enough to take attendance.

She was so desperate for syrupy sweetness she practically jogged down the hall. Almost tripping over her own feet,

Mira grabbed the wall to keep from falling and noticed the watercolor paintings hanging on a string across several bulletin boards. Hers was smack in the middle of the batch. She'd always loved Impressionists — her mother claimed she had to cart her away, kicking and screaming, from Monet's *The Artist's Garden at Vétheuil* at the National Gallery of Art when she was four. Maybe that was why she was always drawn to watercolors and dreamy, pretty pictures of flowers or the sea whenever she was asked to complete an assignment in art class. She thought everyone got As in art, which was why she was so surprised last spring when Mr. Capozo insisted on displaying her watercolor of the boathouse she had painted. Mr. Capozo said Mira had an artist's eye. Her. A girl who rarely painted anything except her nails.

Forget the Coke. Suddenly Mira wanted that painting back so badly, she was willing to steal it right off the wall. She looked both ways to make sure no one was coming before she unclipped the paper. Then she quickly rolled up the painting and placed it carefully in her bag before hurrying away.

"Nothing like a little petty theft to start the school year off on a high note," said a deep voice.

Mira spun around, gripping her bag. A cute guy, wearing a messy clear smock, stood in a doorway a few feet away with his arms folded smugly across his chest.

"It's not stealing if you're taking what's already yours."

Mira tried to sound sure of herself even though she was shaking. She pulled the painting out and unrolled it again, pointing at the elegant script of her signature. "That's my name. I painted this, so technically I should be allowed to take it back."

His green eyes glinted mischievously as he pushed his sandy blond hair off his forehead. "I'm just messing with you. Those pictures were coming down later today anyway. Let's see if yours was worth the heist." Before she could protest, he took the painting from her hands and studied it. She couldn't help but notice his fingers were covered in dried green paint. "Not bad," he said, then frowned. "You could have used a little more yellow in that sunset, though."

Mira snatched the painting back. "No one asked you."

"Touchy." He smiled. "You're good. You'd be better if you took classes. Are you in watercolors or drawing this fall?"

"I can't waste time on art classes," Mira said. Who was he to judge her painting?

The boy shrugged. "Your loss. I've got to get back to my own work. See ya." He started walking away, which only made Mira madder.

"And you think your painting is better?" Mira followed him into the classroom, ready to critique. She stopped short when she realized where they were. This was one of the specialty art rooms, where you could take classes like sculpting and drawing. Mira had opted to get public speaking over with instead. A dozen easels were set up alongside one another, and there was a small stage in the front of the room where models probably stood. The boy was already back at his easel with his paintbrush and a small palette of paint in his hand.

"Wow, that's really good," Mira admitted, coming closer. His work was much more realistic, with sharp angles and dark colors. It was so clear she would have thought it was a photograph of the dolphin fountain right outside the classroom window. "When did you paint that?"

"Just now." He grinned. "Okay, more like in third period and now. I have study hall, so I figured I'd come in here and finish it."

"You can come in here during study hall?" Mira asked curiously.

He nodded. "If you take art classes, yeah. But like you said, you can't waste time on that sort of stuff." He smirked. "What grade are you in, anyway?"

"Tenth," Mira said, sounding standoffish. This guy unnerved her. "You?"

"Eleventh." He laid a long blue-green brushstroke through the fountain pool he was painting. He looked at Mira and she felt her heart stop just a little. He was really cute. "I'm Kellen Harper. I'd shake your hand, but you can see I'm sort of in the middle of something."

"Mira," she said, stopping short of her last name. Once

people heard that, they tended to treat her a little bit differently.

"Well, Mira, maybe if you sign yourself up for a real art class sometime, instead of the standard one where you make papier-mâché heads, we can square off for real." He looked at her seriously. "You'd be pretty good if you worked at it."

Mira blushed. He really thought her painting was good? It didn't matter. Only the Goth theater kids took art electives, and she definitely didn't fit in with that crowd. Kellen didn't look like he did, either, though. She looked longingly at his easel. "I don't have the time, but thanks."

Kellen shrugged. "This is EP. No one has free time. But somehow I manage to mentor for Big Brothers, run cross-country, and do something I really like — paint. Go figure."

Kellen ran cross-country with Hayden? How come she'd never noticed him before? And he did charity work, too? This guy didn't seem like some of the other art freaks, but still, she just couldn't see herself diving into this world. No matter how much she wanted to pick up a paintbrush. She backed out of the room, almost afraid she would be glued to the floor if she didn't. "Nice meeting you, Kellen."

"You, too. And Mira? Don't let me catch you stealing any more paintings," Kellen teased.

Mira just shook her head, but she couldn't stop thinking about what Kellen had said. He seemed pretty cool — okay, for the five minutes they were together — and he took art classes. Would it really be so weird if she did as well? She put a dollar in the vending machine and a Diet Coke tumbled out. No one even had to know, she realized. She headed outside and sat down at the fountain Kellen had just painted. She wondered if he could see her sitting there. Savannah came flying into her, sitting so close she was practically on Mira's lap.

Savannah gasped. "Mira, you look so pale out here! What happened to having a tan — fake or otherwise — for the first day of school?"

Mira's hand went to her face. "I used self-tanner." Didn't she? Did Kellen just see her with a pasty, white face? Why did she care? She had a boyfriend! Savannah's face, Mira noticed, was the perfect blend of blush and bronzer glow even after several hours in the heat. Mira didn't know how she did it.

"Oh, you did?" Savannah asked, looking at Mira with a critical eye. "I guess I didn't notice." She put a hand on Mira's shoulder. "You look so white. But it's no wonder, with everything going on at your house. Are you freaking out?"

"Yeah," Mira admitted, grateful for the chance to finally unload on someone. "One minute I was with you at the club, and the next Izzie was at my house and I was giving her a tour of her new room. My parents didn't even know she existed till a few months ago, and now she's living with us permanently! Apparently we're her only family."

"Yeah, that's what they said on the *Today* show," Savannah told her.

"It's weird having a complete stranger in the house, especially someone our age who I have zero in common with," Mira complained. "I always have to be 'on'!"

Savannah nodded appreciatively. "I can't believe your parents did that to you! They've totally bought into that rags-to-riches story Izzie's peddling."

"Well, actually, Lucas is the one selling the story," Mira admitted.

"So? It's got to be a sham. How could you be her only family? How'd she even find you?" Mira opened her mouth to explain, but Savannah rarely let another person get a word in. "She wants fame! She thinks she's going to ride your dad's coattails all the way to D.C. and make everyone at this school feel sorry for her. Well, she's wrong. The publicity will die down when another sob story hits the news. That's what happened to Miss Teen USA." That girl, coincidentally, went to their school, and Savannah hated her, too. "It doesn't matter how famous she becomes. No one is going to let her into our crowd, you know."

"I don't think Izzie really cares about being popular," Mira said thoughtfully. "I think she's sort of quiet, but then sometimes I'll catch her with Hayden, joking and laughing, and she's a completely different person." The whole situation was still confusing almost a week later. "Did you know she's this incredible swimmer and a lifeguard?"

Savannah's eyes glinted sharply. "I read that, but it doesn't change anything. It doesn't mean our friends are going to trust her."

What does trust have to do with it? Mira wondered. But she knew better than to question Savannah. Her best friend's phone started to vibrate.

"It's my mom. She's away in Hilton Head. I've got to take this. I'll see you at lunch, okay? Mom, hold on." Savannah put a thin hand over her phone and looked at Mira. "Do you have to sit with her, or are you sitting with us?"

"Uh…" Mira hadn't even thought about that. Would Savannah really ban her from the table if she brought Izzie?

"There's no room for her." Savannah winced. "I'm sorry."

"No, I know, but…" Was she supposed to let Izzie eat alone? Even she wasn't that mean.

"Like you said yourself, she has nothing in common with us. Izzie," Savannah said, the name rolling off her tongue tartly, "will be better off when she realizes that. She'll figure out where she belongs at EP." Savannah smiled and started to walk away. "I'm sure the scholarship kids will love her."

She always sounded so sure of herself, but Mira wasn't. If anything, Mira worried she had just made things a whole lot worse — for Izzie and herself.

Seven

Izzie didn't get it. She just didn't get it.

She knew she had been uncharacteristically sullen the last week (Hello? World turned upside down, thank you!), but she really did want to give her new school a shot — even if said school was what she'd imagined Harvard might be like if it had been invaded by *Gossip Girl*. She had met dozens of people as she raced around campus with a map (EP actually needed a *map*!) and all of them were perfectly polite. And yet they seemed… what was the word she was looking for?

Fake?

Every girl she'd met acted like Mira. They were cheer-leaders on Red Bull. Real estate agents in training. It was like they had a secret manual on how to charm a new student. But the minute Izzie attempted to get beyond standard introductions, the room got so frosty she needed a sweater.

What could she have done to tick people off so quickly? She'd barely spoken! It felt like everyone she'd met was in on something she wasn't and Izzie already felt out of place as it was. Her new home situation was a blur, she missed Grams, and now she was walking around a private school with hundred-dollar ballet flats on her feet and an itchy school uniform that made her break out in hives. Carrying a laptop in her messenger bag wasn't doing anything to calm her down, either. She'd never owned a computer before. What if she dropped it? Or someone stole it? Okay, so she could already tell EP was not the kind of place where people got mugged, but still. She was nervous.

"Hey! You're Mira's cousin, right?" a blond girl in a high-pitched voice squeaked when Izzie approached her lab table in fourth period. "Welcome to EP!"

Izzie was starting to feel she needed pom-poms to keep up with all this EP enthusiasm, but maybe Blondie would turn out to be different. "Thanks," she said in a voice that wasn't nearly as high as the blond's. "So do you happen to know anything about swim team tryouts?" Izzie asked tentatively. "I had heard they were next week, but..." She slid into the open seat next to the blond, but the girl stuck her hand out so fast Izzie almost sat on her palm.

"Oops! Sorry, it's just, I usually sit alone." The girl was

sweating as her eyes darted around the room like she was being watched. "Because I, uh, don't do well with lab partners."

Izzie looked at her quizzically, but by this point she was used to the bizarre behavior. "Okay, but you're missing out. I am great with a beaker." Whatever that meant. Blondie looked at her strangely as Izzie placed her bag on a chair at the table in front of her.

Maybe Izzie didn't get the way EP worked yet, but Blondie didn't look like she was at the top of the food chain herself. Mira and her friends definitely held that honor. This Izzie knew by the time homeroom started. Hayden had to be at the top of the popularity ladder, too — and he deserved it. He seemed like a good guy. So then wouldn't people go out of their way to be nice to someone related to the Monroes? She didn't want special treatment, but a lab partner would be nice.

"Where is Ms. Scott?" asked Mr. Preston, her biology teacher, as he took attendance. Izzie raised her hand. "Hello, there. It's nice to finally meet our most famous new student."

"Famous?" Izzie repeated. Mr. Preston looked like Ichabod Crane and his smile was just as thin as he was.

"It's rare I get to read the intimate details about my students' lives before I meet them," he said, staring at her over the rim of his glasses. "I enjoyed reading about your swim merits this weekend while drinking my espresso. Nice photo, too." He held up the front page of the Sunday edition

100

of the *North Carolina Gazette.* Izzie saw a photo of herself in a bathing suit followed by an article that took up the entire first page. She read the headline underneath: **Sweet Charity: Senator Monroe Adopts Impoverished Teen from Harborside.** The color drained from her face.

"We're happy to have you," Mr. Preston continued. Izzie could feel the entire room's eyes on her. Suddenly the room felt very warm. "I know you're living a fairy tale now, but don't think you can rest on your new family's name around here," he teased with a wag of his finger. Izzie didn't crack a smile. "Everyone has to pull his or her own weight. Even the Monroes."

While Mr. Preston droned on about what they would be learning that year, Izzie stared at the newspaper on his desk. She couldn't stop obsessing about that article. An article about her! When he finally asked everyone to get up and gather lab supplies, she made a break for it, swiping the newspaper and hiding it in her notebook till she could read it back at her desk. But when she did, she felt nauseated. Everything — *everything* — down to practically her Social Security Number was in there, from her mother's death to her grandmother's deteriorating health and poverty to how the community had been practically raising Izzie till the saintly Monroes stepped in.

"Cute photo," said a guy carrying a microscope and some slides past her. Izzie tried to hide the newspaper, but then she realized the guy was just making conversation. He might have even been flirting. "I love a girl in a one-piece, but the picture they showed on the *Today* show was hotter."

"The *Today* show?" Izzie quickly returned the newspaper to Mr. Preston's desk and went back to her seat.

The guy seemed to think for a moment. "Or maybe it was *Good Morning America*? I don't know." He leaned on her desk and smiled. "You were on everything this weekend."

So this was why everyone was acting so weird around her. She wasn't just Mira and Hayden Monroe's cousin. She was *that* cousin. The poor one from Harborside. While Izzie had been in Atlanta with her aunt, everyone in EC had been reading about her princess makeover. How could this have happened without anyone telling her? Her uncle was even quoted in this article, which meant he'd probably done TV interviews, too. Did people at EP really care that much about zip codes? She glanced out of the corner of her eye at Blondie. She was whispering heatedly with another girl over a Bunsen burner. When they caught Izzie staring, they stopped and gave a little wave. Yep. Apparently the students at EP did care about geography.

She forced herself to get a microscope even though all she wanted to do was go home. To her *real* home, her old school, her old life. Izzie knew starting a new school was going to be tough, but not like this. She and Lambie (yes, she still had a stuffed animal) had stayed up last night staring at the Pepto-Bismol pink chandelier on her ceiling. She didn't want to have to make new friends, or figure out how to find the gym—excuse me, the Bill Monroe Sports Complex—or worry about where she was going to sit at lunch. She knew Mira would show her around and introduce her to people, but Izzie wasn't an idiot. Mira didn't want her there, either. It was almost as if Mira was scared of what having Izzie around meant. Didn't she realize Izzie was scared, too?

Science may have been her favorite subject, but thirty-five minutes later, Izzie had never been happier to leave a lab. She slipped out the building's side door, pulled out her new phone, and dialed.

Kylie screamed excitedly instead of saying hello. "It's you!"

"It's me!" She felt better just hearing Kylie's voice.

"*Fi-na-lly,*" Kylie drawled slowly. "I got your first text and freaked, and then your second with the new number and freaked some more because you haven't answered this number *at all.* Hot surfer boy has been trying to reach you, too."

Izzie felt her stomach drop. "Brayden?"

"Yeah, he came into Scoops three times asking if I'd heard from you yet. He said he texted you, too, but he must have had your old number. Seemed more concerned than just a friend. I'm just saying. You should call him."

Izzie couldn't help but grin. "I will." She cradled the phone between her chin and shoulder so she could dig out her school map and find her way to lunch. "I'm sorry I've been

MIA. Things got weird, and then even weirder, and then my aunt took me shopping in Atlanta for the weekend...."

"That last part isn't weird. It's cool!" Kylie said, and the nice thing was Izzie knew she'd meant it. "How is the fabulous life treating you, anyway? You're like a celebrity now! Barbara Walters knows your name, Iz! My mom counted this morning — Babs said it three times!" Izzie laughed. "Everyone is talking about you, though." Her voice petered out a little. "The Harborside comments the papers make really blow."

Izzie winced. "I've only seen one article. Is it terrible?"

"Yeah. And it's everywhere."

"Well, while Babs name-dropping me is cool, I wish there never was an article or a TV mention in the first place." She quickly filled her friend in on what had been going on. "I'm so popular in these parts that I'm basically hiding by the side of a building to avoid lunch."

"Ooh, I bet they serve something better than nachos there," Kylie said. "Go! Eat! And don't let those prissy girls boss you around. You could body slam one with your right arm tied behind your back."

Izzie laughed. Her stomach was growling. "Not on an empty stomach. Call you later?"

"You better!" Kylie said.

Izzie felt more upbeat when she hung up, even if she still couldn't figure out the map.

"Where are you headed?" A girl with long, dark brown hair stopped and stared at her. She had deep-set oval eyes and her hair was pulled back in a plaid headband that looked a lot like the one Mira had on that morning. "Hey! You're Isabelle, right? We have bio together. Word of advice: Never sit that close to Preston — he's a spitter."

"Too late. I know," Izzie said. "But thanks." They smiled at each other. Okay, so the second sentence was usually the one that sent people running in the other direction. Time to test the theory. "Any chance you have a GPS handy to help me find my way to the cafeteria?"

The girl chuckled and quickly explained a direct route. "I have to meet with my adviser; otherwise I'd take you there myself."

"Vi! You coming?" A blond yelled to her from the steps of the social sciences building. She had quite the lungs to be heard this far away. "I don't want a late slip on my first day back!"

"Yes, Nicole, I'm coming!" the girl yelled back. She looked at Izzie and smiled. "I'm Violet, by the way. Maybe I'll see you at swim tryouts next week. Enjoy lunch. The mac and cheese is killer."

Violet is a swimmer, too! Maybe things at EP were starting to look up, Izzie thought.

Or maybe not.

The Jack Eunice Cafeteria looked nothing like a cafeteria

and everything like the Great Hall in the Harry Potter movies. Sadly, it seemed nowhere near as fun. Jack Eunice, whoever he was, definitely had put money into the place. Classical music played while students ate shrimp scampi, salads from a chopped-salad bar, and lobster mac and cheese. Izzie was surprised anyone could see what they were eating in the dimly lit room. Why did Hayden have to have a different lunch period? Why? Izzie held her tray of pizza, chips, and Snapple close to her chest and prayed she'd spot someone who looked friendly. She did not want to eat alone. That just looked pathetic. *Second option: Ditch the tray and take the pizza to go,* she thought. She made her way to the French doors on the right side of the room. That's when she heard Mira's sugar-coated laugh.

Izzie glanced at Mira's table before she could stop herself. Mira actually wasn't the one laughing. She was too busy kissing a very tan, tall guy with floppy blond hair. He, in turn, was half kissing Mira and half looking to see who was watching them. Savannah was the once cackling. She saw Izzie and stopped cold, which made Mira look over, too.

"Izzie!" Mira couldn't hide her surprise. Her face was flush and Izzie didn't know if it was because she'd been caught sucking face or because she was embarrassed to see her. "Hey. I looked for you, but — don't you have lunch sixth period?"

"Fifth," Izzie said, stating the obvious since she was, in fact, there during fifth period.

"Oh, okay," Mira said awkwardly. "Let me introduce you to some people. You met Lea, Lauren, and Savannah this morning, but this is my boyfriend, Taylor."

"Hey," he said smoothly, extending a large hand. He pulled it back and motioned to her tray. "I guess you can't shake, huh?"

"Not unless I grow another arm," Izzie joked. She shifted slightly to balance her heavy tray. She leaned it on the edge of the table and Lea looked at Savannah nervously.

"Usually our table is full, but if you want to sit with us *just* for today, you can," Savannah said, extending an olive branch. "We were leaving soon anyway."

Well, that sounded inviting. "Thanks. I'm going to eat outside." Izzie lifted the tray.

Savannah's eyes widened. "Perfect! It's gorgeous out there." Everyone at the table mumbled their agreement.

"I can't believe you grew up in Harborside!" Taylor jumped in, ignoring the awkwardness. "What was it like? Did you have bars on your windows and stuff?" Mira shot him a dirty look. "What? The article in the *EC Tribune* said she grew up in the worst part of town." Izzie winced. She wondered what else some of these articles said. Half of her wanted to run and find a copy of the *Tribune*. The other half wanted to burn every edition of the *Gazette* and *Tribune* out there.

Taylor stared at her expectantly. The guy was so pretty he

looked like he had been un-twist-tied from a Barbie box. Unlike the girls, though, he wasn't trying to be condescending. He just seemed clueless. "My school was definitely different from Emerald Prep," Izzie said, staring at a fifty-two-inch flat-screen TV on the wall that had rolling announcements and a live feed of cross-country practice. "But there was no lockdown or armed guards. It wasn't juvie hall."

"Yeah, but you and your friends probably know ways to get beer, though, right?" Taylor said eagerly. "You must have a fake ID."

"Taylor, God! Leave the girl alone," Savannah reprimanded him, and looked at Izzie. "Sorry. Guys can be so nosy."

Izzie shifted the tray again. "I don't drink, so I never had to worry about a fake ID."

"You don't know what you're missing," Taylor said with a laugh, and Lauren snorted.

Lea was staring at the contents of Izzie's tray. "Are you seriously going to eat that pizza? That stuff has, like, over a thousand calories a slice!"

"She probably burns it off swimming," Savannah said. Her own tray had a small Fage yogurt and a water. "Mira said you placed well on your last team. Good for you!" she said condescendingly. "You must be so thankful your community center had a pool." Izzie's fingers clenched around her tray. "I'll see you at EP tryouts. I'm going to be captain this year."

"Really?" Lauren asked excitedly. "When did they tell you?"

"They haven't officially," Savannah said, and took a swig of her water. "We don't have tryouts till next week, but it's pretty much a done deal." She stared smugly at Izzie. "I'm going to be the one to beat in the water and out this year."

"I wouldn't be so sure of that," Izzie said casually, unable to help herself. "You haven't gone up against me yet." Taylor nearly spit his soda out of his nose. Mira looked mortified, but Savannah just smiled.

Going toe-to-toe with Savannah was exhausting. Izzie felt both an adrenaline rush and a meltdown coming on. "I should go." She grabbed her tray and quickly rushed out of the cafeteria, but she wasn't watching where she was going and plowed right into someone, knocking his tray out of his hands. A sandwich went flying, Baked Lay's hit her in the head, and her Snapple shattered on the floor along with the other person's, too. Both of them landed on the floor. "I'm so sorry," Izzie said as she started grabbing her pizza's remains. She looked up to apologize some more and froze. "Brayden?"

"Iz?" Brayden looked like a statue holding a fork in midair. His woven rope pirate necklace and ball cap had been replaced with a white collared shirt and a tie that now had pizza sauce all over it. Izzie was so happy to see him she had to fight the urge to throw her arms around his neck. Maybe she'd even say she missed him, because she had. A lot.

"You go here? I mean, of course you go here!" she said, finding her voice again. "I can't believe it's you!" She smiled for the first time in days. "I just talked to Kylie and she told me you were looking for me. I got this new phone and I couldn't figure out how to check messages and…"

His blue-green eyes were a mixture of emotions flying at her like those pesky seagulls that always tried to steal her lunch. "I…" he stammered. "Where have you—what are you—"

"Brayden? Sweetie? What are you doing on the floor?"

Izzie heard Savannah's voice and turned around slowly, her butt squishy from the iced tea all over the floor. Mira's best friend was standing in front of them with her arms crossed, looking less than thrilled to see the two of them tangled together in a heap. Lea, Lauren, Mira, and Taylor were looking on along with the rest of the cafeteria, but the only thing Izzie had heard was *sweetie*.

Were Brayden and Savannah a couple?

"It's okay, Savannah," Brayden said, throwing both of their food onto one tray and picking everything up. "I wasn't looking where I was going and I plowed into her. Are you okay?" he asked Izzie. He stood up and offered Izzie his hand.

She didn't take it. "I'm fine," Izzie said, getting up and dusting off her skirt. Her shirt was stained red thanks to the pizza, and she had a small cut on her hand from a glass shard.

"Did you cut yourself?" Savannah draped herself over Brayden, but his eyes were still on Izzie. "B, you have to watch where you're going. You could have killed Mira's cousin."

His eyes widened. "You're Mira's cousin?"

"Small world, huh?" Izzie said. She couldn't stomach watching Savannah hang on him. They were definitely a couple.

"Iz," Brayden said, peeling himself off his girlfriend, "you're bleeding. Maybe you should have your hand looked at."

"I'm fine, Brayden," Izzie said tightly. She felt like the sound was being sucked out of the room. Suddenly she was angry with him. They had spent almost the entire summer together. How could Brayden not mention he had a girlfriend? Or have told her where he was from? Maybe they didn't know each other as well as she'd thought.

"Iz?" Savannah repeated Brayden's nickname for her curiously, her eyes dark. "Do you two know each other?"

Brayden looked at Izzie, and the pain in his eyes was way too obvious. "I...we..."

Izzie quickly cut off his stammering. "No," she said flatly, trying not to sound as hurt as she felt. "We don't know each other at all."

Then Izzie turned and rushed out of the cafeteria before anyone could see the tear roll down her cheek.

Eight

"What happened to you?" Hayden dropped his backpack and plopped onto the leather chair next to Izzie in the den.

Some mindless Fire and Ice show was on and Izzie hadn't had the energy to find the remote and shut it off. She thought watching *The Cliffs* spin-off with Marleyna and Brooke would lighten her mood, but instead it made her feel worse. Marleyna and Brooke reminded her of Savannah, and when she thought of Savannah, she thought about Brayden. She didn't want to think of Brayden ever again.

"Izzie? You in there?" Hayden waved a hand in front of her face. "I thought I was supposed to give you a ride home after third period. I tried your phone three times."

"Sorry." Emerald Prep was the first school Izzie had ever heard of that had parent-teacher conferences the first week of school. It was only her fourth day at EP and yet as she sat on the couch, her aunt was there giving Izzie's teachers the lowdown on her. Izzie wasn't sure if her aunt knew enough about her to talk about what kind of student she was, but she was grateful for the conference all the same. Getting out at eleven fifteen meant she got to skip lunch, which meant avoiding Brayden and the battle to find someone to eat with.

Hayden pulled off his dress shoes and propped his feet on the ottoman. "How'd you get home?"

"I walked," Izzie said as if it were obvious.

Hayden's feet fell off the ottoman with a thud. "It's over two miles."

She shrugged. "The boardwalk is that long, and we walk that back and forth all the time."

Hayden laughed. "You are nothing like the girls in Emerald Cove, you know that? Most would rather get a ride half a block than risk chipping their pedicures."

"Ah, so that's why they want nothing to do with me." The words slipped out before Izzie knew what she was saying. Hayden was watching her and she quickly looked away. She hated sounding so pathetic.

"Hey," he said, touching her knee. "What's up?"

"Nothing." Izzie tried to ignore him by staring at the shampoo commercial on TV. Why did girls on commercials always act like washing their hair was so exciting?

"Liar." Hayden grabbed the remote from the couch and shut off the TV. "I know we barely know each other, but you can talk to me, you know."

Izzie didn't know Hayden that well, but if there was anyone in the house she felt at ease with, it was him. Who else was she going to tell? Kylie didn't get it. She thought taking a swing at a few of the future Miss North Carolinas would solve everything. Grams hadn't been well enough to take a call from her, and her aunt just wanted to make sure Izzie had enough jewelry to accessorize her uniform. Izzie had to trust Hayden because if she didn't unload on someone, she would be crushed under the weight of it all. She didn't have swimming or lifeguarding at the moment, and that had always been her stress release.

She sighed. "Are you sure you want to hear this?"

"Why else would I ask?" Hayden grinned. "Talk!"

"Okay." She pulled a pillow to her chest. "I know I'm at a new school, and I'm not going to win prom queen overnight," she deadpanned. "But I feel like a social leper."

"Seriously?" Hayden looked puzzled. "Because Mira said —"

"People talk to me," Izzie cut him off. She knew she was being confusing, but she was confused, too. She didn't mention Mira's behavior. She had a feeling they wouldn't be the best of friends, but Mira's attitude still stung. "Everyone's almost too sweet when they meet me. But then the minute I try to make actual conversation with them, they brush me off, like they don't want to be caught dead at the same lab table." Her voice sounded pained and she hated that.

"I don't—why would they do that?" Hayden seemed as confused as she was. "My friends all thought you were cool." He winked. "I guess us juniors are just more mature." Then his face clouded over. "Did Mira's friends give you a hard time? Because some of those girls I avoid like the plague."

She felt like she was treading on shaky ground. EP was Hayden's school. Mira was his sister. Should she really be saying these things? "Maybe they're acting this way because of all that stuff written about me in the papers," Izzie said, not looking him in the eye. "I think the fact that I'm from Harborside freaks some of them out."

"That's insane." Hayden sounded annoyed. He leaned back in his chair with a thud. "Did any of them actually come out and say that?"

Hayden was a good guy, which made what she was going to say next that much harder.

"No," Izzie admitted. "It's just a feeling I get. Maybe some of them think I don't deserve to be here." She shrugged. "I can't say I blame them. I did—as the papers say—become an overnight princess." She gave him a look. "But it's not like I asked for any of this. Two weeks ago, I'd never even heard of Emerald Cove. I didn't even know I was coming here. But I'm here, and I'm giving this my best shot. I know Grams would want that, but now…" She felt hot tears spring to her eyes. "Hayden, they know everything about me. My mom's death, how Grams couldn't pay our bills, what my house looked like," she whispered. "Some of these papers even interviewed my old neighbors. It's like I never had a chance."

"Izzie, I'm so sorry," Hayden said, shaking his head. "I didn't think people here would be like that. My friends aren't that way, I swear, but Mira's grade thinks they rule the world already. Or at least Emerald Cove." His face twisted angrily. "When I see Mira, I'm going to—"

"No," Izzie said sharply. "I can handle this. I've never been the kind of girl who just lies down and dies." Her voice regained some of its strength. "I just wanted you to know why I may seem a bit mopey." She had overheard Mira using that word to describe her the night before. "I'll figure things out," she said. "The TV and newspaper stuff just threw me."

"You have to know, Mom wanted to kill Dad over the news coverage and Lucas—I thought she was going to hang Lucas upside down by his Gucci loafers," Hayden said. "She practically strong-armed all of us into not telling you what was going on. That's why she fled with you to Atlanta. She thought you wouldn't find out. Pretty stupid of us, huh?"

"No." Izzie smiled to herself. "It's actually nice." She was touched to think her aunt was trying to protect her. How could she be mad at her about that?

"Dad's a good guy, too. He's just easily swayed by Lucas,"

Hayden said. "That guy has never met a press opportunity he didn't like. But he should have run it by you. They were wrong, just like Mira's friends are. Don't let Mira, Savannah, or their minions get to you." Izzie looked down at the raw silk pillow still in her arms. "You can hang with my friends anytime. We're family. We've got to stick together."

"I don't really feel like family." She was being honest.

"Yeah, well, sometimes I don't, either," Hayden said, making Izzie curious. "Or at least, I have my moments. Dad once told the world my life story at a press conference. He told everyone how he adopted me." Her eyes widened. He picked up his backpack and pointed to the monogram: *HDM*. "Bill is not my real dad. This *D* stands for *Denton*. That was my dad's last name. He was a Marine who died in the line of duty when I was a baby. Mom and Bill started dating afterward and pretty much got married right away. Lucas made Dad use the story in a speech last year." He dropped the backpack on the floor. "Everyone at school was talking about me, too."

"That's so unfair!" It made her angry to think of anyone giving Hayden a tough time.

"I was too young to remember my dad." Hayden stared at the empty fireplace. "But I was more angry that Lucas exploited my story like that." She nodded. "Eventually I got over it. People stopped talking. I never wasted energy on the people who claimed I wasn't a real Monroe. I know who I

117

am. I've got my father's picture in my room, but Bill's the only dad I've ever known," he explained. "Bill adopted me, so I'm officially a Monroe, but I don't always think like one. I still see my dad's family, and they definitely don't have money like this." He looked around the den, which was probably the same size as Izzie's entire first floor at Grams's. "I know how weird it can be living in two different worlds."

"My mom died when I was almost ten," Izzie said suddenly. Her voice sounded foreign to her. "Car accident."

"That's rough," Hayden said. "I'm sorry. You never get used to it, do you?"

"No," Izzie agreed. It turned out she and Hayden had more in common than she'd realized. He might not remember his dad, but she remembered her mom and thought about her a lot. It was hard not to imagine how different her life would have been if her mom were still alive.

"It won't always be this rough," Hayden promised her. "Give it a few weeks. There are a lot of cool people at EP. There has to be at least one person you've met who you like."

Brayden's face flashed in her mind. Why was he there? He hadn't even admitted to knowing her. Before she could think about that question further, she heard the front door open.

The *click-clack* of heels was heard from the foyer. "Hello? Hayden? Isabelle?"

"Thanks." Izzie finally released the pillow she had been squeezing. She fluffed it up in its rightful corner.

"Anytime," he said, standing and stretching. "Watch. In a month, you're going to love it."

"Love what?" her aunt asked, entering the kitchen with two shopping bags. Her blond hair was pulled into a low ponytail, and she was wearing a short-sleeve white sweater and khaki capris. Connor wheeled in a *Star Wars* backpack behind her and was followed closely by Mira, who avoided making eye contact. Things had been sort of awkward between them since their cafeteria encounter. Mira was polite to Izzie at school, but at home Mira hadn't brought up what had happened, and neither had Izzie. If anything, Mira was being overly pleasant at home, especially when they talked about mundane things like toothpaste ("Do you want to use the Colgate Total Whitening or the Crest 3D White? It makes your teeth *so* white!").

Hayden winked at Izzie. "We were talking about the regatta this weekend."

"I forgot to tell you about that, Isabelle," her aunt gasped.

"The preparty is the kickoff of the fall season," Hayden told Izzie. "Great place to be seen, as Mira would say."

Mira gave him a look. "Everyone from school will be there," she said, falling into EC tour-guide mode again. "They have it at the boathouse, and Mom's Emerald Cove Cares Club matches the money raised dollar for dollar. What's this year's cause, Mom?" She took an apple from the fruit basket.

"Cardinals," Aunt Maureen said without a hint of irony. "It is our job to ensure they are well-protected. They are the EC mascot and the North Carolina state bird."

Izzie bit her lip. The last she checked, the cardinal wasn't an endangered species.

Izzie's aunt began unloading containers of fruit and bottles of seltzer. "I'm so sorry I didn't remember to tell you earlier, Isabelle. We'll need to go shopping again." She paused, seltzer in midair. "Forgive me, sweetie, but I went through your closet the other day, and there is not a single dress in there."

Izzie wasn't sure she could handle more shopping, but her aunt seemed to find it therapeutic. They'd spent three hours in Bed Bath & Beyond finding Izzie the perfect comforter to complement her personality.

"You're toast," Hayden whispered, and flipped on the TV. "Run while you can."

"Do I have to wear a dress?" Izzie asked tentatively. "Can't I wear those pants you bought me?"

"Pants?" Her aunt said the word like it was tainted. "You can't wear pants to a cocktail party." She set the bag of apples she was holding firmly on the table. "That's it. Clear your afternoon."

"I didn't actually have anything planned," Izzie said. Until swim tryouts next week, she had nothing going on. She hadn't brought up the club lifeguarding job again. It sounded dull.

Her aunt looked relieved. "Good. We're going shopping!"

"We don't have to," Izzie insisted. This was why she needed to find that girl Violet again and hang out with her — to avoid doing stuff like this. "You got me so much already. The computer and the phone…"

"You needed them!" she insisted. "Just like you need more clothes. Isabelle, you don't have anything appropriate to wear to cotillion practices."

"Cotillion?" Izzie looked at Hayden. He made a strangling motion.

"But I'm getting ahead of myself," Aunt Maureen said, her blond ponytail dancing as she shook her head. "That's not till late fall. For now, we need some Vera Wang and maybe some cashmere." She was talking a foreign language. "Mirabelle, want to come help me whip her wardrobe into shape?"

"I'd love to, but I'm meeting Savannah," Mira said between bites of apple.

"You can meet her anytime," Izzie's aunt insisted. "Isabelle needs us." She sounded so passionate that Izzie would have thought she was talking about her cardinal mission, not gown shopping.

"I want to help," Mira said smiling tightly at Izzie. "But Savannah —"

"— will understand." Izzie's aunt headed toward the front door. "Let's go, girls. Christoff's is waiting."

Mira and Izzie looked at each other. Izzie really thought they did have one thing in common: Neither of them wanted to hang out together.

"Aunt Maureen, it's fine! Really!" Izzie tried one last time. "I'm not really a dress kind of a girl."

She saw the look of horror on her aunt's face and wished she could take the comment back. It was as if Izzie had just told her she was a Communist.

Then her aunt's face relaxed. Her green eyes glowed as she opened the front door and grabbed her keys. "Honey, that's just because you haven't shopped with the right person yet."

Nine

"We'll start with Christoff's, and if they have nothing special, we can go to Saks. Worst-case scenario, we head to Nordstrom tomorrow. If you need something altered, we really need to find it today so I have time to call in a favor with my tailor." Her mom sounded like she was planning a battle as she explained the strategies of dress shopping to Izzie from the front seat of their Range Rover.

Mira had her own battle brewing. Savannah hadn't texted her back about Mira's bailing again on her, and it was making her nervous. The last thing she wanted was to face Savannah's wrath. She had been in a particularly foul mood about Brayden that week. She said she felt like he was acting weird—not that she wanted anyone to know that. Mira closed her eyes just as her phone started to vibrate.

TAYLOR'S CELL: R U coming 2 practice today? Miss U!!!

Mira groaned. *Taylor!* She had forgotten about his practice. She hadn't made it to one yet, but she couldn't tell him why. She hadn't told *anyone*, but she'd decided to take an art class after all. Actually, two classes, if she could make the scheduling work — painting and sculpting! (She had met with her guidance counselor and switched out of public speaking, and painting was during study hall, so hopefully that would work out, too.) Maybe she had an artist's eye, like Mr. Capozo had said, but she wouldn't know if she didn't take the time to find out.

She just had to keep it a secret. Her friends would think she was a total dork if they knew she was hanging out with the art geeks. That's why she already had a plan: She was going to stash her art supplies in a cute bag at the bottom of her locker, and would wash meticulously to make sure she never left the art studio with dried paint on her hands like Kellen had. There was a part of her that hoped he'd be in one of her art classes, but she wouldn't know till she started next week.

MIRA'S CELL: Mom made me go shopping w/her & Izzie (don't tell S). Tomorrow, I swear.

"I don't think we'll have time to get everything today, but we can come back tomorrow after my Emerald Cove Cares

124

meeting and find you shoes, and—sweetie, how are your bras?" Mira's mom asked delicately. Her full lips formed a frown. "They don't look like they're doing their job."

Mira's phone buzzed again. *OK,* Taylor wrote back. *That's it. OK.* Was he mad? She texted him something mushy and tossed the phone in her bag. The Izzie situation was complicating everything. Didn't her mom realize she had her own friends to take care of?

"Bras are bras, right?" Mira heard Izzie say.

Her mother laughed. "Good heavens, no! We have to introduce you to Victoria's Secret. You'll need some supportive, strapless numbers for your new dresses."

"You're doing too much," Izzie insisted. "I'll be fine with one dress, and my bras are doing their job, I swear. And I already have black heels. I got a pair at Payless for a thing with my swim team."

Mira and her mom looked at each other in the rearview mirror. Mira actually felt bad for her mom. In her own way, she was trying to relate to Izzie. Her mother spoke two languages: politician's wife, which included her charity work, and professional shopper. Izzie spoke neither.

"Once you get to Christoff's and see how incredible the clothes are, you won't be able to say no," Mira piped up. "No one knows her Vera from her Stella better than my mom." Her mother smiled.

"I forgot to tell you, girls," Mira's mom said. "Lucas called earlier and told me your father—uncle," she added quickly, "will be able to make the regatta festivities tomorrow night, so he'll want to pull us aside for Isabelle's first photo op. He also wants us to appear at the race on Saturday."

"Mom," Mira groaned. "I have plans. I haven't seen my friends all week!" *Because of Izzie duty*, she wanted to add.

Her mom sighed. "Maybe I can get away with just taking Connor, but remember, Mirabelle, when your dad wins this candidacy, we are going to have to do a lot more public appearances. What about you, Isabelle? Big plans Saturday?"

"I was hoping I could see my grandmother," Izzie said.

"Oh, well, yes, I'm sure I could have a car arrange to take you there." Mira's mom sounded uncomfortable.

"Hayden offered to drive me," Izzie told her. "I wanted to stop by my house while we're out that way, pick up a few things, and show Hayden the boardwalk."

"How about we send someone to get the stuff for you?" Mira's mom suggested. "You can make me a list, okay?" Her chipper voice returned. "And we'll get a car for you so you can visit your grandmother. Hayden has to go to the race, since he works for your uncle."

"Okay." Mira heard the disappointment in Izzie's voice.

Her mom had never come out and said it, but Mira knew she was just as freaked out by the fact that Izzie was from Harborside as everyone else was. (She was just too much of a lady to admit it.) Izzie was still the topic du jour—as long as she wasn't in earshot—among Mira's friends. They wanted to know what Izzie was really like. Did she own a knife? Was she rough and rude? One even asked if Mira hid her Pandora bracelet at night. (Then she immediately took the comment back.) Mira knew they were being extreme, but this was how her friends were. They broke girls down into two categories: those who could afford Louis (Vuitton—no last name needed) and those who could not. Those whose parents had their names on building plaques and those who were on scholarship at EP. "If she thinks she's one of us now that she is becoming a Monroe, she's mistaken," Savannah had hissed when no one but their core group was around to hear it. In public, Mira's friends were nothing but sweet and welcoming to Izzie. But Mira knew what they were really thinking and she felt a twinge bad about how they'd never accept Izzie. Mira wasn't sure if she ever could, either. She wanted to try, but how could you relate to someone so completely different from yourself?

Ten minutes later, they had arrived at Christoff's and were on their way to the formal-wear department. Izzie looked nervous about fanning out to hunt for the perfect gown. Mira was glad she'd changed out of her uniform and into a black tank and a tiered taupe skirt. Both were easy to pull on and off. She knew they weren't *technically* shopping for her, but her mom would never say no if she found something incredible. There were so many dresses that had come out since Mira was there a few weeks ago that she began piling ones she liked in her arms before she remembered they were looking for Izzie. That's when she spotted a silk organza gown with a black sash and metal trim. If Izzie was willing to go funky, this could be to die for.

"Izzie, you have to see this!" Mira carried the dress as carefully as she would a baby. "Isn't it incredible? Look at the way the metal trim pulls the whole look together, and the raw silk flowers with the tiny pulls at the end. Isn't that incredible?" Mira couldn't help sounding excited. It was like a piece of art as far as she was concerned. She eyed her cousin hopefully. One sip of high fashion and Izzie would be hooked.

"That came in this week," said a Christoff's attendant, appearing out of nowhere. She smiled as she gave the group the classic once-over. Mira always joked you had to get dressed *before* you went to buy a dress at Christoff's. Obviously, her mom felt uncomfortable passing along that pearl of wisdom to Izzie, who was in jean cutoffs and a tank. "Isn't it divine?" said the saleswoman, touching the sash. "The bodice has boning, and the metallic fibers completely overlap, giving the skirt a full feel."

Izzie looked at the price tag. "Does that say seven hundred and ninety-eight dollars?"

"Yes. It's a Tadashi Shoji dress," the woman said by way of explanation. "It's imported."

"It's stunning is what it is," Mira's mom said, shifting her weight to hold all the dresses in her arms. Izzie still had none. "My niece just moved in with us, and we want her to shine at her first event. We're looking for something special. This dress could be it."

"Mrs. Monroe, right?" The saleswoman looked at Izzie. "Yes, I think I saw that story on TV." She extended her slender hand. "My name is Catherine. I'd be happy to help you today."

"Izzie, you have to try this dress on," Mira's mom insisted, making no mention of the TV comment. It was a sore subject with her. She didn't talk to Mira's dad for two days after *Good Morning America* aired its piece.

"No," Izzie shook her head, like she was being force-fed fashion. "It's a lot of money."

"Try it." Mira's mom nudged Izzie. "Mira's right. It would look perfect on you."

"I'm sure I have your size. You're a six, right?" Catherine asked.

"I guess." Izzie pressed her hands to her legs, leaving white marks on her knees. "Sometimes I can do a four, or I can wear an eight if I take it in," she added. The Harborside Army/Navy Store was limited on sizes and Izzie usually took what she could get.

Catherine looked a little flustered. "Let's start with a six, then."

"Thank you," Mira's mom said, and put her arm around Izzie. "Let's get you in a fitting room!" As they reached the dressing area, they heard a gasp.

"Maureen, is that you?" Vivian Ingram, Savannah's mom, was sitting on a round ottoman near one of the mirrors. She had one hand on her cell and the other holding her latte. Mira felt the color drain from her face. Savannah must be with her, and Mira hadn't said where she was going.

Mrs. Ingram stood and kissed Mira's mom on the cheek. "How *are* you? I just got back from Hilton Head last night, which is why I missed our meeting on Monday, but I heard all about your new houseguest!" She gave Mira's mom a look of pity. "How are you holding up, honey?"

"I want you to meet our niece, Isabelle," Mira's mom said, pulling Izzie toward her. "We're buying her a dress for the regatta cocktail party. It's her first event in Emerald Cove."

"Isabelle, it's a pleasure to meet you." Savannah's mom extended her hand as she gave her a once-over. "I'm Vivian Ingram, Savannah's mother. I've heard so much about you from my daughter." Mira knew what that meant. Mrs. Ingram shook Izzie's hand limply before turning her attention to Mira. "And you! Congratulations are in order, I hear. Savannah told me you two are cochairing the Butterflies this year. They need these two, don't they, Maureen?"

"Absolutely," Mira's mom agreed. "They run things so differently from when we were Social Butterflies. The same events over and over! The Butterflies have always been known for reinventing things...."

To Mira's horror, instead of waiting patiently for the conversation to end, Izzie started walking around. While Mrs. Ingram and her mom talked about the country club's proposal for a new playground and Main Street's new traffic pattern, Mira watched Izzie sort through a rack of gowns. She pulled out the same navy gown twice before putting it back on the rack. Then she wandered over to the long jewelry case they kept in the fitting room area. The best part about shopping at Christoff's was that the salespeople would bring over pricey shoes and jewelry to try on with your evening wear. But before Mira could stop her, Izzie pulled open the drawer herself and pulled out a long strand of pink pearls, holding them up in the bright fitting room light.

"Miss!" Catherine rushed over, and Mira's mom and Mrs. Ingram's conversation ground to a halt. "Excuse me, miss!" she said anxiously, but Izzie didn't know Catherine was talking to her till she gently took the pearls out of her hands. "You can't just open the jewelry cabinet on your own. These pearls are worth two thousand dollars!"

"Whoa, you should have a security tag on that!" Izzie said. No one laughed. "Sorry. I didn't realize that cabinet was off-limits."

"Where is my key?" the saleswoman asked, looking at the

glass cabinet before feeling her own suit pockets. "I thought this cabinet was locked."

Without meaning to, Mira noticed all eyes turned to Izzie, including her own.

The saleswoman's eyes focused on something near Izzie's right foot. She reached down and grabbed a silver key. "There it is! I wonder how *that* got there."

It was official. Mira was never going to be able to show her face at Christoff's again.

"Isabelle? Why don't you try on your dresses now." Mira's mom pushed her toward the fitting rooms. "Catherine? What room are they in again?"

Who opens jewelry cabinets without asking? Mira thought. She knew Izzie wasn't trying to steal the pearls, but Mrs. Ingram didn't know that. Her eyes were practically shooting lasers into the back of Izzie's head. By tomorrow morning, everyone at school would have heard this story. Mira was so mortified she didn't even want to try on dresses anymore.

"Maureen," Mira heard Mrs. Ingram start to say, "I can't believe—"

"How was the rest of your summer, Vivian?" Mira's mom bypassed the faux pas and slipped back into the old conversation comfortably. "I'm glad our charity season is starting up again, aren't you? I have so many thoughts for Emerald Cove Greeters."

"I heard Bill is taking a hard look at the state restoration project," Mrs. Ingram said, forgetting the pearls for the moment, too. "Holden can't wait to get that off the ground and..."

The fitting room door in front of Mira opened, and Savannah emerged, holding up the bottom of a slightly long gown. With her blond hair and tan skin, the two-toned cream-and-tan dress looked incredible on her. "Hi, girls," Savannah said pleasantly, even as she gave Izzie a sharp look. "Doing some shopping? Mira, why didn't you tell me you were hanging out with Izzie?"

Mira's face burned. "It was last minute. My mom wanted me to help Izzie find a dress for the regatta cocktail party."

"Your first designer dress!" Savannah said, her voice almost mocking. "So exciting!"

Izzie smiled thinly. "I'm going to go try these on."

"Have fun!" Savannah said as Izzie shut the fitting room door behind her. Savannah rolled her eyes at Mira. "I hope she knows to leave her underwear on when she tries on those dresses. Otherwise they'll have to burn the ones she doesn't buy." Mira clutched her dresses tighter. Sometimes Savannah could be downright cruel. Savannah linked arms with her. "I forgive you for ditching me now that you're here anyway. So, shopping guru, tell me: What do you think? Isn't this dress divine? Brayden is going to die when he sees me." Mira noticed half a dozen designer gowns in every color and style peeking out from the fitting room, waiting for their turn to shine on Savannah's slender frame.

Mira watched her give a little spin in front of a small mirror. "Vanna, it's gorgeous."

Savannah admired her own reflection. "Then it's settled. I'm taking it. The others, too. One of these might make the perfect sweet-sixteen dress."

"I thought you already had one of those," Mira reminded her. Actually, Savannah already had several.

"I'm not a hundred percent decided." She spun around again. "This could be a winner, and if it's not, who cares? It will like life in my closet. I can't let Daddy's credit card go to waste."

Mira's parents were cool about letting her get whatever she wanted, too, but she never took total advantage. After trying on several dresses herself, she decided to take the gray chiffon one that made her feel like she belonged on a red carpet. She could wear it to the cocktail party tomorrow night.

"What's the verdict, ladies?" Mira's mom strode toward her and Savannah with Mrs. Ingram. "Vivian and I were thinking we could have dinner together before heading home."

Savannah clutched her nonexistent stomach. "Nothing for me. I need to fit into this dress tomorrow night."

"I'm sure they have salad," Mrs. Ingram said. "Do you want to change so we can go?"

"Where's Isabelle?" Mira's mom asked. "She's been so quiet I forgot she was here."

"I didn't," Savannah casually whispered to Mira.

"I didn't see her leave," Mira said, feeling bad for completely abandoning her cousin. She had been so immersed in her and Savannah's dresses that she hadn't checked on her once.

"Isabelle?" Mira's mom tried again.

A door at the end of the row creaked open, and Izzie emerged in the floor-length navy dress Mira had seen her admiring earlier. The silk strapless gown fit her perfectly, falling to the floor in a cascade of layers. Mira felt her jaw go slack. Who knew Izzie had those curves? She was a knockout.

"Isabelle, you look stunning," Mira's mom said, gaping. "Doesn't she look stunning?"

Mrs. Ingram's and Savannah's lips were pursed shut, but Savannah couldn't take her eyes off her.

"You have to wear that dress to the party," Mira said without thinking, and Savannah gave her a sharp look.

Izzie glanced in the mirror. "You really think so?" Mira could see the corners of her mouth turn upward. It was more than okay, even if she wouldn't admit it. "It's on sale for a hundred and fifty dollars. Is that okay?" she asked Mira's mom as if it was out of the question. "It has a small lipstick stain, so maybe they'll take more off."

"It has a stain?" Savannah repeated, looking from Izzie back to Mira. "Make them bring you a new gown!"

"It's on clearance. There aren't any more," Catherine said, walking up behind them. Savannah resisted the urge to smirk. "And we don't usually do discounts."

"I'm sure we can, uh, talk to the manager about getting a discount if this is the last dress. Right, Catherine?" Mira's mom said slowly. Discounts were something new to her. "It really suits you, but you're going to need more than one dress this season. Are you sure you don't want the Tadashi Shoji as well?"

Izzie shot both girls a look. "I don't need a thousand-dollar dress. I love this one, and if I need more, I'm sure we can find others below the two-hundred-dollar mark. It seems insane to spend more than that on one dress."

"That's very sensible, Isabelle," Mira's mom agreed, as if it were a foreign concept. She looked proudly at her niece.

"Excellent bargain hunter you have here, Maureen," Mrs. Ingram said.

Mira's mom nodded. "You girls change, and we'll meet you by the registers."

Mira's face flamed as she stared at her own dress. It cost over a thousand dollars. Savannah's loot was three times that. That comment was definitely meant for them. She looked at Savannah. Mira thought she was going to start hurling hangers at Izzie like swords.

Izzie didn't say anything, but Mira caught the small smile creep onto her face before the door shut. Savannah saw it, too.

Mira turned to gauge Savannah's reaction. Her best friend hated nothing more than being burned—especially in public. "Vanna, I..."

"Forget it. It's not your fault." Savannah put her arm around Mira and walked her back to her fitting room. "It's *hers*. That little street urchin," she whispered, "needs to be shown her place."

Ten

Izzie wondered if someone else's reflection was staring back at her. How else could she explain the girl in the mirror wearing the expensive fairy-tale gown?

Isabelle Scott did not own eight-hundred-dollar dresses. She didn't even own eight-hundred-dollar dresses marked down to a hundred and twenty-five dollars and fifty cents thanks to a lipstick stain. She loved this dress and couldn't believe her aunt expected her to only wear it once. (Apparently, wearing the same dress twice in a season was frowned upon in EC.)

How could she wear a dress like this only one time? Look how it swayed when she moved! She'd sleep in this dress if she could. Izzie never considered herself a dress kind of girl — and certainly not a heels girl — but now that she had both on, she had to admit her aunt was right: Good clothes made a person feel different. She could almost sense her posture improving and her confidence returning. Emerald Cove was nothing like Harborside, but maybe in a dress that made a person feel like Cinderella, she could make things work.

But she couldn't forget what had happened to Cinderella when the clock struck midnight. The gown may have made her look like a born and bred Emerald Cove kid, but inside, she still felt twisted like a pretzel. One day she felt like she was getting the hang of things, and the next she wanted to take the first bus back to Harborside. At least once a day she asked herself the same question. *What am I doing here?* she wondered again as she looked around her new room.

Her aunt had left catalogs on her bed earlier in the week with a note: *We want you to make your room your own! Just circle whatever you like!* She'd never had a room makeover before. Her furniture at Grams's was her mom's when she was a kid and it had definitely seen better days. But just when she started getting excited, that nagging guilt would return, especially when she flipped through the catalog and saw the prices. Seventy dollars for a lamp *base?* Five hundred dollars for an area rug? She didn't have the heart to circle a thing. How could she ask her aunt and uncle to drop that kind of money on her when they'd done so much already? In one week, she had gotten a computer, a new phone, a bedroom set, and a full wardrobe. She'd never spent this much on clothes. *Ever.*

Her aunt was too smart for her. She saw the folded page in the catalog for the black-and-white floral room that Izzie secretly loved, and two days later it was delivered. Izzie had a new bed with built-in bookshelves, a desk, a black-and-white floral comforter, curtains, and a black-and-white polka-dot area rug. *I hired a painter to paint your room next Thursday to match the one in the catalog!* said a note on her bed. It all still felt like a dream. She had such mixed emotions, though, and she missed Grams so much. She missed her mom, too. Seeing the new bed only reminded her more of the old one. The paint had peeled so badly her mom used to tell her it was because her bed was made from a washed-up pirate ship. For years Izzie had thought she might find treasure buried inside.

"Isabelle?" Her aunt knocked on the door, even though it was slightly ajar. She was wearing an incredible cream silk dress and four-inch pointy heels. Her hair was swept into a bun and her makeup looked professionally done. In her hands, she held two small velvet boxes. "Can I come in?"

"Of course," Izzie said.

"So you like your room?" her aunt asked hopefully.

"I love it," Izzie admitted, looking around again. "Thank you so much."

"You don't have to thank me, sweetie. This room is you."

Aunt Maureen looked at her appraisingly. "And so is that dress. I'm glad you picked that one. So reasonably priced, too, and the dry cleaner did wonders with that lipstick stain. You can't even tell there was one!" She thumbed the fabric.

Her aunt tried so hard, Izzie thought. "It worked like a charm at the Harborside Army/Navy Store."

Her aunt's eyes lit up. "Do you know that place? My Emerald Cove Cares group is partnering with them for a fund-raiser for their community center. They have practically nothing in the way of an arts program, so we're trying to get one off the ground. The whole place is falling apart. They've been holding dance classes with a boom box! Can you imagine?" She shook her head, her chandelier diamond earrings swaying. "We're going to do a fashion show next month, something mother-daughter again, maybe to raise funds for a sound system and art classes. I was hoping to get a floral arrangement class there, too. Knowing how to pair a peony with a sunflower is a definite skill," she said, and Izzie bit her lip.

"You might be wasting your money on that one," Izzie said delicately. "A gymnastics program, on the other hand, would be awesome. We've wanted one forever, but there's no money to buy equipment." She felt herself growing excited at the thought of the community center getting a room makeover of sorts, too. "Art classes are big. If you could get someone to do a class on tagging in murals so people don't do that on fence posts, that would be huge. The boom box works fine for dance class, but what the community center really needs is more teachers. If they had a hip-hop class, do you know how many kids would sign up? There are a ton of kids who want to be there. There just aren't enough programs to go around."

Her aunt looked pale as she slid her tennis bracelet back and forth on her wrist. "I...you...I didn't know that was your community center."

"Only one around. It's not really falling down," Izzie added. "It could use a face-lift, but, hey, at least it's still open. The state keeps trying to shut it down due to lack of funding. If it wasn't for that place, I certainly wouldn't have learned how to swim." That gave her an idea. "If you're doing a fundraiser, I could help. If you want."

Her aunt still looked rattled, but she managed a small smile. "I'd like that. You almost made me forget why I came in here. These are for you." She patted the boxes on her lap. "I thought your dress might need some accessories, and this Swarovski crystal cuff bracelet and necklace might do the trick. I also brought some earrings." She frowned. "Do you have pierced ears?" Izzie held back her hair and revealed double holes and one near the top of her earlobe. "Oh, I only bought one pair, but..." She took Izzie's wavy hair in her hands and pulled it off her face. "They'll work. How do you feel about pulling your hair off your face?"

A half hour later, Izzie felt like a pincushion. By the time her aunt was done with her hair and makeup, even her own reflection didn't recognize her. Izzie felt herself grow hopeful. *Tonight is going to be different,* she thought. If people at the party hadn't been told she was Bill Monroe's orphaned niece, they'd never know she didn't belong there.

Her aunt stood behind her and smiled approvingly. "I think you're ready for your first Emerald Cove party."

Eleven

As the town car inched toward the boathouse valet, Mira got goose bumps. She was a sucker for parties and the first one of the season was always a good time. The boathouse was the perfect venue. It overlooked the bay, which meant there was a chance of catching a perfect sunset, and her mom's charity group had made sure every detail not under Mother Nature's control was set to wow. Catering trucks had been on-site for days, floral arrangements sprouted out of every planter, the valet was jammed with attendants, and there was an orchestra and a DJ. Mira watched as beautifully dressed couples and classmates emerged from town cars ahead of hers (no one drove themselves to these things).

Tonight had all the makings of a perfect evening, and it hadn't even started yet. She didn't have to babysit Connor because he was too young to attend, her mom and dad would be unofficially campaigning, and Hayden was working with her dad. All she had to do was figure out what to do with Izzie. She glanced at her cousin across the seat. Izzie looked like she wanted to throw up, but she had total wow factor going for her in that dress. Mira had to primp for hours to look this good. She'd gone for a spray tan before slipping into the gray cocktail dress and strappy gladiator heels. Her hair had been pinched in curlers for hours to look this bouncy.

"I can't wait to get in there," Mira said as their car inched closer. She checked her phone for the tenth time looking for a text from Taylor or Savannah. They always texted each other when they arrived so they could go in together. So far her phone was silent. "I heard they got DJ Backslide and he's booked a year in advance! I wonder how they pulled that off."

"Dad." Hayden looked back from the front passenger seat. He had on a navy suit and his blond hair was slicked back like he was in *The Great Gatsby*. "The organizers couldn't find anyone major, so Dad called in a favor. He knows Backslide's dad."

"I'm just thankful DJ what's-his-name is for you kids and we have an orchestra." Mira's mom checked her lipstick in a mirror. "The DJs are so loud. I can barely hear myself think."

"Wait. We're not going to the same party?" Izzie tugged

on one of her dangling crystal earrings. Her top two piercings had her usual sterling-silver studs in them.

"The EC party circuit strays from the norm," Hayden explained. "The parents here don't like to mingle with anyone under the age of twenty-one, so sometimes they have two bashes going at once. We have the DJ, and Mom and Dad have an orchestra and casino gambling."

"It's not that we don't want to mingle with you," their mom said hastily, mostly for Izzie's benefit. "We just know, from experience, that you kids enjoy a different atmosphere than we do."

"Keep telling yourself that, Mom." Hayden winked at Izzie.

"This kickoff event is very important to your father," their mom reminded them. She smoothed out the skirt of her dress again and said to Izzie, "He wants to keep his name out there as much as possible before the primaries, and he's been working overtime to make sure this preparty is a huge success. He's on the charity board of directors for the regatta."

"There's more than one party for a boat race?" Izzie looked more confused than ever.

"There are two," Mira counted. "Well, three, but no goes to the actual race."

"*You* don't go to the race," Hayden corrected her. "The rest of us like to see the event that we're having a party for in the first place."

"What is that supposed to mean?" Mira said indignantly.

"Are you okay, Isabelle?" Mira's mom asked, placing her hand on Izzie's.

Izzie nodded and stared out the car window.

Mira's mom looked concerned and shot Mira a look. "You're going to have a fabulous time. All of Mira's friends are going to be here. They'll make sure you have a lot of fun tonight."

Did her mom really expect her to babysit Izzie? She was looking forward to some alone time with Taylor. The few times she'd seen him this week were with the team. Tonight she wanted to slow-dance and hang out on the boathouse dock like they did at last year's party, which is where they had their first kiss.

When the car stopped at the valet stand and an attendant opened the passenger door, Mira emerged first. The driveway was mobbed with attendants wearing headsets and pointing people to the right party. The boathouse was directly ahead of her and she could see people already dancing inside through the floor-to-ceiling windows. To her right was her parents' party. Three white tents housed an orchestra and women in floor-length gowns noshing on appetizers.

"You're right on time, just how I like it." Mira heard her dad's voice, and turned in time for him to give her a kiss on the cheek. A photographer crouched low and took a picture as Lucas stood nearby. "Great dress, Pea." Her dad was wearing a gray suit and a red tie with tiny boats on it—the official tie of this year's regatta. "Have fun in there, okay? But not too much fun. We need to set an example."

Mira sighed. Why was she the only one he said these things to? "I know, Dad." She scanned the crowd for Taylor and Savannah.

"And keep an eye on Isabelle, okay?" he added with a whisper. "Your mother thinks she's gun-shy after all the press, but she seems okay to me, no?" Mira didn't answer him. "Either way, this is her first event with our family, and your mother and I want it to go well."

"It's going to be fine," Mira assured him. She wished Hayden was on Izzie duty. His friends didn't seem to care about Izzie's background, while it was obvious Mira's crowd did.

Izzie was the last one out of the car, and Mira's dad held out his hand to help her. "You look lovely, Isabelle," he said, his voice sort of hoarse.

"Thanks," she said shyly.

Lucas handed her father a clear box, which he gave to Izzie. "I got this for you to wear tonight." He opened it up, and Mira saw it was a pink rose corsage. Her dad hadn't bought her one of those since the sixth-grade dance, when she'd insisted he stop buying them. They were so tacky, but she watched Izzie's face light up. "It is your first official party in town and your first with us, and I thought you might like

148

some flowers. But you don't have to wear it if you don't want to," he added hastily. Mira wasn't used to hearing her dad sound so unsure of himself.

"I like it." Izzie delicately lifted the corsage out of the box and slid it on her wrist. Mira noticed the rose actually looked kind of cool, like a giant cuff. "Thanks."

"You're welcome." He patted her awkwardly on the shoulder. "You kids have fun," he added as Lucas nudged him along. "I'll text you when Lucas is ready for our family photo."

"I'm just going to walk them in first, Dad," Hayden said, linking arms with both girls.

"Why? Where are you sneaking off to afterward?" Izzie asked.

He frowned. "No one told you? I have to man the regatta info booth at the adults' party." Hayden smiled as a photographer took a picture of the three of them. Izzie winced. "Mira is going to stick to you like glue, aren't you, Mira?"

But Mira was only half listening. She had spotted Kellen a few yards away talking to her new art teacher and she couldn't stop staring at him. He looked really good in a tan suit and she couldn't help but notice how his blond hair swayed as he threw back his head and laughed at something the teacher said. Mira unwound her arm from Hayden's. "You can get Izzie settled, can't you, Hayden? I'll meet her inside!"

She didn't wait for an answer. She felt like a magnet being pulled toward Kellen. By the time she reached him, the teacher had disappeared. Kellen saw her and smiled. "Well, if it isn't my favorite art thief."

"What are you doing here? Preparing a heist of your own?" His face clouded slightly. "I'm kidding," she added. He was obviously the sensitive type. "I've been looking for you." She instantly regretted saying that, especially when he grinned coyly.

"Can't stop thinking of me, huh? I get that a lot."

Her face burned. "I meant in the art studio. I, uh, found some free time and I'm going to be starting painting and sculpting next week."

His eyebrows rose slightly. "Is that a fact? Maybe now your work won't be so sloppy." She gave him a nasty look. "So what periods do you have painting and sculpting?"

"Fourth and sixth," she said. Her phone vibrated in her bag, but she ignored it.

Kellen grinned. "Sounds like you can stop stalking me, then. That's when I have those, too."

"You don't say." Mira tried not to sound excited.

"Mr. Capozo is a tough grader," Kellan warned her. "I hope you're ready to face the fire."

"Oh, I'm ready," Mira challenged him. "Are you? Because I don't recall seeing you in the art studio this week at all."

He rolled his neck. "Sorry, I do warm-ups of another

kind. I like to study the masters — Allan Houser, Frederic Remington, Bufano."

"Bufano?" She was impressed that the famous sculptors' names rolled off his tongue so easily. She knew of Michelangelo, of course, but the ones Kellen mentioned she knew only from research she had done to prove to her guidance counselor that she should be in that sculpting class.

"They have some of their pieces at the Gem Museum," Kellen said. Mira knew that. The museum was one of her favorites. "I go there all the time just to chill out. This week I took the kid I'm mentoring for a pottery painting class. They do all these kids programs there."

"I didn't know that," Mira said. "I have a six-year-old brother who would love that."

"You should come one time," Kellen said, leaning against the building. "The boy I mentor is seven. They'd probably get along better than we do." He grinned.

Mira was trying to think of a comeback of her own when she felt a hand on her shoulder. Taylor spun her around and kissed her, wrapping his arms around her waist. She felt her whole body stiffen, and she pulled away without thinking.

"I've been looking for you everywhere," Taylor said. He looked gorgeous in a pale blue dress shirt, a navy tie, and navy pants. "Didn't you get my text?" He looked at Kellen and held out his hand. "Hey, man, I don't think we've met. I'm Mira's boyfriend, Taylor."

"Kellen," he said. If the boyfriend comment bothered him, he didn't show it. But it bothered Mira. She felt like Taylor was staking his claim. Shouldn't she find that sweet?

"How do you two know each other?" Taylor asked, and Mira froze. She couldn't let Kellen tell him about art class. She would be mortified.

"School," Mira blurted out, her voice sort of squeaky. Both boys looked at her strangely. "Kellen is a junior. We met in the guidance office, right? I, uh, had a question about my public speaking class."

"Right." Kellen's mouth twitched slightly.

"Cool." Taylor nodded and slipped his hand in hers. "We should go, babe. Everyone is waiting for us. See you inside," he said to Kellen as he pulled Mira away. She turned around and mouthed "sorry." Kellen shook his head.

Taylor didn't question her about Kellen as they headed inside, so Mira started to relax again. The party was incredible. Girls from her social studies class were clustered in a circle on the dance floor, and people were eating dinner at tables decorated with cupcake towers that had sugar crew boats on them. Real boats hung from the ceiling like piñatas, and official regatta posters, which you could purchase as part of the fund-raiser, hung around the room on canvases. Mira couldn't wait to get on the dance floor. First they had to find a table where they could put their stuff. She headed toward an empty one, but Taylor kept walking.

"Let's take this one," Mira yelled over the music. She could already tell Backslide rocked. The two songs he'd played since they'd arrived were ones she loved. She looked at him rocking out in his DJ booth. Backslide had short, spiky black hair and was tall and wiry, but he couldn't have been much older than she was.

"The guys are waiting for us out back," he yelled. Taylor sighed when he saw her reaction. "Let me guess — you don't want to hang with the team."

"I didn't say that," Mira had to shout to be heard. Riley Danford walked by arm-in-arm with the team's second-string quarterback looking like she'd just won the lottery.

"It's written all over your face," Taylor said loudly. They sounded like they were arguing, but they weren't. Were they? "I thought we've been over this, Mira. It's football season and I'm part of a team. We hang together, on the field and off."

He sounded like he was reading off one of those cheesy motivational posters, which usually pictured a skier or a cat hanging from a tree. She looked away, refusing to yell over the next song to explain herself. This wasn't the place.

"You used to be supportive, but you haven't been to one practice yet," he reminded her. "I want my lucky charm back."

Taylor always called her that. Since they started dating, every game Mira attended, either Taylor scored a touchdown or the team won. The few times she couldn't make it last season — usually because of something going on with her dad's office — the team lost. Call it superstition, but Taylor had gotten hooked on Mira being his shadow. She loved that he wanted her there, but it was nice having her own time, too. With her mom keeping her on Izzie duty, she had been neglecting him completely. Now she felt bad.

She weaved her arms around him. "I'm sorry, babe." She played with a piece of his blond hair near the nape of his neck. "I'm going to be at practice next week and the game next Saturday. I swear."

Taylor smiled, revealing the slight gap between his two front bottom teeth. (He said it gave him character. She had to agree.) "Promise?"

"Promise." She crossed her heart.

He kissed her. "Now can we go out back? This DJ is giving me a headache."

"Don't you want to have one dance first?" she asked wishfully. DJ Backslide was playing a slow song. "Or go out to the docks for a while?"

Taylor looked at the porch. "Maybe later, hon, okay?"

She was starting to think he didn't remember where they had their first kiss. "Okay." She didn't want to sound disappointed. Mira reluctantly followed him outside. Half the football team and their girlfriends were on the porch along with the cheerleaders and some of the swim team. It was quieter out there, and the view at sunset was spectacular, but inside was where the party was. She instantly wished she were there, too.

"Mira!" Savannah threw her arms around her, practically knocking her down. She stroked Mira's head, flattening her hair in the process. She was completely giddy, which wasn't very Savannah.

"Are you all right?" Mira asked, trying to pry Savannah off her. Mira's phone was vibrating again, but now wasn't a good time to get it.

Savannah smiled goofily. "More than fine! I might have had a little something to get the party started." She pointed to the corner where some of the group were nursing a bottle of vodka.

Mira frowned. There wasn't enough at this party to keep them entertained? Savannah practically tripped into Mira's lap and Mira quickly steadied her. "Do you want to sit down?"

Savannah straightened her strapless black-and-white dress. It was short and poufed at her hips. Only Savannah could have pulled that off. "Nope! Brayden went to go get me some Sprite." She rolled her eyes. "He said I was getting sloppy," she said, her speech slurring.

You are, Mira wanted to tell her. She wondered if Savannah would drink like this if she knew what a fool she looked like.

Savannah nudged her so hard, Mira practically fell herself. "Go get a drink!"

Mira shook her head, watching as one of Taylor's teammates passed plastic cups around. Inside they were using real glasses. She felt like she had left the party and gone to a Piggly Wiggly. "No, thanks," Mira said. "My dad is working, so I really shouldn't." She'd found it was easier to lie about drinking than tell the truth—which was that she didn't want to ever act as ridiculous as Savannah.

Savannah rolled her eyes. "You're no fun. Lea, get me another drink!" she called to their friend. "Mira, sometimes you can be so dull," she slurred.

Mira hated when Savannah acted like this. It usually happened when Brayden wasn't around. When he was, she was friendlier than a restaurant hostess.

Lea handed Savannah a drink and draped herself on Mira, too. Her breath was hot and it reeked. "You don't want some?"

"Her dad is working, blah, blah, blah," Savannah said, leaning on Lea now, too. They looked like the Leaning Tower of Pisa. Any second the three of them were going to come crashing down. "Always some excuse. Go get Harborside. I bet she'd throw back a few." Lea giggled.

"She could probably drink all of us under the table, and then when we were passed out, she could take all our jewelry," Lauren added. Obviously a few drinks had made Mira's normally reserved friends let their thoughts fly.

"You should have seen her yesterday at Christoff's,"

Savannah said. A few people were migrating toward them. "She actually asked for a discount on a stained dress!" Lea burped, then burst out laughing.

Mira twisted the ruby ring on her index finger around and around. Did Savannah have to say that in front of everyone?

"At least now she owns a dress," Lauren said, and someone yelled, "Snap!" "She has no class. The other day at EP, she got up and Mr. Preston asked where she was going. She said, 'I have to pee.'"

"Eww!" Lea and Savannah chimed in.

"Who says that?" Savannah said, looking sort of spaced out. "But that's Mira's family now." They all giggled. Even Taylor seemed to find the whole thing amusing.

Mira felt the anger bubble up inside her. If she could have reached any of the silver balloons hugging the ceiling inside, she would have popped them all. All anyone wanted to do these days was talk about Izzie and how much she didn't belong in EC. Didn't they realize Mira had no control over the situation? This was her parents' fault! She wasn't Izzie's keeper and she was sick of them acting like she was.

"I hope your mom doesn't think Izzie is getting into the Butterflies," Mira heard Savannah say, and that's when Mira snapped.

"Izzie is *not* getting into the Butterflies." The Butterflies was hers alone and she wasn't sharing. In fact, she didn't want to share anything with Izzie ever again! Before Izzie had arrived, Mira's life had been perfect. Now it had turned into one hot mess. Look at tonight's party. She had been looking forward to it for weeks, and now it was turning into a disaster. She wished more than anything at that moment that Izzie would just disappear. "If my mother even *thinks* of asking me to let her join our club, I will flip out," Mira said, seething. "Izzie is as much a Butterfly as I am…as I am…" She was so bad at zingers. They never came to her till hours later. "As I am homeless," she shot out. The words tasted bitter leaving her lips.

"Finally!" Savannah said, staring at the heavens. "My best friend sees the light."

Mira was revved up, and she felt an overwhelming desire to be cruel. "You should have seen what she moved in with — a few boxes and a duffel bag! My mom pretty much had to buy her underwear." People laughed. As her friends started to gather around, Mira felt she was in on the Izzie joke for once. "Oh, and get this — the shoes she told my mom she wanted to wear tonight were from Payless!"

Savannah snorted (something she never would have done sober). Her drink sloshed all over her dress and she didn't even notice.

"I'm surprised Izzie is even here tonight," Mira added, enjoying the mean-girl high. She mocked Izzie's deep twang. "What is a cocktail party, anyway? You dance there? Where I come from, you're lucky your house even has a floor."

Savannah's snorting was uncontrollable now. Taylor and the others were laughing, too. Suddenly the laughter died out. Mira instinctively turned around.

Shoot.

Izzie must have come through one of the side doors without anyone noticing. Mira didn't know how long she had been standing there, but she knew it had been long enough. Izzie's face was pale and strained. She glanced around the patio at the others, her eyes stopping on Mira. The hurt on her face was unmistakable. Mira suddenly felt sick. Before she could even think of something to say, Izzie spun around and disappeared inside, leaving Mira to think about how low she had just sunk.

Twelve

Izzie slammed the door behind her, pushing her way through the crowd to get as much distance between her and Mira as possible. Hot tears streamed down her cheeks.

Mira would be a fool to come after her. If she were stupid enough to do it, Izzie would give her the show she wanted. They wanted to see her act like a redneck? She'd show them a redneck. First she'd snatch Mira's pearl necklace from her neck. Then she'd deck her in the teeth. She'd like to see Mira manage a dainty little laugh when she was missing an incisor.

Izzie finally stopped running and leaned against a regatta poster on the wall. Who was she kidding? She would never do that. She thought putting on an expensive dress and wearing her aunt's jewelry might make this crowd start to accept her, but now she realized they never would. No one at

EP wanted to give her a chance, especially not Mira. She had known that she and her cousin were different, but she didn't realize Mira actually loathed her.

Izzie changed her mind. She couldn't be part of this world. Why would she even want to? She dialed Kylie's number, but it went right to voice mail. If Kylie had answered, Izzie would have told her to borrow her mom's car and come get her out of EC for good.

Just half an hour earlier, Izzie had assured Hayden she would be fine at the party alone after Mira disappeared, but the truth was, she felt awkward. Izzie had tried to find Violet or another classmate to talk to, but no one exactly waved her over. Finally she'd asked a girl if she knew where Mira was, and the girl had pointed to the patio. Going out there had been her huge mistake. Now she just wanted to go home. To her *real* home. The one that Barbara said was up for sale and had a bid from someone who wanted to turn Grams's house into a doctor's office.

Izzie stood for a while, watching the girls in designer gowns dance to a song DJ Backslide was playing, and she felt the anger growing inside her. These girls took everything for granted. They probably had no clue how much a ticket to this party cost (two hundred dollars!). They didn't know what charity this party was raising money for (her aunt's cardinals project), and she doubted they'd care anyway. The girls in EC didn't think about anything that went on outside their bubble. Just the thought of spending the next three years of high school with them made Izzie want to gag. Suddenly the tears were coming so fast, she couldn't stop them.

"Iz?" Brayden was walking toward her with drinks. He was wearing a white shirt, a khaki jacket, and navy pants. She would have thought they looked stuffy on anyone else, but Brayden looked like he belonged in the pages of a J. Crew catalog. Seeing her face, he quickly put the drinks down. He touched her bare arm, alarmed. "Iz? What's wrong?"

She shrugged him off, wiping her eyes with the back of her hand. Brayden did not get to call her Iz anymore. "What do you care?" she snapped, surprised at the venom in her voice.

"Whoa," Brayden said, his eyes wide. "Invasion of the body snatchers." She stared at a paper boat named *Emerald Eve* that hung high above her head and didn't say anything. "You're giving me the silent treatment?" He ran a hand through his brown hair. "Okay, you're right. I deserve that, and probably more, like a sucker punch to the stomach. But please hear me out. I'm sorry, okay? I shouldn't have acted like that the other day. I knew it the minute you stormed out of the cafeteria. I've been trying to track you down every day since to apologize in person, but I never see you at school. You're like a ghost."

See? Even Brayden thought she was invisible.

"You're not with Mira, you haven't been at lunch," he added, "and I can't exactly call your house. Your cousin is my girlfriend's best friend. Like *that* would go over well." Izzie finally faced him and saw that his blue-green eyes were pained. "I feel like such a jerk. Iz, I'm so sorry. I'll say it a thousand times if that will help."

Izzie wouldn't look at him. She wanted to believe him, but after all that had happened, how could she trust him?

Brayden continued his plea. "The last place I expected to run into you was at Emerald Prep. I must have been the only person alive who missed your princess story in the papers! We were away in Key West that weekend, but all I could do was think of you," he admitted, and Izzie inhaled sharply. "I was ready to send out a missing-person report! You sent me *one* text to say you were leaving town. I sent you dozens and never heard back. I had no clue where they took you, and neither did Kylie. Then you were standing in front of me at my school. Can you blame me for being thrown?"

"I kind of had a lot going on, if you haven't noticed." She folded her arms across her chest like a shield. "Maybe I should have texted you back, but look how you reacted when you did see me. You acted like you didn't even know me!" She glared at him. "You can admit it, Brayden. None of your friends or your girlfriend are here to hear it. You ignored me because you were ashamed to tell everyone that you spent your summer in Harborside with someone like me." His jaw dropped. "Just what I thought. You have nothing to say. *Again*. You're just as fake as everyone else in this town." She started to walk away, but he yanked her back.

"You've got it wrong," he said, his face a swirl of emotions. "I've *never* been embarrassed to know you, Iz. If anything, I was embarrassed for you to learn more about *me*."

"Why would *you* be embarrassed of where you came from?" Izzie asked incredulously.

Brayden looked sheepishly around the crowded dance floor. "You see what EC is like. It's all about how many cars your parents have or where you spent your last vacation. I've never been the type to get into a pissing match over who has the bigger summerhouse in Maine. *That's* why I started hanging out at Harborside Beach. I was sick of this scene."

An EC party was a scene, all right. The waiters were serving caviar and carrying fruity nonalcoholic drinks on sterling-silver trays. DJ Backslide probably cost a few thousand to book. Izzie wondered if this crew would like Backslide as much if they knew he was from Harborside, too.

"Why didn't you tell me where you were from?" she asked quietly, and looked at her heels as she waited for his answer.

"You were always confiding in me about stuff like buying Grams's groceries. What was I going to do?" Brayden asked bluntly. "Kick in with a story about how my parents had just bought a new yacht? Let's be honest: You wouldn't have wanted to hang out with me if you'd known where I was from, either."

"That's not true," she said, but inside she wondered: Would she have felt as comfortable around Brayden if she had known he was born with a silver spoon in his mouth?

"I should have said I knew you the other day. I know that, but I felt trapped, too," Brayden told her. "My friends and Savannah thought I spent the summer building my parents' boathouse. Not surfing. My parents would freak if they knew I owned a board."

"You didn't want to blow your cover," Izzie finished for him, "so you threw me under the bus. Got it."

"No," Brayden said, looking like he was struggling to find the right words. "It's just, if no one knows where I've been, they can't keep me from going back. I wanted to tell Savannah I knew you, but I didn't know how to do that without giving away my secret, too." He sounded desparate. "I had my plan all figured out before you came along. The boathouse is going to take years to finish, and my parents haven't even asked about the progress. At this rate I can keep surfing in peace for years. When you showed up, I didn't know how to be excited to see you without giving it all away. That beach is important to me, too, you know. I would go there every day if I could," he said wistfully. "Sometimes I want to ditch football practice so I can hit the waves instead. Does that make any sense?" Brayden asked sheepishly.

It did make sense. She was beginning to realize that her former zip code meant as much to Brayden as it did her. More important, though, she realized something that had kind of broken her heart. Brayden wasn't embarrassed of her. He was embarrassed of himself. "I thought you ignored me because you didn't want to be seen with me," she admitted.

"You seriously thought that?" She wasn't sure if Brayden was mortified or hurt. "Iz, you've been a better friend to me than anyone around here lately. And that includes my girl-friend. I feel like I don't even know who she is anymore," he said almost to himself. "I think you're incredible, Iz. I love being friends with you. The last thing I would want is for you to doubt that." His eyes never left her face.

Friends. It's not like they were ever more than that, right? So why did hearing Brayden officially label them that make her so sad? "Friends," she echoed.

"Good." He looked relieved and grinned. "So if we're friends again, then why don't you tell me how I went from seeing you at Scoops to Emerald Cove's kickoff of the fall season regatta party?"

"Don't you have somewhere you should be?" Izzie couldn't get herself to say Savannah's name, but she was dying to ask why he was with someone like Savannah if he felt the way he did. Wasn't Savannah the perfect example of what he hated about EC? But she knew she didn't have the right to ask him that.

"No one will even notice I'm gone." He motioned to two chairs at an unmanned table and smirked. "I'm all yours, so start talking."

Izzie wasn't sure how long she and Brayden sat there, but by the time she was done, DJ Backslide had gone on a break. Brayden had already known about Grams's condition, so he wasn't shocked to hear that Grams was now in a nursing home. What did floor him was how alienated she felt at school.

"Hayden is a great guy and Mira is nice," he said carefully. "She and Savannah have been best friends for as long as I've been with her."

"Maybe they've rubbed off on each other," Izzie said lightly, then stopped herself. She did not want to bash his girlfriend to him. "Mira surprised me, I guess. I didn't realize how much she resented my being here. She can't stand me, and after tonight, I don't think I can stand her, either. She doesn't care about anyone but herself."

"The Iz I know wouldn't let her get away with that kind of behavior." Brayden smirked.

She closed her eyes tightly like she was preparing to rub a magic lantern. "I just wish I was on the beach right now. That's the only place I can ever make sense of things."

He sprinkled some of the confetti lying on the table around her hands. "I can't take you to Harborside Beach, but I think I have the next best thing." He held out his hand. "Follow me."

She was curious so she let him lead her out a side entrance and past the catering tent, where they were nearly run over by a waiter trying to get someone's lobster tail to his table. He wove around the adults' party and led her down a wooden dock where tall green grass grew on both sides of the path. A few minutes later, they were staring at the darkening sky and — even better — the water.

"It's not the ocean, but at least you can dig your toes in the sand," Brayden said, staring at the bay. Lights from a town across the water were bright in the distance against the orange-hued sky. "Come on, take a dip. It will make you feel better." He pulled off his shoes.

Izzie slipped off her heels and waded into the bay, hiking her dress up above her knees. The sand felt good against her toes. She hadn't realized how much she'd missed the water till she was in it. She'd swum laps in the Monroes' pool a bunch of times to get ready for tryouts, but it wasn't the same thing. She breathed in the salty night air and kicked the water with her foot, her dark cranberry pedicure barely visible in the low light. "God, I would kill to swim right now."

"Then why don't you?" Brayden nudged her forward, getting the bottom of her dress wet.

"Dude, I'm in a ball gown!" She laughed.

She shoved Brayden back, getting his pants wet. They splashed around for a few minutes, and by the time they were back on dry land, Izzie's updo had fallen out and her dress was soaked. Brayden's shirt looked like it had just come out of the wash, and he had water marks up to his thighs. But she didn't mind. Brayden always put her at ease. She'd been mad at him an hour before, but now she felt lighter than she had in weeks.

"There's the smile I remember."

She hadn't realized Brayden was looking at her. He wrapped his sports coat around her shoulders. He had wisely removed it before their water fight.

"You're going to be okay, Isabelle Scott," he said softly.

"You think?" She could barely breathe. He was standing so close she could smell his cologne.

"Yes," he told her. "Because the girl I know has guts. You won't let this place beat you. If anything, you're going to turn this town on its head. I just know it." She smiled to herself at the thought.

A second later the moment was gone, and they were laughing about something stupid. They'd barely reached the top of the beach walkway when Izzie saw Lucas striding toward her. She almost dropped the shoes in her hand when she saw how peeved he looked.

"We've been searching for you everywhere," he said sharply, looking disdainfully from her disheveled appearance to Brayden's. "Don't you check your phone? I have the photo set up and the press ready to go. I've spent the whole night making sure your introduction to the community goes perfectly, and now look at you! The whole family is waiting for you in front of the boathouse."

Her phone was in her bag, Izzie remembered. And she'd left her bag at coat check. It hadn't occurred to her to keep it on her. "I'm sorry," she said, that feeling of being an outsider flooding back to her. She instinctively touched her wet head. "Just give me a few minutes and I'll pull myself together —"

Lucas cut her off. "I am not letting you ruin things for this campaign. You cannot get into a picture with your uncle for the first time looking like that! No. I'll tell them I couldn't find you." His brown eyes were on fire. "Clean yourself up before anyone else sees you," he snapped, and walked away.

Izzie started shaking. It took a lot to rattle her, but Lucas definitely could. She looked at Brayden.

"What a jerk," he mouthed. She pulled his jacket tighter and shrugged, embarrassed.

"Oh and Isabelle?" Lucas said, turning around. She looked over at him. "I don't *ever* want something like this to happen again. You're a Monroe now. You'd better start acting like one."

Thirteen

Izzie stood at the edge of the pool and waited for the signal. At the sound of the buzzer, she dove into the cool water and zipped across the lap lane doing the breaststroke, her specialty.

Just swim, she told her body. *Forget about Coach Greff and whatever she's going to write on her clipboard. Block out the three dozen girls sitting on the bleachers, watching your every stroke. Ignore the giant ticking clock that is counting the seconds till you reach the end.* She heard her mom's voice inside her head: *No guts, no glory, kiddo.*

She swam as hard as she could. When her hands finally hit the wall, she removed her Speedo goggles and looked at the clock.

Christie Greff, the EP swim coach, grinned. "Just under

a minute and ten seconds. Nice." The petite blond crouched at the pool edge, the whistle around her neck hovering above Izzie's head. "Are you always that fast?"

"Yes," Izzie said, slightly winded. "My personal best is even a few seconds quicker."

"Good to know." Coach Greff scribbled on her pad. "Think you can do it again?"

"Yes," she said, trying not to get too excited. She knew the Emerald Prep swim team was highly competitive. They'd won their division the past three years, and most of the team was made up of juniors and seniors. She was lucky they had four slots to fill. Izzie desperately wanted one. She had been thinking a lot about what Brayden had said the night of the regatta party. She'd never been a quitter and she wasn't about to start now. She had to show this town they couldn't beat her.

The coach looked over Izzie's info sheet. "I see you placed at the Harborside Community Center for diving. And the breaststroke. And you were a lifeguard this summer? You seem pretty qualified for the team." She frowned slightly. "As long as you get those grades up this year."

Izzie nodded. She knew the Cs she got at Harborside wouldn't cut it here at EP. Her aunt and uncle had told her that when they'd squeaked her by admissions. She also knew she had more time to study now that she wasn't working. (*Or taking care of Grams*, she thought guiltily.) She could do better. She *would* do better, which was what she told Coach Greff.

The coach smiled. "Okay, then, take a seat, and we'll have you challenge one of the girls in a few minutes. I'd love to see what you could do with an IM." An IM was an individual medley that included four laps, each with a different stroke: freestyle, breaststroke, butterfly, and backstroke. The IM was one of Izzie's strongest races after breast.

Izzie pulled herself out of the water and wrapped a towel around her waist before walking the long way around the pool and over to the bleachers. She kept her eyes locked on the bench to avoid the piercing stares of some of the other swimmers. Whether they were impressed with her swimming or just making a snide comment, she didn't know. She was getting used to the staring, but that didn't mean she had to like it. Savannah's whispers echoed off the high ceilings. She was the hardest to ignore. She was dressed in a lime-green one-piece and a navy-blue swim cap with green polka dots. *Even her swim caps are trendy*, Izzie thought. Izzie sat on the bottom bench, feeling the steel against her legs, and looked down at her toes. She had painted them green for luck. Green was her community center team's color. As she was examining her less-than-stellar pedicure skills, she felt someone slide down the bench next to her.

"Hey. Nice breaststroke." It was Violet, the girl who had stopped her on the way to lunch on the first day of school.

At least Izzie *thought* it was her. It was hard to tell when her hair was hidden under a swim cap, but there was no mistaking the girl's deep-set, dark, oval eyes.

"You're Violet, right?" Izzie asked, and the girl nodded. "Good, because I feel like I've been stalking you unsuccessfully—but not in a creepy way," Izzie added quickly. "You're one of the most normal people I've met at EP, and I've only talked to you once. It makes for a pretty lonely existence."

Violet laughed. "Well, I'm glad to hear I'm one of the select few who fall into the normal category." She leaned closer. "Although I totally know what you mean about this place. This is Nicole," she said, motioning to a blond girl, who slipped as she descended from the seat above them. Nicole was so beautiful and Amazonian in stature that it would be easy to be intimidated, but Izzie also knew the girl was a klutz, which brought her back down to earth. Whenever Izzie saw Nicole on campus, she was tripping or dropping something, and that morning she'd actually mixed the wrong chemicals during biology and smoked out the class.

"You're Mira's cousin, right?" Nicole said, not waiting for a reply. "I heard about you and Brayden Townsend! Were you two really hanging out the night of the regatta party? Savannah is so peeved." She whispered conspiratorially. "She was whining to Mira about it in the locker room before gym. She thought I was tying my sneakers with my iPod on, but I 'forgot' to press Play and heard everything."

"Nic, 'Hi, nice to meet you' might have been a better 'hello,'" Violet deadpanned.

Izzie heard Savannah's laugh, and her chest tightened. She was not scared of the girl in the least, but she also didn't want to give her any more ammunition with Brayden.

"Don't worry about Savannah," Violet assured her, reading her thoughts. "Karma's a killer. She's made a lot of girls' lives miserable — including mine and Nic's. I'm glad to see something finally go wrong in her otherwise perfect life. One time she had me locked out of the cafeteria because I was carrying the same lunch bag she was," Violet said. "Where I come from, they'd stuff you in a locker for a stunt like that. I can't do that here. I'm on scholarship."

Izzie was comforted by the fact that Violet couldn't afford the twenty-thousand-dollar yearly tuition, either. "Have you gone here since sixth grade?" she asked.

Violet fiddled with her watch, which looked like an orange. "No. We moved here last year from New York. It's okay, I guess. A little too much open space and a few too many debutantes." She grinned. "Savannah was fine with me at first. Then she realized that just because I'm from New York doesn't mean I'm a 'Gossip Girl.' We couldn't have lived farther from the Upper East Side."

"I got in because I'm a founder's great-granddaughter," Nicole admitted. "It's practically written in the school code that they have to admit Jameses."

"Thank God, or you would have flunked out your first week of sixth grade," Violet said, and the two started to bicker playfully.

"I wasn't with Brayden at the regatta party." Izzie felt the need to say that. They stopped and looked at her. Izzie glanced quickly at Savannah. If she was upset about Brayden, she didn't show it. She was deep in conversation with half the team and barely came up to take a breath. "I mean, I was with Brayden, but not like that. We're friends." The word *friend* still stung even after a weekend of letting it sink in.

"You must be good friends, then," Nicole said. "He left Savannah half the night to hang out with you. Well, that's what she told Mira. Brayden's one of the coolest guys in the grade. Why he's still with Savannah, I'll never know."

"Jedi mind powers," Violet said knowingly. "He can't see how evil she is because she acts like a peach whenever he's within ten feet of her. Is he in one of your classes?"

How could Izzie explain the connection when there really wasn't one? Not here in EC, anyway, and she couldn't tell them about Brayden hanging out in Harborside. "I know him through the Monroes," Izzie said, trying to sound convincing.

Nicole looked disappointed. "Bummer. I was dying to know how he rated as a kisser."

"You're better off not knowing the answer to that question," Violet told Izzie. "Savannah is pretty possessive. She thought Nic was flirting with Brayden last year during a bake sale and Savannah dropped a blueberry cobbler in Nic's lap."

"She knocked my latte over, too, and it spilled all over my new rain boots," Nicole complained, pursing her lips. "God, thinking about that makes me wish I had a coffee right now. I usually hit the coffee bar after eighth period, but today Coach Greff wanted us here early."

"I can't believe the school has a coffee bar," Izzie said. Some things still amazed her.

"It's a little much, right?" Violet agreed. "Welcome to Emerald Prep."

EP's coffee bar was actually a Starbucks inside the Walburn Library. Izzie hadn't gone to it. An iced mocha was $4.50. She couldn't stomach spending her aunt's money on that. She couldn't believe she had spending money in the first place when she no longer had a job.

"We prefer the coffee bar in town," Violet told Izzie. "It's not an EP magnet like the school one is." A buzzer went off behind them and another girl dove into the water for her first tryout. Violet motioned to the pool. "So, it looks like you are a shoo-in."

"I hope so," Izzie said wistfully. "I was on a team at my community center. My old school didn't have swim team. But you probably know all that already."

"About you being from Harborside? Big deal." Violet

shrugged. "That doesn't scare me. I'm from Brooklyn. Besides, you don't look like you could beat me with a pipe." Izzie raised an eyebrow.

"You don't beat people, though, do you?" Nicole bit a strand of hair peeking out of her swim cap. Violet nudged her. "What? My mom says I have great bone structure, and I'd hate to mess with that."

"I don't beat people," Izzie assured her. "But it's nice to finally hear someone be honest! Everyone else pretends to act nice to me when what they really want to know is if they train us in Harborside to be criminals." Nicole looked anxious. "The answer is: They don't."

"Now that would be an interesting after-school club," Violet joked.

Izzie laughed. Finally, she had found girls she could talk to. Where had they been hiding?

Maybe they hadn't been. Maybe she was the one who had been doing the hiding.

"Whoa," Violet said, and Izzie looked up. The swimmer had already reached the other side of the wall. Her freestyle time was fifty-eight seconds. "She's going to make the team for sure."

One less slot for me, Izzie thought as she watched the freshman.

Violet nudged her. "Don't sweat it. You're going to make the team. Did you see some of the girls who tried out? Coach

Greff is lucky they know how to blow bubbles out of their nose."

"Next, I'd like to have Isabelle Scott, Savannah Ingram, and Millie Lennon down front for an IM," Coach Greff announced with her megaphone.

"Good luck," Violet said as Nicole clapped wildly.

Izzie walked to the edge of the pool to take her place next to Millie, the girl who had nailed the freestyle. She looked terrified. Savannah quickly blocked Izzie's path.

She smiled coolly at Izzie. "Look at you swimming like a pro. At least you're meant to get wet today." She leaned in close and whispered in Izzie's ear. "I have no idea what you were doing with my boyfriend at the regatta party, but you *won't* be doing it again. Got it? Stay. Away. From. Him. I will make you supremely sorry if you don't."

"Get ready, ladies," the coach said. Each girl walked to her mark, and Izzie kept her head down. She wasn't about to argue with Savannah now. She had to concentrate.

"Hi, Savannah," Izzie heard Millie nervously introduce herself. "I'm Millie. You're really good."

"And you're not," Savannah said flatly. "Better luck next year." Millie looked miserably at a puddle on the floor.

"Okay, girls, we're going to do an IM to see how you race," Coach Greff said through a megaphone from across the pool. "Savannah holds the record, so I'd like to see how you two stack up against her. Good luck."

"You're going to need it," Savannah said under her breath as she took a graceful position on her starting block and adjusted her swim cap.

Izzie put on her goggles, got on the diving block, and waited for the buzzer. When it sounded, she exploded off the diving block and swam freestyle down the first lap. The water churned from her kicks and arm strokes, and her head turned quickly in and out of the water for breaths. There was no time to see where Savannah and Millie were. She just had to swim as hard as she could and count the laps in her head. Two for freestyle...two for breaststroke...two for the butterfly...and then she hit the wall and quickly turned onto her back for the last two laps. Now she could hear the screaming again. It sounded like it was getting more frantic and louder, but she couldn't be sure and she couldn't waste a second to check.

When her hands finally hit the wall, Izzie looked down the line at the other lap lanes. The water churned choppily around her. When she saw that Millie was already at the wall, her heart sank. But where was Savannah? Izzie heard the buzzer sound again. That meant the last person had reached the wall, and it wasn't her! Izzie saw Savannah angrily rip off her swim cap.

"Times," Coach Greff announced. "Millie Lennon: two minutes and fifty-four seconds. Isabelle Scott: two minutes and fifty-six seconds. And Savannah Ingram, still a personal best at three minutes." She shook her head in amazement. "Girls, that was incredible! Millie and Isabelle, I think it's safe to say you've officially made the team." A round of cheers went up from the bleachers as Savannah glared at them, her chest rising and falling rapidly. "I'd also like to congratulate Holly Abrams, sophomore, and Carly Banks, junior. The rest of you, thanks for trying out."

Izzie felt like she was going to burst. She wished she had someone to share this excitement with. She could call Grams and tell her, but her grandmother hadn't recognized her when she visited last Saturday, and it had been upsetting. She'd call Kylie instead the moment she dried off. Brayden would be happy for her, too, but she couldn't call him, could she? She wiped her face with a towel and thought about texting him. That's when she felt the towel get ripped out of her hands.

"Welcome to the team, fish!" Violet yelled as Nicole hugged Izzie. "We're taking you to Corky's to celebrate."

Izzie remembered Corky's from her first ride into town. She heard people talk about the popular hamburger haunt all the time. Mira was a regular. Up until now, Izzie hadn't had anyone to go with. She grinned. "You don't have to twist my arm. I'm in."

"Forget Corky's," Izzie heard someone else say, and she turned around.

Savannah stood with her hands on her hips, but she was actually smiling at Izzie, which was sort of disturbing. "Congratulations on making the team! I knew you would."

"Uh, thanks," Izzie said, and waited for the punch line.

"If we're going to be teammates, then you should come to the Tryout Day celebration," Savannah told them. "We're having a pool party and ordering dinner at the EC Country Club. It's sort of an EP tradition. A welcome-to-the-team sort of thing."

Nicole frowned. "I don't remember being invited last year."

"You weren't," Savannah said simply. She looked at Izzie. "Look, I got a little territorial before. If you and Brayden are really just friends, I'll get over it," she said with a shrug. "But the swim team means a lot to me and this is a new year, new team. Might as well all get used to each other, right?" She smiled at Violet and Nicole. "Millie's coming and a lot of the other girls' teams will be there, too. So are you guys in?"

Izzie glanced at Violet and Nicole questioningly. Was Savannah actually extending an olive branch? She really did want to fit in and feel like part of the team. *No guts, no glory.*

"Okay," Izzie said to Savannah, who smiled. "We're in."

Fourteen

By the time Mira got to the Emerald Cove Country Club, the Tryout Day party was already in full swing. Girls from field hockey, swim, and cheerleading (better luck getting an invitation next year, cross-country team) had changed out of their practice clothes and were sitting on lounge chairs and floats or were at the edge of the pool. Navy and green balloons were tied to every chair, and there was a long table full of green gift bags (courtesy of Savannah's mom) that held sunscreen, goggles, and exclusive Tryout Day beach towels that would be paraded around school afterward by those fortunate enough to be invited. Mira was collecting hers when Savannah caught up with her.

"Where have you been?" she demanded, looking peeved but beautiful in a green one-piece that was almost identical to the pink one Mira had on (they had bought them together).

Mira knew her cover, but she hesitated when she saw Savannah's stony expresssion. "I..."

I was working on a still life of a water lily that I botched in painting class today was the real answer. And the truth was, she wished she was still at the art studio with Kellen instead. She could have listened to him wax poetic about painters like Paul Gauguin all afternoon, but after three texts and two frantic calls from Savannah, Mira knew she should get to the club before things turned ugly.

"I've been waiting for you for an hour!" Savannah complained. "Didn't you get my texts? You were supposed to help me set up." She looked at Mira suspiciously. "Where were you, anyway?"

"Science lab," Mira lied, glancing at her hands for signs of paint. "I had to finish that stupid experiment on sound effects on plants, and I guess I left my phone in my bag. Sorry, Vanna." She nudged her pouting friend playfully. "Looks like you did a great job without me, though. Everyone is having a great time." She shook her goody bag. "Love the towel."

Savannah's face relaxed. "It's cute, right? But that's nothing compared to this afternoon's entertainment." She pointed out four girls sitting at the edge of the pool.

Mira recognized Violet and Nicole in their team swimsuits right away. The third girl with them was definitely a freshman, but it was the fourth girl who surprised Mira the most. It was Izzie, and she sat in the middle, her mouth going a mile a minute while her slender legs swished back and forth in the water. Mira watched her cousin throw her head back and laugh. She'd never seen Izzie laugh at anything before. She looked comfortable for once, Mira realized. *And she did it all without my help.* An arctic freeze had settled over the two girls since the regatta party. Izzie wasn't stupid. She knew Mira didn't like her and she was steering clear. Not having to pretend anymore should have been a relief to Mira, but instead she felt haunted by her behavior. She kept seeing the pained look on Izzie's face that night on the patio.

"Today is phase one," Savannah declared, watching the girls. "It's payback. We're going to sink Izzie before she even learns how to swim. Figuratively, of course."

Mira's stomach felt like it had dropped out of her bathing suit. "How so?"

"She's a total embarrassment to you and your family, Mira. Let's face it—having her around takes your class factor down a notch." Mira winced. "What's worse is her messing with *my* life." Savannah glared at Izzie. "Beating my time on the IM today? Hanging out at the party with *my* boyfriend?" Her voice rose. "It's humiliating! I can't have her undermine me like that! Brayden had the nerve to tell me that I have to get used to them being friends. Can you believe that?" Her voice was shrill. "He *never* talks back

185

to me like that. Never. I don't get it. Why would he care so much about being friends with a girl he just met?" Her brown eyes looked sad as she added in a whisper, "Don't tell anyone, okay? I would die if people knew Brayden and I fought over *her*."

Mira had never seen Savannah so flustered. So Brayden and Izzie were really friends? She'd heard what had happened that night at the party, but she just assumed the two bumped into each other and the story got spun out of control. But if Brayden was laying claim to the friendship and not worrying about Savannah's wrath, then something had to be going on. "Vanna, don't freak out. You know he adores you," Mira insisted.

Savannah's emotions turned off like a switch, and her sly smile returned. "Of course he adores me. And once he realizes what a troublemaker Izzie is, he'll probably never mention her name to me again." She smoothed her hair with one hand but kept her eyes on Izzie. "That change starts today." She motioned to Lauren and Lea, who were lounging nearby. "Let's go say hi to Mira's cousin," she told them. Mira followed, feeling like a reluctant puppy. As soon as Izzie saw them coming, her face clouded over. "Hi!" Savannah squealed. "How are you guys? Having fun?"

"This is a little bigger party than you'd described." Violet looked around in wonder.

"It reminds me of an episode of *It's My Party*," Izzie said.

186

Mira noticed that the way Izzie said it, it didn't sound like a compliment.

"I love that show!" Nicole and Violet said in unison, and the three of them laughed.

"I'm pretty much a shoo-in for next season," Savannah told them confidentially. "My mom has been in talks with them about it for the last year." She took a seat by the edge of the pool, and everyone still standing followed suit. "I'm just glad you guys were willing to come today. Fresh start, right?" Savannah looked at Mira. "Did Izzie tell you? She made the team. She's amazing." Izzie's eyes were wary.

"That's great, Izzie!" Mira said, and she meant it, but Izzie didn't say anything. And why should she? She was doing fine on her own.

"This is our other new recruit, Minnie," Savannah added, pointing out the tiny brunette.

"It's Millie," she said. She had to be a freshman. Only a freshman would correct Savannah.

"Now that everyone is here, it's time to start the initiation," Savannah told them.

"Initiation?" Izzie repeated, not looking convinced. Neither was Mira. As far as she could recall, they never played games or had initiations on Tryout Day. Come to think of it, other than the hazing that went on during cotillion season, EP didn't have any sort of initiations at all.

"It's been a tradition at EP forever," Savannah told Izzie,

her expression never wavering. Savannah was an excellent liar. "Since the school started, practically, but the Tryout Day one is sort of new. "

"Are all the teams involved? Or just the swim team?" Izzie asked. Mira couldn't help noticing a change in her cousin. She didn't know if it was because Izzie made the swim team or had finally made a few friends, but she suddenly had no problem standing up to Savannah.

"Each team has its own initiations, and some teams do them another day," Savannah said. "But the swim team one always happens here. What better place to be initiated than the pool?"

Millie looked like she might break out in hives. "What do we have to do?"

"Steal the club's emerald choker," Savannah said as if it was the easiest task in the world. "Take a picture while wearing it at the pool, then put it back."

Mira knew the prank was a death sentence. Both the town and the country club were named after a priceless jewel for one reason: Victor Strausburg, EC's founder, made his fortune mining emeralds and other gems in North Carolina's Blue Ridge Mountains. He had his first haul of baubles made into a necklace for his wife, Audrey. It was worth millions, but it had been passed down for generations and was now guarded at the club in a temperature-controlled, locked case.

"No problem! Maybe I'll just hold on to the necklace to wear to the first Butterflies formal, too," Violet deadpanned. Violet turned to Izzie to explain how dicey the situation actually was. "This necklace she wants us to steal — "

"Borrow," Savannah corrected.

" — is under lock and key," Violet told Izzie. "This town worships that stupid necklace so much they voted down a request from the mayor to wear the emeralds to the Governor's Ball last fall." Violet shot daggers at Savannah. "It can't be done. That necklace has more locks on it than the vaults in Gringotts."

Savannah sipped her lemonade. "Don't be so dramatic. Do you really think we'd ask you to snag it if was impossible to pull off? I know where they keep the key."

Izzie's eyes narrowed. "How?"

"Does it matter?" Savannah asked. "The point is, I can get you to the key, you can do your initiation, and we can go back to tanning." She gave them a bored look. "You guys are really making this more complicated than it is."

"And ruining the fun," Lauren said, swirling the water with her finger. "Just get it over with already."

"It's a suicide mission," Violet said. "If we got caught, my family would be kicked out of the club, and my mother would die of shame, be shunned at her book club, and blacklisted from Emerald Cove Cares. She'd rather move than lose her favorite things." Lauren pretended to shed a tear.

"We'd also be kicked off the team," Izzie reminded them. "I'm not risking my spot for a childish dare."

"Don't be such a whiner," Savannah said. "You could do this game blindfolded. And then you get to do what the rest of us never have — try on the necklace." Savannah looked wistful while Millie appeared on the verge of throwing up. "I got to wear it once for a split second, and it made me feel like a queen."

Izzie didn't take her bait. "Well, you'll have to keep dreaming about the day you land Prince Harry so you can wear it again. We're not playing along, Savannah."

Good, Mira thought. She couldn't say it in front of Savannah, but if Izzie got caught stealing Strausburg's emeralds, her parents would not only go ape and be mortified, but Lucas would go postal.

"Suit yourselves," she snapped, her tone changing. "I just hope the rest of the team doesn't ban you over this. Everyone on the team has been initiated but you four." Savannah glanced at the other swim team members hanging out near the diving board. "Might make swim practice uncomfortable. The swim team is a sisterhood, and sisterhoods have rituals."

Lea spoke up. "This is a cakewalk compared to what the seniors made me do last year. I had to streak through the boys' locker room after football practice. I didn't eat for a week leading up to it."

"You see?" Savannah said. "This is easy." The girls didn't

budge and Savannah stared at Millie ruefully. "Fine, don't play. Leave. Seriously. No initiation, no party." Millie's eyes widened. "You may be club members, but this is an invitation-only affair. Your names have just been crossed off the team party list permanently."

"I think we'll survive." Izzie stood up and grabbed a towel. Nicole and Violet did the same. "Come on, Millie."

Millie's butt was glued to the pool edge. She swung her legs in the water, not looking up at them. "Maybe we should do this. I don't want to be a whipping post all season. It's a long season! And besides" — she looked around — "I want to be invited back here."

"Freshmen," Violet mumbled. "They're so easily swayed."

"I'm usually easily swayed," Nicole said. "But even I think this has disaster written all over it."

"Look," Savannah said soothingly, "we don't want you to get caught. This is all in fun. It's almost five thirty. The club closed early for the party. The grounds crew is out on the course. No one is even in the building. You just go in, get the necklace, bring it here, click, click, click, bring it back, and done. We'll never ask you to do another dare again."

"The answer is still no," Izzie said with a steely gaze, and the girls turned to leave.

"I'll do it," Millie said. Izzie and Violet did a double take. Millie pulled herself out of the pool and crossed her skinny arms across her chest. "Where do I find the key?"

Savannah looked impressed. "In the main room there is an aquarium. Reach your hand underneath, and the key is taped to the bottom of the tank." Mira didn't want to know how Savannah knew that. "You should be back here in time for finger foods. We're having sushi."

"Where is the aquarium again?" Millie hesitated. "My family just joined the club last week."

Izzie groaned. "Fine! I don't know where I'm going, but I'll take you." Millie looked so happy, Mira thought she might cry. "You have *botched job* written all over you."

"Don't do it," Mira blurted out. Had she said that out loud? Izzie looked at her strangely. Mira could feel Savannah's nails digging into her arm. She quickly looked down at the water.

"There is no way you're doing this alone," Violet told Izzie. "You haven't even been inside the club yet." Nicole nodded. "We're coming with you, too." Izzie didn't argue with them. Instead, she actually smiled. She wasn't alone anymore.

"Great, you're all one big family," Savannah said. "So get in there, already! I want a photo of me wearing that necklace as my phone screensaver. Once I have that, you can all give me your addresses so I can send you invites to my sweet sixteen. It's not for another few weeks, but it's worth the wait."

"You can save my stamp," Izzie told Savannah. Mira had never heard Izzie this fired up before. "I'm only doing this to save Millie's butt."

Savannah held her heart. "That's so sweet. Have fun!"

Mira's heart felt like it was on vibrate mode as she watched the girls leave the pool area. Savannah was right. The club was practically deserted at that hour. All the golf carts were back, dinner had been served on the outdoor terrace, and most of the club staff were gone for the night. They should be able to snatch the necklace and have it back again before anyone even noticed it was missing. But for some reason, Mira felt uneasy, and she should have known why.

Savannah watched the girls head inside the clubhouse door. "Make the call," she said quietly.

Lauren reached for her bag near the pool ledge and pulled out her phone. "Hi, Mr. Matthews? This is Lauren Salbrook, Parker's daughter," she told him, her voice bubbling with sweetness. "I'm at the Tryout Day bash and this is so awkward...." She looked at Savannah gleefully. "I'm okay, it's just...I heard some girls talking about stealing the Strausburg emeralds."

Mira stared at Savannah in horror, but she was busy watching Lauren's Emmy-worthy performance.

"Oh, you're still here at a meeting?" Lauren's eyes widened. "Yes. I would head downstairs right away. They're probably in the club lounge right now." She hung up and squealed. "He's calling the police."

"Savannah." Mira yanked her arm. "What are you doing? If Izzie gets caught —"

Savannah pulled her wet arm from Mira's grasp and started to get out of the pool. Mira scrambled after her. "I thought you wanted her gone as bad as I do."

"I do," Mira said. But is that what she wanted? She'd never thought about Izzie being run out of town—just sort of tucked away enough not to embarrass her anymore. She didn't want her to land in jail.

"But I don't want it to happen like this. If the press finds out what happened, my dad's campaign brownie points will be gone." She thought quickly. "That means your dad can kiss those coastal revitalization plans good-bye."

Savannah's dad was in charge of some major low-income makeover project in North Carolina. Mira didn't know the details, but her parents had mentioned it in passing, and she knew that Savannah's dad, who owned a big commercial contracting firm, wanted to build new housing, hotels, and storefronts in impoverished areas. Seemed like a slam dunk, but apparently Mr. Ingram had to knock down important town buildings to get the job done, and some communities were still balking. If Mr. Ingram didn't get Mira's dad's backing on this, it might not happen.

The color drained from Savannah's face. "You've got to learn to open your mouth, Mira. You're supposed to keep me in check, remember?" she whispered. "Now look what you've done!"

"What I've done?" Mira ran a hand through her hair. This was not good.

Both girls stared across the lush green lawn at the clubhouse doors, willing them to open. After what felt like an eternity, the four girls bolted out a side door and raced across the lawn toward the pool. Mira could see Millie cradling the necklace in her hands like she was holding a baby. Her face was beaming triumphantly, but Mira noticed that Izzie looked apprehensive. That's when Mira heard the sirens. She turned her head in time to see three cop cars screech to a halt by the club gates. The girls hesitated for half a second, unsure where to turn. Then Izzie's eyes locked on Savannah, and she started charging for her just as Mr. Matthews, the club manager, appeared on the club lawn with two officers in tow.

"This is it," Lea said gleefully as Savannah's and Mira's faces turned pale.

Izzie is going down, Mira thought, *and I've done nothing to help her.*

"You set us up!" Izzie yelled as she raced into the pool area, stopping inches from Savannah's face.

"What are you talking about?" Savannah said coolly, eyeing the approaching cops and Mr. Matthews as they descended on the pool area.

"I can't believe I fell for this!" Izzie glanced at Mira, too. "You wanted us to get caught!"

"Izzie, just stop talking, okay?" Mira pleaded. "I'll call my parents. They'll get you out of this mess."

But Izzie was too enraged to stop. "You got me *into* this mess!"

"No, I…" Mira hesitated, her face burning, and she looked at her pedicure.

Violet, Nicole, and Millie ran up behind Izzie, sounding out of breath. Millie held out the necklace. "Quick! Hide this!"

Savannah stepped back. "No way. I'm not putting my fingerprints on that."

Violet looked like she wanted to strangle her. "You little…"

"It's those girls right there, officers!" Mr. Matthews ran his hand over his toupee, which had flapped out of place in the wind. "I saw them! I don't know how they found the key to the case, but they have the emeralds." His hand shook as he pointed at Violet, Nicole, Millie, and Izzie. Millie quickly handed over the necklace, her face the color of beets.

"Mr. Matthews," Savannah spoke up, her voice sweet like honey. Savannah's family had practically been founding members of the club, so if the manager was going to listen to anyone, it would be her. "These three didn't do anything," she said, pointing to Violet, Izzie, and Nicole, who looked at her strangely. "I overheard the whole thing before it happened. Millie Lennon is the one who wanted to steal the necklace. The other three tried to stop her."

"That's not true!" Millie squeaked. Big tears plopped down on her cheeks.

"Wait a minute," Violet said.

"Don't cover for her," Savannah cut her off. "The rest of us heard her say it." She looked at Lea and Lauren, who mumbled their agreement. "We all know the truth."

So did Mira, which was why she was so torn. On the one hand, this could be good—Izzie wouldn't have to take the fall—but on the other hand, Millie was only a freshman. Now she was going to be known for the next four years as the girl who stupidly tried to steal Strausburg's emeralds.

"Officers, if you would lead this young lady inside, I'd like you to write up a report while we call Ms. Lennon's parents," Mr. Matthews said.

Millie started full-out sobbing. Violet put her arm around her and looked at Nicole and Izzie worriedly. Mira glanced at Savannah, who winked at her as if to say, "See? We're saved." But Mira didn't feel saved. She felt terrible.

"Wait!" Izzie yelled as a cop started to lead Millie away. "You can't book her. She's not the one who stole that."

Mira felt her stomach start to swirl like a Jacuzzi.

"If you're arresting anyone," Izzie said, sounding not the least bit nervous, "it should be me. I broke into the club. And I stole the emeralds all by myself."

Fifteen

"Isabelle?"

Izzie heard the knock on her bedroom door, and she closed her eyes, wishing she could disappear in a cloud of smoke.

"Can we talk to you?"

They didn't wait for Izzie's response. Two seconds later, her aunt, her uncle, and Lucas were standing in her doorway looking less than happy to see her, even though they were the ones doing the intruding. They were all in black tie for a silent auction at the school that evening. Her aunt's pink floor-length gown shimmered as she rocked nervously on her heels.

"We're trying to understand what happened today," her aunt said, making a swishing sound as she crossed the room and sat on the edge of Izzie's bed. "We know you didn't steal the club's prized emerald choker on your own. What really happened?"

Izzie stared at her comforter. There was no point in telling her aunt the truth. She could tell by the way Lucas was staring at her that he already had her rap sheet memorized. What was the use in speaking up now? EC was not going to give her a chance to show who she really was. That's why she took the rap for Millie. It wasn't a stretch to think that Izzie would steal a necklace, but if Millie had been blamed, her family's reputation would have been ruined. Izzie's already was. She just wished she hadn't been stupid enough to believe making the swim team would change things.

"Is there more to the story?" her aunt asked hopefully. "Did someone put you up to this, perhaps? If you know something that could clear your name, you have to tell us."

Izzie shook her head, and she could see the disappointment written all over her aunt's face. It made Izzie want her mom so bad she could taste it. She'd been thinking about her mother all day today, which wasn't surprising. Today was her birthday. Or, at least, it would have been.

"Isabelle," Lucas said her name sharply, "you have nothing to say for yourself? Nothing?" He looked like he was on the verge of having to breathe into a brown bag. He put his hand over his face. "Bill, this is the sort of thing that can sink your campaign before it even officially starts."

"It's not *that* big of a deal, Lucas," Izzie's aunt started to say. "Kids make mistakes."

"Maureen, she's an underage kid from Harborside," Lucas snapped. "Her third week living with you guys, she steals a priceless piece of jewelry! How do you think that is going to look to your campaign boosters?"

Izzie winced. She hadn't thought about how this would affect her uncle.

"Are you sure there is nothing you can add, Isabelle?" her uncle pressed. "Mira told us there were other girls with you, but your statement says you acted alone. That's a little odd."

He knows I'm lying, Izzie realized. *How nice of Mira to mention Violet and Nicole, but leave out the part about how her best friend had orchestrated the whole dare.*

She hadn't had a chance to shower yet and she sat shivering in a tank top and shorts over her damp bathing suit. She wasn't sure if she was cold or just lonely. It was funny how she could be in a room full of people and still feel empty inside. Seeing her mom wasn't possible, but she'd give anything for the old Grams to be by her side.

"Do you think this is funny, Isabelle?" Lucas must have seen her smile at the thought of Grams, and now he was furious. "I had to move mountains to sweep this mess under the rug! I just got off the phone with Mr. Matthews at the club, and he's agreed not to press charges." He ran a hand through his hair. "I practically had to agree we'd bankroll the club's next function to keep him quiet. We cannot have this sort of thing getting out to the press, not when we're this close to securing that nomination. You're very lucky, Isabelle. The least you could do is act appreciative of what this family has done for you."

"Lucas," Izzie's uncle said sharply. "That is enough. Why don't you both wait for me downstairs. I'd like to speak to Isabelle alone."

"Bill." Lucas's face paled, but Izzie wasn't sure why.

Her uncle cut him off. "I said I need a minute, Lucas."

Izzie's aunt hugged her before leaving the room. "Put a sweater on, sweetheart." She touched her cheek. "You're shivering."

"I feel like I owe you an apology," Izzie's uncle said once they were alone. "Today is my fault. Maybe if I'd been around more…" he trailed off. Izzie didn't think he was making sense. "I'm sure you wish Chloe were here right now. I do, too." Hearing him say her mom's name made a lump form in her throat. "Maybe she'd know what to say to get through to you. This is your new beginning. We want you to have the best of everything EC has to offer, but we can't help you if you don't trust us enough to tell us the truth." He looked down. "What happened today is done. Hopefully it was just a misunderstanding, which is why we've decided not to ground you." Isabelle couldn't believe what she was hearing. Her uncle moved to the door. "I'm always here, though, Isabelle, if you want to talk some-time."

She knew he was trying to get through to her. She just didn't have anything left to give. The day had left her emotionally exhausted.

"Well, I guess I'll give you a chance to get ready for the auction," he said when she still had nothing to say.

Did they really expect her to show her face after all that had happened that afternoon? No one wanted to see her. She'd only tarnish the Monroe name more if she went. "Actually, I don't think I'm going to go," she spoke up. "I'm not feeling very well." She glanced at the purple wrap dress hanging on her closet door that her aunt had bought for the occasion. "I'll catch the next one."

Her uncle actually looked disappointed, which made Izzie feel worse. "I understand. Feel better and get some rest." He closed the door behind him.

Izzie flopped back on her bed, ready to sleep for a week. She thought about calling Kylie but then decided she needed to take a shower first. The whole world seemed brighter after five minutes under hot water. She hadn't eaten or drunk anything since lunch, so after she blow-dried her hair, she headed downstairs. The house was eerily quiet. Izzie opened the refrigerator, grabbed one of her aunt's sparkling waters, and drank it with the fridge door open. The cool air was just what she needed to decompress.

"Thirsty, Isabelle?"

She spun around, letting go of the fridge door, which hit her head as it closed. "Lucas." She rubbed her head. "I thought you guys went to the auction." There was something about the way he was staring at her that was unnerving.

Lucas walked toward her. "You caused quite the scene this afternoon. I hope you're happy with yourself."

"Look—" Izzie started to say.

"No, you look." Lucas's voice was as sharp as a knife. "You're leading a pretty charmed life here, kid, one I'm not sure you deserve, so for all our sakes, don't screw it up!"

Izzie almost let the water bottle drop and spill all over the floor.

"I've been working on this campaign with your uncle for months, and I will not have some kid come in here and blow our chances of winning," Lucas said menacingly. All Izzie could think about was the fact that Lucas had used the word *our*. Whose campaign really was this? "Keep. Your. Nose. Clean. Got it?" He leaned in and Izzie stiffened. "If you pull another stunt like the one you did today, or the one you pulled at the regatta party, ruining my planned press photo op, well, this relationship of ours isn't going to be so pretty anymore." He flashed a thin smile. "I can make your life hell. How do you think Grams is in such a nice nursing home, anyway? Do you really think she could afford to pay for a place like Coastal Assisted Living?" Izzie felt her face pale. "I don't want to have this conversation again because if we do, you and that frail grandmother of yours are going to regret it."

As Lucas walked out of the kitchen, a cold sensation swept over her and this time it had nothing to do with the fridge. It wasn't till the front door slammed a few minutes later that Izzie felt like she could breathe normally again. She couldn't believe what had just happened. Had Lucas really threatened her? Threatened Grams? The Monroes' house suddenly felt very small, like the walls were closing in on her, and that's when she knew. She had to get out of there. Pronto.

She pulled out her cell and dialed. "Kylie?" she said, sounding choked up. "It's me....No, I'm not fine. I really need to talk to you. You're where? The boardwalk?...I don't know if I can get over there."

The idea was so tempting, Izzie could taste it. She was an outcast at school and in this house, and she couldn't handle it anymore. She needed to be with people who understood her, and there was only one place where she'd find that.

Home.

Her aunt and uncle would freak if she went to Harborside without telling them, but it was only seven thirty. Did they really even have to find out? She'd be home before the auction even ended.

"Okay, give me an hour," Izzie said, feeling determined. "I'll meet you there."

Forty minutes later, she was walking as quickly as her legs would take her to a place she could find blindfolded. She ducked under the boardwalk near Fourth Street and grinned. It was a Friday night, which meant that everyone she knew in Harborside was there. Her friends were bundled up in sweatshirts sitting around a large bonfire. Just the sight of the fire was soothing.

Kylie looked up. "*Iz-Whiz!*" She ran over, practically knocking her down. Izzie laughed as Kylie put her hands all over her face. "Is it really you or am I seeing a ghost?"

"It's me," Izzie said, and squeezed her tightly. "You have no idea how good it is to see you. I've been trying to reach you all week!"

"I've been pulling double shifts at Scoops." Kylie frowned. "Duke quit and —"

"Look what the tide washed up." Their friend Molly approached and removed her gray hood, revealing her pink hair. She surprised Izzie by giving her a quick once-over. Izzie thought only EC girls did that.

"Hey, Molly," Izzie said. She and Molly Boone were friends, but Izzie wouldn't exactly call them close. To put it in perspective, if Izzie someday made the Olympics swim team, Molly might be the tenth or eleventh person she called — if she even remembered to call her. Molly never forgave Izzie for winning the only open spot on the swim team all those years ago, and their friendship had definitely suffered because of it.

"Pete!" Molly called to a guy lying on a beach towel. "Look who showed up. Iz-Whiz!"

"Look at that! Hey, Iz-Whiz." Pete Booker had a new dragon tattoo on his forearm. Knowing Pete, that's why he was in a tank top when it was only sixty degrees — he wanted to show it off. She had forgotten how cold it was down by the shore at night and she wished she'd brought a jacket. "We were taking bets on whether we'd ever catch you around here again," Pete said, glancing at Molly.

"Of course you were going to see me again," Izzie said. It had only been three weeks. Three very long weeks. "I've really missed you guys."

Molly kicked the sand. "Missed us, huh? We heard about your new digs. Pretty sweet gig you've got going for yourself. I heard you even go to private school now."

"She's gone high-class on us!" Kylie joked. "Izzie goes to Emerald Prep with that hot surfer boy." She nudged her and Izzie blushed. "Does that mean you two can finally go out now?"

Izzie shook her head. She wanted to tell Kylie everything, but she didn't feel comfortable in front of the others. "It's complicated."

Pete stuck his hands in his pants pockets to warm up.

"People from EC don't do complicated. When you have money, nothing's complicated."

"It's not my money," Izzie reminded them.

Molly startled her by running her hands through Izzie's hair, her sterling silver rings scraping Izzie's scalp. "Maybe it's not technically your dough, but they've still given you quite a makeover. This isn't a cut from Lemon Tree."

"New haircut, new makeup, better clothes." Pete walked in a circle around her. "Look who got a princess makeover."

"Ha-ha." Izzie was starting to feel uncomfortable as they dissected her like a frog. "It's still me."

"How much are those jeans you're wearing, princess?" Molly asked, thumbing Izzie's thigh.

"Guys, back off." Even Kylie was getting annoyed. "You're acting like jerks."

Molly touched the bag over Izzie's shoulder. "And whoa…what is this? Do you know how much we could get for this bag?" Molly yanked the bag toward her.

Izzie pulled the bag roughly from Molly's grasp, and the others stared at her. Her aunt had given Izzie the bag as a gift before her first day of school. She felt funny having an "it" bag, but she hadn't received a gift in years. This bag meant something to her. "This was a present. I can't hock it."

Molly rolled her eyes and zipped up her oversize sweatshirt. "Whatever, princess. You just want that bag so you can pretend to be one of them now."

Kylie's eyes narrowed at Molly. "You wish you had someone to buy you a gift like that." Then she smiled at Izzie. "I think it's cool that they're being so good to you. You deserve it."

"We all do," Molly said. "Can't we tell your new 'rents my family disappeared so they can take me in, too? I'm kidding. You know I'm kidding, right, princess?"

"Sure," Izzie said quietly. She wasn't, but she wasn't about to rock the boat. She was just happy to be with her real friends, somewhere she wasn't judged.

Oh, wait.

But they were joking with her, right? "Do you guys want to do something?" Izzie asked, hoping to change the subject.

"We *are* doing something," Molly said, looking around the dark underside of the boardwalk.

Izzie looked around. There was a couple sucking face on a beach blanket, some guys singing with a guitar by the fire, and others just burying each other's feet in the sand. If nothing was going on at the community center — and even that was hard to drag her friends to sometimes — hanging out under the boardwalk was what they did every weekend. Weeknights, too. She had already forgotten how quiet it was down here. There was no DJ Backslide blasting the latest hit, overpriced lattes, or girls smack-talking someone whose gown was so last season.

But Izzie also realized as she looked around her that there

wasn't much to do under the boardwalk, either. She wanted to do more than sit on the sand every night for the rest of her life. She didn't want to wear Vera on a daily basis, but there had to be more than this. And that's when it hit her. She'd only been in Emerald Cove a few weeks, but apparently it was changing her. She didn't fit in there, but she wasn't sure she belonged here, either. She didn't belong anywhere. Suddenly she felt more depressed than ever.

"I should probably get going," Izzie said hastily.

"You can't go yet," Kylie begged. "You just got here! We haven't even caught up yet."

"I know, but…" Izzie trailed off.

"When you said you were coming, I got everything together," Kylie told her. Izzie looked at her strangely as she began pulling things out of her purse. She held up a lighter. "I didn't forget what today is, Iz."

"None of us did," Molly said quietly.

Izzie bit her lip. "You remembered?"

"We'd never forget, babe." Kylie pulled out a plastic bag with a smushed cupcake.

Izzie didn't want to cry, but the mushy pink frosting was too much for her to handle. Izzie slowly sank onto the sand. "My mom would have been forty-one today," she said, staring out from under the boardwalk at where the water should be. Kylie sat down and put an arm around her. "That's so young," Izzie said. "She's missed so much." She took some sand in her hands and let it slide through her fingers. "I wish she were here to tell me what to do right now."

"Is it six years?" Molly asked, rubbing Izzie's shoulders.

"Almost." Izzie winced at the memory. The phone call at Grams's house, the crowded and very loud ER, the way Grams broke down…she hated thinking about that day. Her mom had died right before she'd turned ten. Her mom loved birthdays, which was why today should be celebrated even if she was gone.

Kylie pulled out her lighter and stuck a candle in the cupcake as Pete cupped his hands around it to keep the candle from blowing out.

Molly held the cupcake out to her. "Make a wish for your mom. And make it a good one. No guts, no glory, remember?"

Molly had hung out at the pool with Izzie's mom, too. Maybe things were changing among all of them, but Izzie realized they were still there for her when it really counted.

"We won't force you to sing this year," Kylie said. "You can just blow out the candle."

Izzie closed her eyes and made a wish for her mom. It was sort of a wish for both of them. She wished that they'd both be happy, even if she wasn't sure that was even possible. Then she blew out the candle and took a little frosting off the top with her finger. "Thanks," she said.

They all smiled, even Molly.

"You're welcome." Kylie hugged her and didn't let go.

Izzie wasn't sure how long they sat huddled together like that. A guy was playing something angsty on his guitar, and she stared at the flames of the bonfire. Then Pete said something funny about rocker wannabes and they all laughed. It felt awkward being there with them, but they were trying to make things okay for her, even if she did look different, and she tried to fit in with them, even if she felt different. Molly was the one who started the questioning about EC again.

Molly used a stick to draw in the sand. "So, what is Daddy Warbucks like?"

"He's okay. He works a lot, but he's been really nice." Izzie didn't say what his job was. That would have just made them rib her more. If Molly read the papers, she'd find out anyway.

"I wish my dad was never home," Molly mumbled.

Home. Izzie jumped up. "What time is it?"

Pete laughed. "Why? We haven't had curfews since we were twelve."

I do now, she thought. Hers was eleven and she hadn't even gotten permission to go out tonight. *Please let it be ten. Please let it be ten.*

Kylie squinted at her watch. "I can't see the time. I think it's…"

Izzie didn't wait for the answer. She reached for her small bag and pulled out her iPhone.

"Geez, you have one of those now, too?" Pete asked.

She had forgotten to turn the phone on. When she did, their little patch of sand got bright. The time was 11:52 PM. The "new voice mail" alert popped up before she could figure out what to do first. She had four new messages. Izzie didn't have to listen to them to know whom they were from. She was doomed. She knew what they said.

Sixteen

Mira's dad was laughing harder than he had in weeks. "I had no idea Lucas and I were bidding against each other," he said as he opened the front door and flipped on the lights. "You should have seen his face when I won the Hank Aaron autographed baseball!"

The Monroes had just come from the annual EP silent auction and Mira was glad to see her dad's mood had lifted after what had happened earlier that day with Izzie. Winning was always an endorphin booster for him. There had been three baseball items to bid on that night and her dad had won two of them. The third was an autographed home plate from a World Series game her dad had played in, but since he had donated it, he obviously didn't plan on winning it back (it sold for $2,450).

"You have me to thank for your haul," Mira's mom said as she carried in their winnings. "The only reason you won is because no one knew you were using my maiden name to bid. All night people kept asking me if I knew who Bill Horn was." Both of her parents laughed.

Mira was glad her parents were speaking again. They'd had a huge fight on the car ride to the auction. Her mom was furious at the way Lucas had spoken to Izzie earlier, and her dad had tried to defend him. "You owe her so much, Bill!" she'd snapped. "Don't you think I know that?" he'd yelled back. Parts of the argument hadn't even made sense. Hayden and Mira had sat silently waiting for the fighting to end. Mira was just glad that Connor wasn't there to hear it — he was too young to attend the EP auction so he'd stayed at a friend's house. But Mira had heard it, and all she knew was that her parents had never fought like this before Izzie had come into their lives. Thankfully, her mom had calmed down when they reached the school gates. Maureen Monroe knew it wasn't smart for her to freeze out the senator in public, especially after what had gone down at the country club.

Mira, unfortunately, couldn't enjoy herself. She felt sick to her stomach all night, and she was sure it had nothing to do with the chiffon dress she had squeezed herself into. Aside from the usual introductions her dad always made, she didn't have to glad-hand many people. Taylor had an away varsity football game, Kellen was nowhere to be found, and Savannah was so thrilled with her power play at the pool that she spent the night recounting the story to anyone who would listen. Millie Lennon's family's table cards sat untouched on the welcome table all night. So did Izzie's.

You got me into this mess. Isn't that what Izzie had said to her? It was sort of true. Maybe she hadn't planned what happened, but she had *let* it happen. Which was worse? In the past, Mira had always laughed along with Savannah's pranks, but they had never involved anyone close to her before. Like it or not, Izzie was family now and she couldn't believe she had let Savannah do that to Izzie. Why didn't Mira tell the cops the truth? Why didn't she stand up for Izzie? Or for herself? *Because you never do,* she heard a voice in her head say. She always let other people dictate her life. Isn't that why she was hiding the fact that she was taking art classes from all her friends?

Her mom had gone upstairs and was already on her way back down while Mira stood in the foyer thinking about these things. "I checked on Connor at his friend's house," her mom said. "They're not asleep yet. Surprise." She smirked. "I haven't seen Isabelle, though. She must be in the den. Maybe she's hungry. These filet mignon kabobs smell heavenly."

"I should go pack," her dad said, and grimaced. "Lucas is bringing the car at four thirty AM so that we can take a private jet to Maine. I've got a rally at eight tomorrow morning."

Hayden patted him on the shoulder. "No rest for the weary, Senator."

Two seconds later, they heard their mom yell. "She's gone!" she said, rushing back into the foyer and looking panicked. "Isabelle! She's not here!"

"What do you mean she's not here?" Mira's dad frowned. "I thought she was sick."

"I checked her room, all the rooms downstairs," Mira's mom said. "She's not here! And curfew was over an hour ago!"

"Let's not panic. Maybe she forgot the time and is out with friends," Mira's dad suggested. Everyone looked at him oddly. "Doesn't she have any friends yet?"

"She's been having kind of a tough time," Hayden said.

"She wouldn't miss curfew," Mira's mom insisted. "It's almost midnight. Do you think she's run away?" Mira's mom's hand went to her necklace and she thumbed it nervously.

Run away? Mira grabbed the coatrack for support. This was her fault. She had to tell them what had really happened at the pool. They needed to know Izzie covered for Millie.

"Try her phone," Mira's dad suggested.

Mira's mom dialed, then shook her head. "It goes right to voice mail. I knew we shouldn't have left her alone tonight." She threw the phone on a chair. "After the things Lucas said to her and what happened today, she was probably humiliated."

"Maureen, it wasn't that bad," Mira's dad said. "I'm sure

she just went out for a walk or something to get some air. We'll spread out and look for her, okay? Mira, Hayden, call your friends. See if anyone who wasn't at the auction tonight has seen Isabelle. I'll call Lucas and tell him what is happening." Her dad walked into the living room, but Mira could still hear him. "Hi. It's me. Isabelle is missing.... No, I didn't call the police.... Yes, I know, Lucas," he sighed.

Her mom's face was aghast. She looked at Hayden and Mira. "Isabelle really doesn't have any friends?"

"She came to the pool this afternoon with a few girls from the swim team," Mira said, hoping that would keep her mom from asking how Mira and her own friends felt about Izzie.

Her mom's eyes darkened. "You mean the girls she got in trouble with? Those are the only girls she's been seen with?" Her mom shook her head. "Today's incident was unfortunate, yes, and I still don't think she's telling us the whole story, but I thought Isabelle was starting to like Emerald Cove. Barbara visited just the other day, and she was saying how well-adjusted Isabelle seemed."

"I know you've been trying to help her, Mom, but she's anything but happy," Hayden said, sounding angry. "EP hasn't exactly rolled out the welcome wagon, you know. She's been here almost a month and the only person she really talks to is me." Mira felt Hayden's eyes on her. "Ask Mira how her friends have been to Izzie. And by *been*, I mean how awful."

"Mira, is this true?" Their mom looked crushed and Mira quickly glanced away. "That can't be possible. She's a Monroe! Why wouldn't people like her?"

"Do you want to tell her, Mira, or should I?" Hayden asked, and Mira felt her face burn. "People say she's not really a Monroe," he told their mom, not waiting for Mira to respond. "You know, the she-doesn't-deserve-the-new-life-she-got bit. Harborside comes up a lot, too. Those news stories about her life did a number on her chances. Izzie is not ashamed of where she's from, and that only bothers the kids at EP even more." Hayden's green eyes darkened. "Don't look so surprised, Mom. What happened at the club today is probably just the beginning of the Izzie hazing."

Their mom still looked confused. "But I thought Mira had taken her under her wing. You're one of the most well-liked girls in your class. Why wouldn't they like Isabelle, too?"

Maybe it was Hayden's confession or maybe it was the guilt getting to her because instead of having a normal reaction, Mira completely lost it. "I did not sign up to be Izzie's babysitter!" Mira said shakily, and her mother gaped. "I did like you asked, tried to help Izzie when she got here. I bent over backward telling her about EC and how things worked, but she basically ignored me. I'm sure that's what she does to everyone else at school, too. It's got nothing to do with Harborside, Hayden," Mira said, and even as the words were coming out of her mouth, she knew they were a lie. "She never tried to fit in, so now she doesn't. That's why people ignore her."

"Maybe Izzie ignores you because she sees right through you and your friends. She knows a fake when she sees one." Hayden's words were like a slap in the face. "But why would you care how Izzie feels? The only person you care about is yourself."

Mira hated the way Hayden was looking at her. They hardly ever fought, and when they did, Mira got sick over it. She trusted Hayden more than anyone in the world and now he thought she was as bad as Savannah. Well, she was, wasn't she? She bit her lip so hard she tasted blood. There was no way she could tell them that Izzie took the fall for Millie now. Hayden would really hate her then. What had she turned herself into? She wasn't always this way. When had things taken such a wrong turn?

"She's not coming back, is she?" Mira's mom's voice was small. She looked at Mira's dad, who had reentered the room. "Why would she when things are as bad as you say they are?" That's when they heard the key in the front door.

When Izzie saw them standing there, she jumped so high that Mira thought she was going to hit her head on the ceiling. Her face was blotchy, like she'd been crying, and her bob was windblown. Mira noticed her jeans had sand stuck to the knees. Mira's mom embraced her, crying, which was a shock to both Izzie and Mira. But Mira felt another emotion, too: relief. Izzie was okay. Physically, at least, she was okay.

"Don't ever do that again!" her mom told Izzie. "We thought you'd run away."

"Run away?" Izzie looked surprised. "I'm sorry. I just lost track of time. I took the bus back to Harborside to see my friends and I didn't realize how late it was."

Mira's mom and dad looked at each other. "You were in Harborside?" Mira's dad said. "You told me you were too sick to go to the auction." Izzie didn't say anything. "I understand that there may be some things you don't want to do with this family, Isabelle, but you can't just go off without permission. Especially to Harborside. What if something happened to you?"

Izzie's laugh was bitter. "I think I'm in more danger here than I ever was in Harborside."

"Your aunt was very upset," Mira's dad said, ignoring Izzie's comment. "You're our responsibility now, and that means you need to abide by this family's rules."

"I can take care of myself just fine. I've been doing it for years," she said, her eyes getting watery even as her voice maintained its sharp clip. "The people in Harborside aren't anything to be scared of. They are decent and kind. They always had my back. No one judges me the way everyone does here," she snapped.

Izzie had never come back at Mira's parents like that before. No one knew what to do next, probably because they knew Izzie had hit a hard truth.

"You're right. We shouldn't judge Harborside like that," Mira's dad said quickly. "Old money can be...shall we say, stuffy. Believe me, I know. But I also know your mother would want you to try harder here in Emerald Cove."

"My mother would have been forty-one today," Izzie whispered almost to herself. "I shouldn't be blowing out candles on a cake without her. I want her here!" she yelled at no one in particular. "I don't want to live in Emerald Cove. I want to go home!" Izzie broke down, and Mira's mom tried to hug her.

All the times Mira had thought about how much having Izzie around inconvenienced her own life, she'd never thought about Izzie's old one. Izzie had a life before EC. She was someone's daughter, too. Mira couldn't imagine what her life would be like if she didn't have her mom in it.

"I'm sorry, Isabelle. I didn't — we didn't know what today was." Mira's mom looked desperately at her husband. Hayden hugged Izzie, too, but Mira couldn't move. She felt so conflicted.

"I'm so sorry," Mira's dad said awkwardly. "We'll make things right."

Izzie wiped her eyes. "I'm fine," she said like she was repeating a mantra. "Someone reminded me recently that I'm a fighter, and I am. Maybe I forgot that today, but I won't again," she warned. "I'm not going to let this place break me."

"I know people are going to love you once they get to know the real Isabelle Scott," Mira's mom said. "You've got the swim team now, and you know what would be really fun? If you joined the Social Butterflies."

Izzie and Mira looked at each other. "Yeah, I'm not so sure that would be good," Izzie said.

"I think it's a great idea," Mira's mom looked encouragingly at Mira, like she hadn't heard a word her daughter had said earlier. "Don't you, Mira?"

Lucas walked in before Mira could answer. His gaze locked on Izzie and she noticed her cousin's face change. "Isabelle, you're here. Thank goodness. Everything okay, I hope? There's no *new* problem we have to deal with, is there?"

"No, we took care of it," Mira's dad said, smiling at Izzie. "We're just glad she's back."

Lucas kept his eyes on Izzie. "Yes, me, too," he said quietly. "We certainly don't need any more surprises, do we?"

Izzie actually answered him, sounding much calmer than she had a few minutes ago. "Not at all, Lucas."

"Good," Lucas said, but Mira felt uneasy.

Lucas was being especially creepy, even for him.

Seventeen

Hot yoga class or frozen yogurt machine for the cafeteria? The Butterflies' adviser, Mrs. Fitzgerald, was perplexed as she listened to the passionate debate among the thirty-odd girls assembled for the club's first fall meeting. The group had already doubled its donation to Save the Children thanks to last year's carnival, but now it still had a small stash of cash left over. Usually that was spent on the end-of-year party, but last year's lavish bash had been sponsored by Savannah's parents (some said in a bid to get her elected club president that fall), which meant the Butterflies now had money to burn, and in EC, money never sat idle for long. So now their adviser was being tortured with this yoga-versus-yogurt debate. Lea was in the middle of her speech on why the cafeteria needed a dessert that had less trans fats when Mrs. Fitzgerald heard a welcome knock on the door.

"Hi. Is this where the Social Butterflies meet?"

Mira heard Izzie's voice and immediately looked up from the meeting agenda. She couldn't believe Izzie was actually taking her mom's advice to join the Butterflies. But there was her cousin, standing in the doorway wearing her school uniform and holding her swim bag over her shoulder. Izzie looked like she wasn't sure if she wanted to come in or bolt.

"Is it too late to join?" Izzie asked tentatively.

"Of course not!" Mrs. Fitzgerald said, practically yanking Izzie in by the arm. "I'm Mrs. Fitzgerald, or you can call me Mrs. Fitz. There is only one requirement for this club," she said, her voice adopting a serious tone. "We need to know why you think you are right for a butterfly transformation."

The only thing annoying about this group Mira adored so much was Mrs. Fitz's need to turn the club's name into something more meaningful. She was constantly talking about the girls' metamorphoses and how they related to the good the girls did in the club. When it came to anything Butterfly-related, Mrs. Fitz took matters seriously. Even a discussion on what color paper club flyers should be printed on turned into a cause for reflection and celebration.

"Um, I'm not sure I get what you mean." Izzie leaped to the safety of Violet and Nicole, who were sitting near the front.

"What. Is. She. Doing. Here?" Savannah hissed, practically spitting in Mira's right ear.

"I don't know," Mira admitted. Was Izzie trying to fit in after all? Ever since Izzie talked about her mom the other night, Mira couldn't stop thinking about what it was like to be Izzie. It was the first time she had put herself in her cousin's shoes since Izzie had arrived and it had been an eye-opener. Mira was starting to realize how hard it had to be leaving behind everything Izzie knew and starting over in a place where she didn't know a soul. No wonder Izzie sometimes came across as standoffish. It made Mira feel guiltier than ever for the things she had said that night to Hayden and her mom.

"We'd love to know what would make you a good Butterfly," Mrs. Fitzgerald tried to explain again, and flapped her arms for effect. "Our group is all about metamorphoses."

There was that word again.

"And we like members who want to help save the world, one day at a time."

Club motto.

"We've been doing that since 1944, the first year girls were allowed to matriculate at Emerald Prep," Mrs. Fitz added, tapping the insignia of the club that was stickered on her folder. "Isabelle, have you done anything that would qualify as Butterfly behavior?"

Savannah leaned over to Lea and Lauren. "Does being on

the receiving end of club donations count?" The girls snickered.

"Well, I…" Izzie looked at Nicole and Violet, who nodded encouragingly. "I taught free swim lessons at our community center."

Mrs. Fitz clapped excitedly. "That's perfect! You are definitely Butterfly material."

Savannah, smelling like the honeysuckle perfume she had spritzed on during an after-school touch-up, leaned over to Mira. "This makes zero sense. Why would Izzie want to be a Butterfly? Unless she's trying to find a way to get back at us for Tryout Day."

"Maybe she likes the club." Mira shifted uncomfortably.

Savannah's eyes narrowed. "No, that's not it. She's up to something, and I'm going to find out what it is."

"Before you arrived, Isabelle, we were discussing what to do with our 'fun' money from last year," Mrs. Fitz told her. "We can't decide between a yoga class or a frozen yogurt machine, and the vote is tied." She looked hopeful. "Maybe you could be our tiebreaker."

Lauren groaned. "What does she know?" she whispered to Mira. "She's probably never had the money for either."

"I don't know if anyone here really wants my opinion," Izzie said, turning her head slightly toward the sound of Savannah's giggling.

"Of course we do," Violet told her.

"Okay, well, to be honest, I wouldn't do either," Izzie said. "If the Butterflies really are a charity club, then why not give the extra money to another charity? Or buy a frozen yogurt machine for a school that doesn't have a lunch program?"

Savannah applauded Izzie mockingly. "Mrs. Fitz, I think you've found the Butterflies' new spokesperson!" The sarcasm was lost on Mrs. Fitz, who beamed proudly.

"You're right, Savannah. This is the type of Butterfly leadership I'm talking about, ladies," Mrs. Fitz said. "It's settled, then. We'll buy a machine for another school." Lauren moaned. She kind of had her heart set on that hot yoga class. Mrs. Fitz looked at Savannah and Mira. "Let's move on to our next topic. New club presidents, do you want to fill Isabelle in on this year's first fall event?"

Mira tucked her hair behind her right ear and looked down at her notes. "We've reserved the Monica Holbrook Arts Center on Saturday, October eighteenth, for our event. That gives us a three-week lead on the Emerald Cove Country Club's Founders Day party."

"EP's football game is during the week, so we pretty much have a lock on the weekend," Savannah added, reading from her own notebook. "Not that we'd have competition anyway. Everyone would rather come to a Butterflies event. We just need a killer idea for a party that will blow the town away." Mira and Savannah had spent weeks trying to imagine the perfect fall mixer, but Savannah's head was so wrapped up in her own sweet-sixteen planning that all she could think about were fire jugglers and henna tattoos (Savannah's sixteenth was going to have an Arabian nights theme).

"It can be difficult," Mrs. Fitz said, nodding. "We've had such winners in the past. Any suggestions?" She smiled at Mira. "We need something worthy for our esteemed senator. He already cleared his calendar to join us and, word has it, might say a few words about his upcoming run."

Nicole shot her pale hand into the air. She was the tallest girl there, so her hand was the highest. "What about a variety show?"

"I don't think we have enough time to get one together," Mrs. Fitz said sadly, pursing her pink lips. "Maybe in the spring. I'm already working on a lovely twenty-minute piano piece."

Think of a great excuse not to have Mrs. F. do a piano solo, Mira jotted down in her notebook.

"Plus, we've done variety shows, like, six times already," Savannah said, sounding bored. "No one wants to hear someone sing 'Defying Gravity' off-key again, Nicole. Mira and I want our first event as copresidents to be different. Come on, girls. We need new ideas!"

"Game night?" suggested Lauren.

"Country club is already doing one," Savannah said as if it were obvious.

"We could do different games," Lauren huffed, "like Old Maid, Go Fish…"

"We need an idea that appeals to people over five," Savannah spoke over her.

"What's your idea, Savannah?" Violet asked sweetly, playing with her dark brown hair.

Savannah gave her a look. "I've come up with our last *four* events, including the spring arts and crafts fair, and our carnival games day, which raised over five thousand dollars to help reopen a girls' school in New Orleans that had been closed since Katrina."

"Most of the profits came from the dunk tank," Nicole told Izzie proudly, then frowned. "I don't think I was dry once in the eight hours I was at that booth."

"Maybe Izzie should come up with our next event idea," Savannah said, a small smile spreading across her lips. "I'm sure being our newest Butterfly she's come armed with loads of ideas." She leaned back in her chair just far enough that Mira and the back row could hear her. "Like that girl would have any idea how to raise money instead of *steal* it."

Izzie's eyes narrowed. Mira knew she'd heard Savannah. "What about a hoedown?"

Savannah bristled. "Did you just call me a —"

"I said a hoedown," Izzie repeated slowly. "It's like a barn dance. They're pretty typical for fall. My aunt's *Martha Stewart* magazine this month features one that looks pretty cool."

"You read *Martha Stewart?*" Lea gave her a harsh once-over.

Mrs. Fitz's gray bun bounced up and down on her head excitedly. "I saw that article! I love barn dances! We used to have them all the time where I grew up in Tennessee."

Izzie thought hard. "You could put hay on the floor, have hay bales for seating, get pumpkins, ask the art classes to paint murals. We could get a band to play and do barbecue food and…"

"Last year, Georgia got her uncle at Sony to fly down Tyler Donovan to host our mother-daughter fashion show. Do you know any celebrities we could use?" Savannah asked.

"A good event doesn't have to be fully fleshed out by one person, Savannah," Mrs. Fitz reminded her. "I guess the first question is whether everyone likes the idea. Show of hands."

Several hands flew up. Those closest to Savannah put theirs up slowly, but even Mira raised hers. Savannah stared moodily at the traitors. What could Mira say? Izzie's idea was good, and so far, Savannah's and Mira's weren't. (A circus? Lame.)

"Well, then, it's settled," Mrs. Fitz said, jotting the word *hoedown* in her notebook. "Now let's choose a charity. Who do you want to raise the money for, Isabelle?"

"Isabelle?" Savannah said in surprise.

Mrs. Fitz slapped her own cheek. "I forgot! Headmaster Heller and I came up with a wonderful twist for the club this year. We decided that whoever picks the theme of an event also picks the charity we raise money for." She looked embarrassed. "He got a little tired of always supporting whatever organization the mothers in this town were already working with. Sometimes they can be a tad pushy."

"My mom wanted me to suggest EC Greeters!" Lea complained.

"Do you have a favorite charity, Isabelle?" Mrs. Fitz asked.

"Her own?" Savannah whispered.

"Well, this isn't exactly Save the Children," Izzie said, sounding a little excited, "but the Harborside Community Center where I used to go needs help. They have some great programs, but there's never been any money left over to patch up walls, get new equipment, or spruce up the day care." Izzie looked thoughtful. "The whole town relies on the center not just for the programs, but also for a sense of community. It's the one place everyone could always go to that was safe and fun and…" She trailed off. "Anyway, I know what it did for me. I don't think I could have stayed out of trouble growing up if I didn't have the community center to go to. Maybe if other kids saw how great the place looked, they'd hang out there more, too. Giving the money to them would help so many people."

Mira couldn't help being touched by Izzie's speech. Mrs. Fitz obviously felt the same. "Giving back to the local community is a glorious idea, and Headmaster Heller will love it. Think of the publicity." Mrs. Fitz looked at Savannah and Mira again. "Presidents, what do you think?"

"Sounds great," Savannah surprised Mira by agreeing. "Izzie should help us plan, too. Since she came up with the event idea and a charity to raise funds for, I think she should be honorary chair."

What is Savannah doing? Mira wondered. Izzie must have been thinking the same thing based on her skeptical expression.

Mrs. Fitz frowned. "I don't know. Isabelle's new. I'm not sure..."

"She'll delegate, get donations. It is easy, right, girls?" Some of the girls nodded, and Savannah looked at Izzie pointedly. "Unless Izzie doesn't think she can get the job done."

Izzie stared at Savannah for a moment before answering. "I can do anything."

"We'll help," Violet offered, referring to herself and Nicole.

"Me, too," Mira said, without thinking. Izzie looked at her oddly.

Mrs. Fitz smiled. "With that much support, how can I say no?"

After the meeting, girls began to file out, heading to sports practices or to Corky's. Izzie was deep in conversation with Violet and Nicole, but Mira lingered. She'd already told coach she'd be a half hour late to field hockey practice. She just needed everyone to clear out so she could get to the art studio to finish working on her water lily still-life assignment. It was due tomorrow. Savannah, however, was in the middle of her own impromptu meeting with Lea and Lauren, and she wasn't leaving till she was done talking.

"Can you believe Izzie said yes?" Savannah laughed. "She almost made it too easy for us. How is *she* going to put a party together? Even with those friends of hers helping, she'll never get the right caterer or find enough donations. And revamping a lame community center?" She rolled her eyes. "Who wants to waste money on that? We need to make sure Izzie goes down in flames. Between the four of us we know enough people in this town to make sure no one helps her. She'll be so humiliated, Mira's mom will have to pull her from EP to save face." Savannah nudged Mira. "Brilliant move offering to help her, though. She'll never suspect we're sabotaging her if she thinks you're on her side."

Mira's heart sank. Her offer had been genuine. A tiny part of her thought helping Izzie might be a way to mend the growing gap between them before it became a gorge. But she could see that Savannah was never going to let that happen. "This is our first event as presidents," Mira reminded Savannah. "Don't we want this party to work?"

"It will," Savannah assured her. "Once Mrs. Fitz finds out that Izzie's plan has blown up in her face, we'll swoop in, save the day, and come up with triple the money to donate to a *worthy* cause. Not to a building about to be torn down." Mira looked confused. "That community center Izzie keeps jabbering about is first on the list of places in Harborside my dad wants to tear down to build new hotels and condos. It's part of the coastal revitalization planning bill he wants *your* dad to pass."

"He's tearing down Izzie's community center?" Mira's fingers wrapped tightly around her notebook. It hadn't occurred to her that Izzie's center could be a part of that project. "She's going to be devastated."

"I know," said Savannah with a vicious glint in her eye. "Which is why when she can't pull this event off and save her precious center, she'll completely crumble."

"You're brilliant, Vanna," Lea said. "I'm totally in."

"Me, too," Lauren said, and followed Lea out the door.

Mira fidgeted with the silver ring on her right hand. She couldn't be part of a plot to sabotage Izzie again. Not after the way she had treated Izzie already. "Vanna, I don't think I can do this," she said anxiously. "It's one thing to embarrass Izzie, but this is downright cruel. It will crush her. I don't think she can take much more." She hesitated. "She's had it really rough. I never realized how rough, actually."

Savannah gave her a look. "We're doing her a favor. People like her are a product of their environment. She's never going to fit in at Emerald Prep or in Emerald Cove. Once she leaves your family and goes back to Harborside, she'll be much happier and so will we."

"She doesn't have anything to go back to," Mira said softly.

Savannah pursed her lips. "She's making your family look like fools. I've been trying to protect you, Mira, but people are talking. They think your parents are bringing down EC by having someone like Izzie move in with them." Savannah fixed her plaid skirt, pinning the flap in the fabric tighter around her tiny waist. "They're worried Izzie's friends will start hanging out here soon, too, and then crime will go up, and, well, there goes the neighborhood."

Mira laughed. "Come on. Who would think like that?"

Savannah was serious. "Izzie is bad news. You know that. Do you really want her to sink your dad's campaign, too?"

Mira stopped laughing. "Could she?"

Savannah's brown eyes seemed to singe Mira's forehead. "My dad said that no one wants to fund-raise for a guy whose niece is more trouble than *Jersey Shore*. If Izzie keeps stealing priceless jewels and ruining your dad's reputation, no one will want to back his bid for U.S. Senate. Who is going to trust a man who can't even control his own family?" Savannah put a finger to her lips. "And if I'm not mistaken, your dad gets more seed money from the Ingram Commercial Contracting Group than any other company I know. It would be a pity to lose those campaign funds."

Savannah's words quickly sunk in and Mira felt clammy. Her best friend in the world was threatening her.

Savannah walked out of the classroom ahead of Mira. "Don't screw this up, Mira." She turned around and her face softened. "You're my best friend. I'm trying to help you here," she stressed. "You'll thank me later."

Mira watched Savannah's tiny body disappear down the hall. *Savannah's plan could work*, she thought. But would she ever forgive herself if she stood by and let it?

"You know you're going to get frown lines if you keep making that face," said Kellen. Mira hadn't noticed him standing nearby watching her. He had already changed into his paint clothes, and his jeans were a rainbow of paint marks. She glared at him. "Ah, the diva look. That's more like it."

"Can we skip the usual banter?" She had grown comfortable enough around Kellen to come right back at him. Once he knew she was a Monroe, the real ribbing had begun. "I've had kind of a rough afternoon."

"Oh, man. Did the Butterflies turn back into caterpillars?"

Mira hit him in the arm with her notebook. "No, but they did give the art club a new assignment," she said as he rubbed his elbow. "You guys have to paint backdrops for our fall event." She couldn't bring herself to use the word *hoedown*.

"You mean *we*, don't you?" Kellen asked as they started down the hall. "Seeing as how you're one of us art geeks and all." She kept her eyes on the door ahead of her, but Kellen stopped short. "You still haven't told anyone? Geez, Mira. I'm kidding. Art classes aren't that lame."

"I didn't say they were lame. And I did tell people. Just not the Butterflies." She looked away sheepishly.

He shook his head. "And you think I'm the one who has issues." She hit him again. "Ow!"

They both started to laugh. Kellen was right. She *did* have issues. Why was she so afraid to let people know she had taken up art? Just because her friends weren't into painting or reading up on Claude Monet didn't mean she couldn't do those things.

"So let me ask you this: If you get an A on this painting, are you going to make Mr. Capozo hide it away in a locked cabinet? Because usually he likes to hang these things up in the art gallery. I was so psyched that I got put up there that I made the cross-country team take a field trip to see my sculpture of a galloping horse." EP's administration building had its own mini museum with works from students both past and present. Mira didn't answer him.

"Oh, so that's the field trip my brother was talking about that he thought was lame," Mira said.

Kellen smirked. "I've been on lamer. Ever suffered through a four-hour tour of the governor's mansion with your mother?"

Mira grinned. "I've actually always wanted to go there."

"Good, you can go with my mom next time she wants another tour," Kellen said. They left the building and headed across the quad to the Monica Holbrook Arts Center. The sky had turned an ashen gray. "It looks like it's going to pour any second."

"Fine by me," Mira said. "I could use the afternoon off practice." Her mind was racing with a million different thoughts. Would Savannah really blackmail Mira's family?

Mira and Kellen had been meeting up almost every afternoon to work on their projects in the art studio, and she was really starting to look forward to it. Some days Kellen brought her a latte or a lollipop. Today his hands were empty. She could have used some chocolate. Savannah's threat was completely freaking her out.

"You're extra tense this afternoon, Ms. Monroe, even for you," Kellen said as they heard a rumble of thunder in the distance. "Does this have anything to do with what went down at the country club last Friday?"

"You know about that?" Mira said, surprised.

"Everyone knows about that," Kellen said drily.

"It was a misunderstanding," Mira said quickly. "Izzie was just pulling off a dare that went sour. We sorted it all out."

"That's good." Kellen bounded up the arts center steps ahead of her. "I'd hate to think your cousin did that stunt to try to fit in here. You know how EP is — people can't handle anyone who isn't cut from the same Oreo cookie mold as themselves." He held open the door just as a giant raindrop plopped onto her nose. Several more came down before they made it inside. The rain started coming down so fast and hard that she could hear it on the roof.

"Izzie isn't like that. She can hold her own," Mira said, slowly realizing that herself. She and Kellen had been talking a lot lately, but EP class wars had never been a topic before.

"I heard Savannah Ingram is freaked out by her," Kellen said.

"Savannah's not afraid of anyone."

Kellen shrugged. "You'd be surprised who people are threatened by."

When they walked into the art studio, the conversation was dropped. Several other students were already there working on paintings or sculptures, and someone had hooked up an iPod to speakers for background music. People said hi to Mira and Kellen as they sidestepped easels to get to open ones. Mira went straight to her art folder and pulled out her work. She had only about twenty minutes till she had to be at field hockey practice, if there was practice. The rain was still coming down really hard. Mira had just taken a seat and thrown her paint-splattered smock over her when she heard loud voices. She looked up and froze. Football players, looking like drowned rats, were filing past the art studio doors. Ryan Hodgkins peeked his head in before Mira could duck. He was one of Taylor's teammates whom Mira couldn't stand. The guy was a complete hothead.

"What the heck is this place?" Ryan said loudly. "Hey, B! T! You got to look at this."

Brayden walked in and looked around. "It's the art studio, you moron. You couldn't figure that out?"

"No, why would I know what this place is?" Ryan picked up a ruler and twirled it around.

Mira tried to hide her head behind her easel as the conversation continued volleying back and forth. What were they even doing in the arts center, anyway? Weren't they supposed to be jogging around campus to warm up at this hour? Another roar of thunder rumbled overhead. They apparently had been forced indoors.

"Well, if we're here, we might as well check this stuff out," Mira heard Ryan say, and she cringed. He hovered over a girl's shoulder. "Freaky stuff. What is that? A giraffe?"

"It's a skyscraper," the girl said.

"Doesn't look like one," Ryan said. "T! Come look at this giraffe!"

"I have to run to the bathroom," Mira told Kellen. "I'll be back in a few minutes." If she hurried, she could still make it out the other exit before Ryan reached her. The rain started to sound like golf balls hitting the roof.

"Hey! Mira, what are you doing here?" Ryan asked.

Mira turned around and smiled brightly. "Hey, Ryan! How are you? Practice get rained out? Hey, Brayden."

"Hey, Mira," Brayden said, looking curiously at her easel. "Is this yours?"

"No," she said quickly, jumping in front of the half-done painting of the water lily.

"It's really good," Brayden said, staring at it closely. "It kind of looks like your backyard."

"Mira!" Taylor said, coming straight toward her, practically knocking down another guy's easel. "What are you doing in here?" He came in for a kiss and rain dripped off his jacket and onto her shirt. "Did you guys get trapped in the storm, too?" He looked at her paint smock. "What are you wearing?"

"You mean you haven't told him, either?" Kellen asked.

"Told me what?" Taylor looked from Kellen to Mira and his face darkened. "Kevin, right?"

"It's Kellen," he corrected him easily.

"Whatever." Taylor shouldered up next to him like he was still on the field. "Could you give me and my girl some space?"

"Actually, you're in my way," Kellen said, surprising Mira. "Literally. I've got to finish working on this and get to cross-country."

Taylor pulled a paintbrush out of Mira's tray, dipped it in orange paint, and ran a thin line across Kellen's painting. "Now you're done."

"Mature," Kellen said, staring at the stripe. "But it works. Gives the painting some depth, don't you think?"

"I can't believe you did that!" Mira snapped at Taylor.

"You're sticking up for this guy, Mira?" Taylor asked. "What are you doing in here with the art freaks, anyway?"

"Hey," Brayden warned Taylor. "Cut it out."

"No, I want to know why she's in here." He stared crossly at Mira. "Are you hanging out with this guy?"

"No. I...had to drop something off for the Butterflies," Mira lied. "It was raining, so I stuck around and painted something for fun." How fake did she sound? Taylor *had* to know she was lying. She tried to get Kellen's attention, but he stared at the ruined work on his easel.

"I think you've had enough *fun* for one day, don't you?" Taylor said, still staring down Kellen. He took Mira's hand. "You can wait out the storm with the team instead. Let's get you out of here."

But Mira didn't want to leave. She wanted to stay there with Kellen. That's what she wished she'd said even as she let Taylor take her hand. She knew she was making a choice right then, and as she walked away with Kellen watching her, she had a feeling she was going to regret it.

Eighteen

Izzie felt like a spy sneaking behind enemy lines. She looked the part (EP school uniform — check!), she had backup (new friends, Violet and Nicole — check!), and she had secured the plans (Butterflies' list of potential event vendors — check!). But whether she could survive her first mission on Main Street was another thing entirely.

Izzie was learning very quickly that EC's town square was much more of a shopping experience than Harborside ever was. Here, people got dressed up to spend nine dollars on a tiny gelato. (Better yet, they sent their nannies in to buy the gelato for them.) The street was crowded with hired help pushing strollers with screaming tots while serene-looking mommies walked a few paces behind them, chatting on their cell phones. Most clothing stores were boutiques rather than chains, sale signs were nonexistent, and parking your BMW or Range Rover for twenty minutes would set you back fifty cents. Any town that had an Apple Store on its main street knew it had money and wasn't afraid to flaunt it. Izzie just hoped those stores were willing to part with some of their cash for a good cause.

Mrs. Fitz had given Izzie till the following Friday to secure a list of vendors, and there wasn't a second to waste. The hoedown needed to be a success. Correction: the Falling into You Fest had to be a success. ("Headmaster Heller is a bit concerned about having the word *hoe* on an official school invitation," Mrs. Fitz had said in explaining the name change.) Whatever this party was called didn't matter. It was Izzie's chance to prove she was cut out for EC and she wasn't going to fail.

"It's time to get people to pony up some free stuff," she declared to Violet and Nicole, looking around the crowded street. "The question is: Where do we start?"

"Where's Mira?" Violet asked as she flipped through the folder looking for the vendor list Mira had given them. "I thought she'd volunteered to help us."

"Yeah, I think what actually happened was she hiccuped and it came out like a 'me, too'. There is no way Mira would face the wrath of Savannah to help us. Besides, she's been out sick." She'd been out the last two days, actually, and as far as Izzie could tell, she hadn't left her bedroom. Izzie was going to check in on her, but then she thought better of it. Why be fake like Mira?

"I heard Mira's been out sick to keep Taylor from dumping her," Nicole said, as she sent a lightning-fast text message. "They had some sort of fight after practice the other day. They were yelling at each other in the pouring rain outside the arts center."

"What were they fighting about?" Violet asked.

Nicole shrugged. "No one actually *heard* them fighting. They could just see them making crazy arm gestures between lighting flashes."

"You must have heard wrong, then," Izzie told Nicole. "There is no way that guy would dump Mira. He's always all over her and calling her babe. Or she calls him babe." Izzie made a face. "It's kind of nauseating."

"Well, whatever is going on with her, at least she remembered to give you the vendor list," Violet said, and pulled it out of the folder. They huddled around the paper to read it. "Crystal Coast Catering always helps us. Then we can move on to Pick a Petal for flowers and hit a few dessert shops. Most of these stores have worked with the Butterflies before, so we shouldn't have any problem getting this done in an hour."

"And they're going to believe we're booking this huge party for EP and need free stuff?" This part of the equation still left Izzie incredulous. Where she came from, people tried to pull fast ones like this all the time. And they never would have signed a contract with a teenager.

Violet laughed. "Yes! EP students ask for stuff all the time, and when they don't, the parents are the ones who work the charity angle. I know it sounds crazy, but there isn't a day that goes by at EP that my mom doesn't have to open her checkbook. This week she paid two hundred dollars to buy *one* ticket to the spring booster dinner. And then she has to pay five hundred to put our family name in the program. It sounds insane, I know, but this is EP. You either give, give, give, or we take, take, take."

Izzie broke out laughing. "This place is insane!" she yelled at the heavens, startling a mother on a phone call walking by. "But fine. I'll go with it. Let's get this party started"—she frowned—"even if I've never planned one before. Come to think of it, I've never even had an actual birthday party."

Nicole's eyes widened. "Never? That's tragic. I had one every year till I was twelve, and we always had a pony." She frowned. "Actually every party I went to back then had a pony."

"No ponies for me," Izzie said, twisting a piece of her damp hair around her finger. The group had just come from swim practice. "It was cupcakes with my mom and grandparents and one or two presents. No one I knew really had parties, and the ones who did probably wouldn't qualify as Butterfly-worthy. Savannah had to have known this when she picked me. Did the *Gazette* article mention my lack of party skills?" she joked.

"No, and even if it did, who cares what Savannah thinks?" Violet told her. "You got this gig because you're the first one to come up with something different for the Butterflies to do for a change. I don't think we've worked on anything not carnival- or formal-dance-related the whole year I've been a Butterfly." She pulled her long hair up off her neck into a ponytail. "And as far as charities go, we never picked anything meaningful and mainstream like you did." She gave the girls a look. "The Butterflies donate to causes supported by George Clooney or the stars of *The Vampire Diaries.*"

Nicole sighed sadly. "Last year we came *thisclose* to winning a group guest spot on the show, but then those prisses at St. Elizabeth's did a bikini calendar and won."

Violet raised her eyebrows. "See? The Butterflies need you and so does your grandmother." She put her hands on Izzie's shoulders and looked into her eyes like she was performing hypnotism. "Being a Butterfly is distinguished, and you need something like that to keep that creep off your back."

Izzie felt she had to tell someone about how Lucas had threatened her, and she knew she could trust Violet and Nicole not to spread the story like wildfire. Violet was right. Being a Butterfly — especially one who was in charge of the Falling into You Fest — would help things continue to work for Grams. Izzie had spoken to her night nurse yesterday, and Grams was doing better at the home than she could have hoped. She couldn't let her down. Armed with the Butterflies, maybe she could also help Harborside in the process.

"You're right," Izzie said, feeling energized. "Let's do this. We'll split the list by category. We can tackle it faster that way. Vi, you go to the caterers. We need them the most. Nic, you go to the florists, and I'll wrangle us some desserts." She took the page with the addresses of all the dessert shops. In Emerald Cove there were four. "We can meet back here in an hour. Sound good?"

"See? You sound like a Butterfly already," Violet said. She and Nicole headed in opposite directions. "This will be a piece of cake!"

Turned out, it wasn't. Not even close.

"If you could just let me speak to your boss, I could explain everything," Izzie pleaded with a bored, obnoxious girl behind the cookie counter at Baked with Love. She'd been arguing with the girl for ten minutes and was growing tired of explaining herself. "I'm with the Social Butterflies. We work with your bakery all the time."

The girl placed a pink, girlie-scripted sign on the counter that said *Be Back in 10!* and glared at Izzie. "You are not a Butterfly, and if I'm wrong, then that group has seriously lowered their standards."

Izzie's jaw dropped before she could stop it. What was that comment about? Before she could come back at her, the worker smiled at a dad holding a toddler who was pointing frantically at the cookies. "Now if you'll excuse me, I have an actual customer."

I Scream for Ice Cream (clever name, Izzie had to admit) wasn't any better.

"We're not interested," the man behind the counter said. Izzie had barely stepped onto their ice-cream-cone-shaped welcome mat.

She let the folder in her hand drop. "I haven't even asked you anything yet."

The guy was wearing a blue shirt and a tie with a dizzying amount of ice-cream cones on it. He wouldn't make eye contact, but that could have been because he was making ice-cream flowers on a big sheet cake. "You don't have to. We don't do solicitations."

"But you must, because you work with my group all the time," Izzie said, feeling self-conscious. What had she done wrong? "I'm a student at Emerald Prep, and my group, the Social Butterflies, usually — "

He cut her off. "I'm. Not. Interested. I don't care whose niece you are. Try someplace else." A couple eating ice cream by the window looked up in surprise.

God, how could she have been so stupid? Of course the shopkeepers knew who she was! Everyone knew Bill Monroe in this town, which meant everyone knew Izzie's rags-to-riches story, too.

But this was no time to be embarrassed. *I'll win him over anyway*, Izzie thought.

"We love your store! It's got such great…" She hadn't had his ice cream yet, but she could fudge a bit. "Such great flavors that would be a perfect addition to our party. If you'd just let me explain…"

"I'm not interested," he repeated. "Do I have to repeat myself twenty times?"

This is ridiculous! Izzie thought as she stormed out of the store and headed in the opposite direction, not sure where she was going. She hoped Violet and Nicole were having better luck. They'd probably booked the whole party while she couldn't even get past "Hi, I'm Isabelle" without someone realizing who she was and showing her the door.

When Izzie looked up, she saw she was standing outside the third stop on her list: Butter Me Up. She took deep breaths before opening the shop door. She fixed a huge, fake smile on her face and even pinched her cheeks, like her aunt had hilariously suggested she do to add color before her school picture last week. *A slight improvement*, she thought as she looked at her reflection in a window. *You've got this, Izzie. Don't take no for an answer.* She opened the door as quietly as she could so that they wouldn't know she was coming, and walked inside.

Butter Me Up looked more like a department store than a bakery. There was music playing, and couches sat in front of an electric fireplace. Cupcakes of every color were arranged artfully on cake plates behind a glass counter. A young woman in a yellow apron with a tiny embroidered cupcake on her chest was the only person there.

"Hi! My school club at Emerald Prep is planning our first event, the Falling into You Fest." God, that sounded dorky. "It's sort of like a hoedown, and we're looking for food donations." Having not been interrupted, she kept talking. "The money raised is going to a great cause this year, the renovation of a community center."

"Now that's different," the woman said. She was so busy making huge swirls of pink frosting on each cupcake that she still hadn't looked up. "We don't usually do donations. We've got at least a four-week waiting list just for orders over a dozen, but that does sound pretty cool."

Izzie felt suddenly hopeful. "It *is* cool."

The woman picked up a bowl of little white crystals and began sprinkling them on the cupcakes. Her name tag said *Amy*. "What community center are you working with?"

"Uh…" This was silly. Was she really pausing to decide whether she should say Harborside? She had never been ashamed of where she grew up before, and she wasn't about to start now. "Harborside. It's this beach town about twenty minutes from here."

As soon as Izzie said the word *Harborside*, the woman's demeanor changed. "I'm sorry," she said flatly, interrupting

Izzie before she could continue. "I shouldn't have gotten your hopes up. We are back-ordered for at least *two* months. I can't help, but thanks for thinking of us."

Noooo! She had been so close. She couldn't let the woman back out now—whether the woman knew who Izzie was or not. She had to get through to her. "I know your bakery has only been around for a year and another cupcake shop is opening down the street," Izzie said, thinking of her notes. "Working with an organization like the Social Butterflies would really keep your name out there."

"We're pretty well-known already," the woman said. "I have to get back to work now. I have to finish an order that is going to the senator's family." She stopped, blushing. "If you don't mind, please let yourself out. Thank you!"

Izzie would have laughed at the irony, but she was too tired to move her jaw. She thought she had been getting close to receiving donations from Butter Me Up, but once she'd mentioned Harborside, the woman had shut her down. She knew people at EP were weirded out about her hometown, but would stores really not want to work with her for the same reason? If the Butterflies were as esteemed as Violet said they were, these places wouldn't keep themselves from being part of a major EC event just because Izzie was the one doing the asking, would they? Izzie dug in her heels.

"Listen, Amy," she said, trying to keep the emotion out of her voice, "I know your cupcakes are the ones everyone in town is gaga over right now and they're selling faster than you can make them. But if you're doing that well, can't you spare a few dozen for charity? Whether you like me or not, the Falling into You Fest is a great cause. Wouldn't you like to help me and get some good karma out of it?"

The woman stuck her pastry knife into a cupcake and looked flustered. "It has nothing to do with Harborside. I just…" She sighed and shook her head. "I can't, okay?" she said quietly. "I'd like you to leave, and please tell the rest of the Butterflies not to bother coming back, either. I'm too old to play games with my business."

Izzie left the store without another word and plopped down on a nearby bench. What did Amy mean by games? And why was she acting so weird when Izzie mentioned Harborside? Whatever Amy's deal was, there was only one thing that really mattered: Izzie had failed. Miserably. She still had fifteen minutes to get to the fourth store, something called Mooo To You, but she didn't have the heart. She closed her eyes in disgust, wishing she could erase the afternoon from memory.

"Well, this is an interesting place to take a nap."

She opened her eyes. Brayden was standing in front of her in his EP school uniform. He sat down next to her, smelling like a mix of soap and Tide. "What are you doing here and why do you look like someone just ran over your puppy?" Brayden asked. "Or in terms you can understand — like someone ran over your favorite pair of swim goggles?"

She smiled. That summer a crazy cyclist had smashed Izzie's favorite goggles after she'd dropped them on the boardwalk. She'd been so upset, and then Brayden had surprised her with a new pair. At the moment neither losing her favorite goggles nor Brayden's joke seemed funny. "This sucks on a level that goggles can't compare to," she said miserably.

Brayden put his arm around the back of the bench. "Want to fill me in?"

She was embarrassed to tell him what seemed to be happening, but knowing Brayden, he wouldn't quit till she had. "I'm chairing the first Butterflies event," she said, and he looked surprised. "I know, me a Butterfly. Weird, right? But that's not the upsetting part. I'm supposed to get all these donations, which every Butterfly in the history of time has apparently gotten blindfolded, and every store I ask keeps turning me down flat." She pushed her hair behind her ear self-consciously. "It's because I'm from Harborside," she said, and stopped him from butting in. "Don't say I'm being insane, because it's true. As soon as they realize I'm the girl from the papers and remember where I'm from, no one wants to deal with me. I can't get over how shallow people in this town are," she grumbled.

Brayden's eyebrows rose. "Shallow yes, but stupid no. Stores around here aren't going to miss out on an EP event just because you're the one who is selling it."

"That's what I thought, but then why would they turn me down?" Izzie asked.

"I don't know." Brayden shook his head. "But something is off. I don't love everything about EC, either, but not everyone here is bad news, Iz. If you give some people a chance, you might find out they're pretty decent." He smirked. "What are you doing joining the Butterflies, anyway?"

She sat up straight. "Why? You don't think I'm Butterfly material?"

"I just didn't think you were wrapped up in that sort of thing," he told her. "Charity work, great, but the Butterflies are, well, like the name says, 'social.'"

"Your girlfriend is a Butterfly," Izzie said without thinking.

His smile seemed to fade. "As I said, the title of the club includes the word *social*. She's as social as they come."

"Why are you with her, Brayden?" Izzie asked quietly, surprising herself and him at her frankness. "You could do so much better than her. You know that, right? Savannah is so…" *Whoa.* What was she doing? "Sorry. That was rude." She looked down, embarrassed, but Brayden didn't say anything. "I should go. I still have one store that hasn't turned me down yet."

Brayden stood up. "I'll go with you." Izzie started to protest. "I'm not taking no for an answer. This is something I know I can help you with."

"Okay, you can witness them turn me down firsthand, " she said.

"What store did you just come out of?" Brayden asked. "Butter Me Up?"

Izzie nodded. "But Brayden, there's no point in —"

Too late. Brayden was already dragging her back toward the entrance. He pulled her inside. Amy saw him and grinned. "Hi, Brayden! Did your mother like the bonnet cupcakes I made for her mother-daughter tea last week?"

Izzie looked at Brayden curiously. Did he have a sister she didn't know about?

"She loved them," Brayden said smoothly. "Which is why we're here. You know you're the best, Amy, which is why I can't believe you would turn my friend away when she's letting you in on the event of a lifetime. The Social Butterflies put on the best Emerald Prep events of the year."

Amy looked at Izzie nervously. "Yes, well, I'm sorry I can't help." She smoothed her apron. "We're back-ordered for at least a month."

Hmm…I thought you'd said two, Izzie thought to herself.

"Amy, you're superhuman!" Brayden charmed her. "You squeezed in my mom with a day's notice. I'm sure you can whip up a hundred cupcakes with a month's notice."

Amy looked trapped. "I could, but…"

"Izzie is a good friend of my family's, and she also goes to

256

Emerald Prep," Brayden continued. "As she tried to explain, all the money raised goes to charity. How can you say no?"

"It sounds like a great cause, but I don't have time to commit to yet another function when I already have a calendar full of them. The situation is complicated," she added vaguely.

Izzie's heart sank. Even Brayden couldn't sway her. She was just too much of a liability.

"That's too bad. I'll have to make sure my mom lets her friends know you're overbooked and aren't taking new orders." Brayden looked at Izzie. "Let's go to MoooToYou! and tell them they can have the event after all." He took her hand. It felt warm and sticky against her own. "Mooo is going to be thrilled. They've been dying to do a Butterflies event."

"Wait," Amy said. "I don't want to upset your mother. Maybe I can shift things around."

Brayden gave Izzie's hand a squeeze, and she got chills. "That would be awesome."

Ten minutes later they were both jumping up and down outside Butter Me Up and laughing. Izzie held the pink contract in her hands. The bakery was officially signed on to the Falling into You Fest and was donating *two* hundred cupcakes. Brayden made Amy double the offer when he slyly let it drop that his mom would be disappointed to hear how Izzie was treated.

"You were a rock star in there!" she told him, feeling so happy that she could burst.

"I aim to please." Brayden bowed. His face grew serious. "But I'm sorry I had to step in like that. They should have listened to you, Iz."

She shrugged. "True, but I'm getting used to it. I'm not backing down."

"You shouldn't," he insisted. "You deserve better than that." He seemed to hesitate. "Listen, about me and Savannah."

At her name, Izzie inhaled sharply. Were they really going to have this conversation? She so wanted to, even though it scared her.

"I want you to know that ever since I met you, I've felt…" Izzie held her breath, waiting to hear more.

"Izzie! Izzie!"

Violet and Nicole ran across the street and Brayden let the half-finished sentence die in the air. Izzie tried not to look too disappointed. Maybe this wasn't the right time to discuss what-ifs. She held up the pink contract proudly. "Two hundred cupcakes from Butter Me Up. You can thank Brayden."

Violet didn't look as excited as Izzie was about the score. "At least we'll have cupcakes. Nic and I were turned down by everyone on our lists."

"What?" Izzie said, shocked. "How can that be?"

"I don't know. As soon as they heard what event we were

doing and where we were from, they basically showed us the door," Violet said grimly.

Nicole shuddered. "I feel so dirty."

So maybe getting shot down had nothing to do with Harborside, after all. But if Izzie wasn't the reason, who was? What would people have against the Butterflies? "All these places are ones the Butterflies have used before. Why would they want to stop working with us now?"

Violet inhaled sharply. "Maybe someone put them up to it."

"Who put together the vendor list?" Brayden asked.

Izzie looked at the bottom of her paper again. That's when she saw a name that she hadn't seen before. She pointed it out to Violet and Nicole. The three of them said the name at the same time.

"Savannah Ingram."

"What?" Brayden asked, and ran a hand through his hair. "She wouldn't... Are you sure?"

"Her name is right here in small print," Violet said, showing him the page.

There was only one explanation for why they'd been shut out everywhere: Savannah had gotten to them first. Izzie was peeved, of course, but something else was bothering her, too: Mira had been the one who'd given her the vendor list in the first place.

After all that had happened between them, would Mira really go out of her way to make things worse?

Nineteen

Mira's mom dropped her off down the block from Corky's just as the rain let up. It had been pouring all day, and the cobblestone street was one giant puddle. Normally you couldn't pay Mira to be out in that kind of weather, but that night she was going to do something she should have done sooner. It was time to face Izzie, spill the beans about Savannah, and say sorry for being such a coldhearted...well, you know. If Izzie was ever really going to fit in with their family, then Mira had to try (not fake try) to get to know her. If that heart-to-heart went well, then part two of her confessional road trip included meeting up with Taylor and dropping a huge bombshell on him, too.

First things first: Find Izzie. Mira's mom had said she was at Corky's, but that sounded off base. Half of EP hung out at Corky's, which meant Izzie would probably steer clear. Mira and her friends loved it there. The diner was fun and loud and known for its gravy fries and kitchen sink full of ice cream that waitresses delivered on roller skates. It was the last place Mira would have expected to find her cousin, but she decided to give it a shot.

The place was mobbed, but she thought she saw the back of Izzie's head across the room. She breathed in the smell of sweet-potato fries as she moved across the room to the beat of the Rihanna song playing on the jukebox.

"Mira!" She heard Savannah's voice and stopped dead in her tracks. Savannah was sitting at a table with Lauren and Lea, and Mira's heart sank as her best friend waved her over. Savannah had on a thick cream headband that matched the fitted sweater she wore with pearls to a tee. Mira had picked out the top for her last week. "Sit!" Savannah said. "What are you doing here? Why aren't you out with Taylor?"

Mira sank in the seat next to her, feeling like she weighed a thousand pounds. "I'm not meeting him for another hour. I came down here early to, uh, do some shopping."

"At Corky's?" Savannah looked at Lea. "Can you check on those fries?"

"We just ordered them," Lea said as she stirred her vanilla Coke with a spoon.

"So?" Savannah sniped at her. "I'm hungry, Lea. Can you check on the fries and take Lauren with you?"

Lauren rolled her eyes at Mira as she and Lea slid out of the booth.

"Thanks!" Savannah sang and turned to Mira, her face full of worry. "I can tell when something is wrong with you. What's going on?"

Mira bit her lip. She was going to have to tell Savannah eventually. She was telling Taylor tonight. "All right. The reason I've been so weird lately is because I've been hiding something." Savannah's brown eyes darkened. "I dropped public speaking and study hall to take painting and sculpting classes." There. She'd said it.

Savannah started to laugh. "That's your dark secret? You're joking, right? Art classes are so cheesy."

"They're not," Mira insisted, and immediately her mind went to Kellen. She felt like he had been avoiding her since the other afternoon in the art studio. He hadn't come after school to work with her once. She thought about going to a cross-country meet but worried he wouldn't speak to her. She had screwed up with him, too. "You know how you're always making fun of me for paying so much attention to the hemline on a skirt or to a flower in your mom's garden? I think I do that because I think of everything as art. I figured it was time to find out if I can actually paint what I see in my head." She smiled. "It turns out I can." Wow, getting this off her chest was better than she had imagined. No more sneaking around. No more worrying about what her friends thought....

Savannah pursed her lips. "Have you told Taylor that you're an artsy chick yet?"

"I was going to tell him tonight." Mira tugged on one of her dangling crystal earrings. "I don't know how he's going to take it, though. He sort of freaked out when he found me in the art studio the other afternoon with Kellen."

"Kellen Harper?" Savannah asked, her eyebrows raised. "How do you know him?"

"He's in two of my art classes," Mira explained. "He's cool."

"You better not say that around Taylor," Savannah said, her mouth twitching slightly. "In fact, I think you should forget about saying anything about art to him tonight or ever." She touched Mira's hand. "Sweetie, taking art is kind of, I don't know, a waste of time, don't you think?"

"No," Mira insisted, her face reddening. "And if Taylor has a problem with it —"

"If you say 'Taylor and I are breaking up,' I will freak out," Savannah told her. "I already sent the party planner my seating chart, and you and Taylor are sitting with me." Savannah's sweet sixteen was on Saturday. Everyone in their class had clamored for an invitation. Less than half got one.

Mira looked at the table. "I didn't say we were breaking up. I just want things to change."

Savannah sipped her soda, leaving a lipstick mark on the straw. "Mira, you're dating one of the hottest guys in school. He's the quarterback, for God's sake. Things don't change.

You do." She looked at her suspiciously. "What's this really about? This doesn't have anything to do with Izzie, does it? Tell me you're not feeling bad for her again."

Mira's mouth felt dry. She decided to ignore the Izzie comment. Savannah could only handle so much in one conversation. "This is about Taylor," Mira said. "Vanna, he's not the guy I thought he was when we started dating. He wants a girlfriend who looks pretty and waves an EP flag at every game and practice. Like a trophy wife. I am so not a trophy wife in training! I want him to know that. I'm tired of things always being about him."

"We all get sick of the guys sometimes, but they get sick of us, too. It doesn't mean you're going to break up. You're just having a rough patch." Savannah looked far, far away as she played with a strand of her blond hair. "Whenever Brayden gets whiny with me about my attitude, I tell him he can't dump me. Our parents would kill him." Brayden and Savannah were practically an arranged marriage waiting to happen. Their parents joked about a wedding all the time. "Now cheer up and stop stressing about Taylor and trophy wives," Savannah added, a devious smile returning to her face. "We're making headway on the Izzie front. It pays to have parents who have the most lavish parties in town. Every restaurant in EC is afraid to tick them off! I told the vendors that if they wanted to keep my parents' business, they'd say no to Isabelle Scott. And it worked! Izzie's got no caterer and no flowers. Butter Me Up caved for some reason, but she can't plan a party with cupcakes. I give it two more days before she waves a white flag."

Mira grabbed Savannah's Coke and took a sip. Mira's mom was so excited about Izzie's Butterflies chair position, she'd already told Mira's dad and all her friends about it. She thought it was a sign of Izzie starting to fit in. If Savannah's plan failed, and they linked it back to Mira, she didn't know how her parents would react. "Savannah, listen. I…"

"I saved the best for last." Savannah leaned in confidentially. "I'm having my mom book something at the arts center that conflicts with our event! Some big, splashy party for Dad's coastal revitalization project. She'll offer the school so much money they can't say no." She looked like she'd won the lottery. "Oh, and on top of that, I got Wave Machine to agree to deejay for Izzie's event. They're going to cancel on her the week before," she said gleefully. "Am I despicably clever or what?"

Mira felt nauseated. This was going too far. "Savannah, I…we can't do this. I'm serious. This is taking things too far." Mira felt stronger just saying the words out loud, but Savannah looked like she could spit fire.

Lea and Lauren appeared at the table out of nowhere. Mira had never been happier to see them, even if they did look like they had just come from a funeral. "Vanna, we have to talk to you."

265

"I told you to stay busy." Savannah glanced at their empty hands. "Where are my fries?"

Lauren pulled at her chunky necklace and looked nervously at Lea. "Brayden's here."

Savannah's face brightened. "Really? I didn't know he was coming tonight." She sat up on her knees, seeming to forget about Mira's betrayal, and looked around. "Did you tell him I'm here, too?"

Lea shook her head. She seemed sort of frightened. "We didn't talk to him."

"Why not?" Savannah started to get up, but Lauren blocked her path.

"He's with Izzie," Lea said quietly.

"He's with Izzie? At Corky's?" Savannah sat down again, momentarily deflated. "Alone?" The girls nodded. Savannah looked around the room anxiously. "Can you imagine what everybody is thinking right now?" she whispered. "This is so humiliating. My boyfriend is hanging out with *her* while I sit on the other side of the room with my friends." She glared at Mira. "This is your fault. You were trying to stall me so that I wouldn't find them together!"

"I didn't know they were here," Mira said, watching Savannah unravel in front of her.

"You just said you're on her side!" Her voice rose, making people stare. Savannah was never anything but refined in public, which made her being this unhinged a sight to be seen.

266

Lea cleared her throat. "This isn't the first time we've seen them together, either." She glanced at Lauren. "We weren't sure if we should tell you, but yesterday, we saw them walking on Main Street." Savannah's face turned pink. "He, um, took her to Butter Me Up."

Mira was paralyzed. Brayden must have gotten Butter Me Up to agree to help Izzie.

The thought wasn't lost on Savannah. "You told him about our plan, didn't you?" Savannah glared at Mira. "You tried to turn him against me!"

"Savannah, calm down," Lea said, knowing the last thing Savannah wanted was a scene.

"Savannah, lower your voice. I didn't do anything!" Mira tried to steer her out of Corky's before she regretted it, but Savannah pushed her away and turned to Lea.

"Where are they sitting?" she asked calmly.

Lea pointed to a booth near the jukebox, and Savannah strode across the diner before Mira could stop her. She moved so fast she almost knocked down a waitress as she glided by on roller skates. Mira, Lea, and Lauren followed, watching as Savannah stopped short a few feet from Brayden and Izzie's table. They were leaning into each other over a plate of potato skins, and they looked like they were having an intense conversation. Izzie was shaking her head and starting to get up. That's when she saw Savannah.

"You. Go. Now," Savannah hissed to Izzie in a quiet, menacing voice that was almost impossible to hear over Jay-Z. Izzie looked from Savannah to Mira and began to walk away without a fight, which surprised Mira.

"Savannah, what..." Brayden's face looked guilty. He slid out of the booth, and she put up her hand to stop him.

"Girls, we're going to need some time alone. You go deal with *this*," Savannah said, pointing at Izzie's retreating frame.

"My pleasure," Lauren said, her eyes narrowing at Izzie as she headed for the door. Mira grabbed Lauren's arm before she got too far.

"I'll go," Mira told Lauren. "She'll listen to me."

She headed after Izzie before the others could stop her. Izzie was already halfway down the block by the time Mira reached her. She ran through the puddles. "Izzie! Wait up!"

Izzie turned slowly, her arms crossed. She was wearing a tan hooded sweater and cute jeans with sneakers. Mira wouldn't be caught dead in sneakers off the field, but the look worked for Izzie. She would have told her that, but Izzie was furious. "What do you want?"

"I want to talk to you," Mira said, and realized as she got closer that she had no clue what she was going to say. Most of the stores along Main Street were closed, and the street was deserted. She could still hear the jukebox playing faintly from Corky's. "What was going on back there?"

Izzie stared at a large puddle. "You can call off your minions. Brayden and I are just friends." Her voice sounded strained. "And that's all it's ever going to be."

"Good," Mira said, and Izzie's face darkened. "I just mean he's taken. If Savannah thought anything was going on between you two, she'd make your life hell."

"Aren't you two doing that already?" Mira winced. "I'm not an idiot. I know you two called all the stores and told them not to work with me. Thanks for volunteering to help."

Mira shifted uncomfortably. "I didn't know how far Savannah was going to take things. I came here tonight to warn you. I wanted to confess," she explained. "I want to help you."

"And why would you want to do that?" Izzie asked. "I know you don't like me." Now it was Mira's turn to look away. "It's fine, but stop pretending. The pep squad act has got to go."

Mira's eyes narrowed. "I was trying to be nice. It's called being a good hostess! You're the one who didn't want to give me or our family a chance. They've been nothing but good to you since you got here, and all you've done is make a mess of everything!"

"With your help!" Izzie shouted back. Their voices echoed in the empty street. It had started to rain again, and they stood there, staring each other down. Izzie wrapped her arms around herself. "You really think I want to muck things up, Mira?" Izzie asked quietly. "I've been killing myself to make things work with your family, but you and your friends sabotage me at every turn! My family is at stake, too. I don't want Grams kicked out of her nursing home. Where else is she going to go?"

Mira didn't understand what Izzie was talking about. This is how it was with Izzie—one moment Mira wanted to strangle her, the next she wanted to give her a big hug. Having her around left Mira with such a mixed bag of emotions. She thought about how she could make things right, once and for all. "Look, we don't have to like each other, but let me help you. I'm sorry about the stores, okay? I'll book catering. Just say the word. But watch yourself with the DJs." Izzie's eyes narrowed. "Wave Machine is going to call you. Savannah told them to cancel on you right before the event."

"Why should I believe you?"

"Because I'm telling the truth," Mira insisted. "I know how Savannah works. That's why I'm warning you about the DJ and about hanging out with Brayden—"

"Forget Brayden!" Izzie sounded exasperated. "Worry about your own screwed-up relationship!"

"Excuse me?" Mira said, the anger kicking in again.

"Your relationship with Taylor is sweet, but it lacks substance. Just like you," Izzie said smugly. It was the first time Izzie had ever said something cruel to her, and Mira did not like being on the receiving end. "You're like a puppy, always at Taylor's and Savannah's beck and call. You never stand up for anything, not even yourself," she kept going. "The world has been handed to you in a pretty Tiffany box and you have no idea what to do with it. You have no guts, and no guts means no glory."

"I have plenty of guts!" Mira snapped. She pulled her coat tight as the rain fell harder.

"I know what I see," Izzie said, her tone changing from anger to sadness. She pulled her sweater hood over her head and without another word disappeared down one of the alleys behind a shop, leaving Mira alone with her thoughts.

She was still shaking when Taylor's mom's BMW pulled up to the curb, sending water splashing in every direction. Mira jumped back to avoid getting mud all over her new jeans. Taylor slid out of the front passenger seat and grinned at her. Mira hadn't seen him in three days. She'd stayed home sick ever since their fight.

"Babe, why are you out here without an umbrella? You're going to get sick again." He opened an umbrella and held it over them as the rain pelted down on the plastic. Mira leaned into his chest, feeling dazed. *You're like a puppy, always at Taylor's and Savannah's beck and call.* Was that really how she behaved? She couldn't get Izzie's voice out of her head. "Are you okay?" Taylor asked.

"I just had a huge fight with Izzie," she said. "It was awful. I came down here early to make things right with her, but it

271

blew up in my face." She sighed. "Twice. Before that, I had a fight with Savannah, too. She said I was conspiring with Izzie and Brayden behind her back."

"Were you?" Taylor rubbed her shoulders.

Mira pulled away. "No. How could you even ask me that?"

He hesitated. "It's just... You've been a little off lately. Making amends with Izzie? Why would you do that?"

"She's my cousin, Taylor," Mira said as if it should have been obvious. She stepped into the rain, away from the shelter of the umbrella, almost as if she couldn't stand another second by his side.

"Okay, forget it." Taylor pulled her hand. "I don't want to fight. Ryan is saving a booth for us at Corky's. We should get going." They began walking down the street as if the matter were resolved, but she felt annoyed. Why was she letting Taylor dictate again? And why was she listening?

"I thought we were spending tonight alone," Mira said, hearing the sound of a lone car as it splashed through the puddles. "I really wanted to talk to you in private." She stared at his blue eyes. She had messed things up with all the boys she cared about, including Hayden. He was still mad at her for what had happened to Izzie on Tryout Day. Taylor was her boyfriend. She had to try to fix things.

Taylor kicked at a puddle near them. "Seriously, Mira. More talking? We tried talking after I found you with those art geeks, and look where that got us. Can't we just

272

go out with the team like we used to and have a good time tonight?"

That was not the response Mira was looking for. "I just thought —"

"You thought." He shook his head. "You think this relationship is all about you and your feelings." He sounded more annoyed than she would expect. "Well, it's not. My life is football. You used to watch me play, hang with the guys' girlfriends, be with the team." He ran a hand through his hair, which she used to like so much. Now she thought it looked oily. "But now, you'd rather hang out with those art geeks. What were you doing in there, anyway? Ryan's girlfriend says —"

Mira wished she could knock him on his butt so hard that he couldn't get up. But she was too much of a lady to do that. "I don't care what Ryan's girlfriend says!"

Some of the guys' girlfriends were okay, but it was their life's mission to worship the team. They were the first at every pep rally, the first to make posters for the games, the first at every victory celebration at Corky's. Didn't any of them want their own lives? Mira had been wondering a lot about that lately. She liked having space. If Taylor wanted to be that suffocating, then maybe, she realized, she didn't want to be with him.

"I'm not Ryan's girlfriend," she said, her voice softening. "I'm yours, and I should be allowed to do what I want, too.

You're right. I have been hanging out with the art geeks," she admitted as he looked at her strangely. "I'm taking art classes. Two, actually, and I haven't told you because I didn't know what you'd say, but you know what? Now I don't care." If she had to tell him about it on a street corner before they met the team of annoying pep squad girlfriends, then fine. "Mr. Capozo says I'm really good, and if I work at it, I could someday make a career out of it." She was getting pumped up. "Maybe I could illustrate children's books! There's so much I haven't thought about before." If that wasn't guts, she didn't know what was.

"Who are you?" Taylor asked, letting his arm drop and the umbrella in the process. They both felt the rain pelt their faces and Taylor quickly held the umbrella up again. "You've been taking art classes and you didn't tell me? What does that say about our relationship?"

"Um, well, you're the one who keeps throwing around the words *art geek*," Mira said, her voice tight. "Can you see why I would be afraid to tell you?"

"God, Mira!" He walked around in a huff, and Mira flinched. Boyfriends were not supposed to yell at their girl-friends that way. "I have enough stuff to deal with," Taylor growled. "I don't need the guys ribbing me about you now, too."

"You're not the only one who has stuff going on," she said, getting upset. "It hasn't exactly been easy having a new person live with us, especially when my dad is getting ready for the biggest campaign of his life. But of course, we don't talk about that stuff because you don't come to any of my family events." She couldn't resist the jab. Her heart was racing. This conversation was spiraling out of control. She felt like she was on a train and she couldn't signal the conductor to let him know it was her stop.

She exhaled deeply and tried to clear her head. When she looked at Taylor again, she felt like she didn't know who he was anymore. "Maybe we should take a break," she admitted to him and to herself at the same time. It hurt saying the words out loud. "This isn't working."

"This isn't working for me, either," he said stiffly, even if he did look a little wounded.

"Dude! What are you doing out here?" Kyle Warnes, the team's second-string quarterback, and his girlfriend, Riley Danford, walked up behind them, cuddling under a polka-dot umbrella. Both Mira and Taylor were startled. "Ryan's got us a booth and he says it's jammed. You guys coming?"

"Yeah," Taylor said, staring at Mira. He at least handed her his umbrella. "I'm coming alone."

Kyle and Riley looked back at Mira questioningly, but she stared straight ahead and watched the back of Taylor's football jacket disappear down the street. Her heart was pounding and she was still shaking, but for the first time in a long time, she finally felt like she had done the right thing.

Twenty

"Iz, I think I have feelings for you," Brayden had said.

Two seconds before that they had been laughing so hard that her milk shake was coming out of her nose, and then Brayden had stopped laughing and had said *that*: "I think I have feelings for you."

Izzie's head was still spinning a day later. Brayden was all she could think about. She kept playing the evening over and over again in her head and wondered if there could have been a different outcome.

Corky's was Brayden's idea. Izzie had purposefully avoided going there after Violet had told her the diner was a popular EP hangout, but Brayden had insisted, saying they had to celebrate.

Izzie had just booked a venue for the Falling into You

Fest. Make that a *second* venue as an alternative to the school arts center. After all the problems she had the day before with booking vendors, Izzie suspected Savannah would mess with the event location, too. She had been played in the past and she wasn't going to let it happen again, which was why she was determined to find somewhere cool to hold the party even it killed her. Trouble was, she didn't know many places, Violet had left that afternoon to visit family in New York, and Nicole had her zillionth family party (she was one of five kids). So Izzie had gone to one of the only other people she trusted.

"I need to find a barn," she had said to Brayden, stopping him at his locker. He smelled like coconut, which reminded her of summer, his suntan lotion, and surfing all in one. The effect was dizzying.

Brayden's mouth twitched. "A barn? Let's rewind. 'Hey, Brayden, how are you?'"

"Sorry, but I need help and fast." She looked away as a few football players walked by and stared at her. "I have a feeling the arts center is going to fall through, and if I don't have a plan B, then those cute Butter Me Up cupcakes will have nowhere to be served."

"That would be tragic," he agreed. He put his history and math books into his backpack and looked at her oddly. "Does the arts center falling through have anything to do with Mira and Savannah?"

"Friends rule number one, remember?" She leaned against his locker. "No discussing the S word." They'd agreed to that after what had happened at Butter Me Up. Brayden was pretty upset when he realized Savannah had been sabotaging Izzie, and Izzie still felt bad for questioning his choice in girlfriends. It seemed easier to avoid the topic completely.

Brayden ran his fingers through his hair and grinned. "Forgot our friends rules already. So a barn, huh? What about the one on campus? EP has its own farm, you know."

"You guys have your own farm?" Izzie was incredulous. Her new school got stranger and stranger by the minute.

"We have a garden, too." Brayden picked up Izzie's book bag, which she had dropped at her feet. He slung it over his shoulder along with his own, and she didn't protest. It felt kind of nice having him hold her stuff. "They use the milk, lettuce, et cetera, in the cafeteria. EP is all about being ecofriendly."

"This I've got to see," she said, and then they walked for what felt like miles, past all the buildings, past the soccer field and the Bill Monroe Sports Complex, and over a hill where there was the nicest barn Izzie had ever seen. It looked like it had been ripped out of a catalog — it was a large, new building with oak floors, big windows that overlooked a pond, and a massive, high ceiling with exposed rafters. The cows were munching happily on hay in a corner, but the bulk of the space was empty, as if the rest of the animals had found better lodging. She wondered where that would be. The barn looked as five-star as a cow could get.

"Can I help you?" a man asked. He didn't look like a farmer. He was wearing the male EP teacher standard—dress shirt, dress pants, and oxfords. He did have on an apron, though.

"Hi, my name is Brayden Townsend, and this is my friend Izzie Scott, and we were wondering if we could book this place for a school function," Brayden said so effortlessly that Izzie was jealous.

"Mark Baker. I oversee the farm." He frowned. "I didn't think EP held events in places like this."

Brayden nudged her to jump in, but she was afraid of screwing things up like she had the other day on Main Street. *Act friendly, be truthful, talk fast*, she told herself. "They do now," she said with a smile. "The Social Butterflies are raising money to redo a community center, and our first event is a hoedown. What better place to have a hoedown than in an actual barn?"

"I like hoedowns," Mark said. "Used to have them all the time when I was a kid." He cocked his head. "I don't think I've ever seen one in this town, though."

"This will be the first," Brayden told him. "We need the space for a Saturday night, so we'd have to find someplace to put the cows on Friday so we can clean it out and then we could have the place back to you on Sunday."

Izzie tried not to focus on the word *we*. Did that mean he was going to help her with all this? He had so far. What would she do without him?

Izzie tried not to laugh. "The event is still under wraps," Izzie added, "so we just ask that you don't mention it to anyone till the invitations go out." She was going to keep this location a secret till the last second. Anything to keep Savannah from stealing it away.

"Well" — Mark still looked skeptical — "I guess it wouldn't be too much of an inconvenience to let you use the place. You did say it was for a good cause."

"A great cause," Izzie assured him.

"Okay, we have a deal," he said, and before Izzie knew it, he had signed an official contract.

Brayden and Izzie were still staring at the contract as they sat across from each other at Corky's hours later. Izzie wanted to pinch herself she was so excited. She was booking things on her own (with Brayden's help), and being an honorary Monroe or a Harborside refugee had nothing to do with it.

"What are you thinking about?" Brayden asked her after they had ordered.

"I was just thinking about how we're going to get people from the school gates to the barn," Izzie said. She was trying not to look around too much. Corky's still made her feel uncomfortable. Seeing her classmates in regular clothes was more intimidating than their uniforms. Designer bags hung off every girl's arm, they all had on the same must-have jeans Mira wore; and each girl was prettier than the next. "What do you think of getting someone to donate horse-drawn carriage rides for an extra fee?" she asked Brayden. "Obviously if they don't want to pay, we can get a school Hummer to take them up there, but I bet some of the parents would go for something exclusive like that."

Brayden laughed. "Look at you, speaking the EP language!" Izzie must have looked confused because he repeated her words. "*Extra fee* and *exclusive*. They live for that around here. I think you're getting the hang of being a Butterfly." He winked at her. "I think you may even like it."

A waitress placed a platter of potato skins in front of them. "I don't know about that," she said as she pulled a gooey one off the plate. Laughter from the football team's table floated over. They were having a fry-eating contest and had drawn a huge crowd. "Why don't you hang out with the team more?" Izzie asked quietly. She'd seen him play and she knew he was good. The Monroes had gone to the first football game of the season the previous weekend. It had felt like the whole town was there. Football was like a religion in Emerald Cove. "Everyone likes you," she added. "That's obvious."

Brayden shrugged. "I guess I never fed into the football God complex. Some of these guys"—he looked over at

Ryan, whose jaw was so packed with fries he looked like he might explode — "think playing for the team means they can treat everyone else as throwaways. Even their girlfriends." He shrugged. "I never wanted to be like that. After high school, I'm hanging up my helmet and applying to a school in California where I can surf in peace."

Izzie wagged a fork at him. "I'm going to hold you to that. If you start getting an ego, I will whip your sorry butt."

He smiled. "Is that a threat or a promise? Because I think you really could whip my butt."

"You know I can!" She took a sip of her milk shake, which had just arrived. "Both in the water and on dry land." Just the thought of her fake beating up Brayden made her laugh.

Brayden started to laugh, too, and a piece of potato skin flew out of his mouth. His face reddened, which only made Izzie laugh harder. That's when her milk shake started to fly out of her nose. The two of them laughed so hard a waitress actually skated over to ask if they were okay.

Brayden stopped laughing and looked serious. "Iz, I think I have feelings for you."

He said it, just like that. And that made Izzie stop laughing. She thought her heart might pop out of her chest, it was beating so fast. She grabbed a napkin from one of the dorky record-shaped holders and wiped her nose. "What?" she said, as if she didn't hear him, but she had.

"I said, I think I have feelings for you." Brayden's blue-green eyes were boring into her skull. "I think I've known that for a while and didn't want to admit it to myself. I know it's complicated, but I can't pretend I don't want to be with you."

"Brayden, don't do this." She stared at the half-eaten potato skin on her plate. "Savannah..."

"Savannah and I don't belong together anymore," he insisted. "I've thought that ever since I met you. Savannah and I are so different, but you and I aren't."

Izzie wavered back and forth. She did not want to be the cause of Savannah and Brayden's breakup. She could not add to the list of reasons Mira already disliked her. But if Brayden wasn't with Savannah...could they actually be together? As she thought about what to say to him, she saw Lea and Lauren. If their eyes were lasers, Izzie would have melted like the nacho platter at the table across from her. Lea actually mouthed "You're dead" before storming off somewhere. Whatever foolish dream Izzie had just imagined disappeared in thin air.

She was kidding herself again. People at EP would never accept Brayden and her as a couple, especially if it came on the heels of a Brayden-and-Savannah breakup. Savannah would exile Brayden the same way she did Izzie. She looked into his heartbreakingly cute face and made a decision. She wouldn't let him feel like the outcast she did every hour of every day. He didn't deserve that.

"We're great friends, but that's all," she said, even though the words killed her.

Brayden looked at her searchingly and Izzie tried to tune out the mushy song in the background. It only made her want to cry. "If things were different, do you think we could be more than friends?" he pressed.

She dug her nails into her knees. "No. You and Savannah work well together. You come from the same world, and I don't," she said flatly. "Real life isn't *Cinderella* or *Pretty in Pink*."

Brayden's face crumbled. "What's that got to do with—"

"You belong with her," Izzie cut him off, and started to get up. She couldn't look at him. Not when she hurt this much. "I didn't grow up with this life. It's not me and it never will be."

Brayden tried to stop her. "Iz," he started to say, and that's when he looked up.

Izzie stopped cold. Savannah, Mira, Lea, and Lauren were standing in front of their table, forming a blockade. Mira's brow was furrowed anxiously and Savannah looked angrier than Izzie had ever seen her.

"You," she hissed at Izzie. "Go. Now."

And without another word or a glance at Brayden, she did exactly as she was told.

Twenty-One

"Name?" asked the man guarding the door to the Shore Harbor ballroom. Loud music was thumping behind the double doors and she could barely hear his question.

"Mirabelle Monroe," she said, peering at his long list as she stood on her tippy toes in clear heels. He found her name at the top of the second page and checked her off. "Escorted by Taylor Covington?" he asked, glancing at the empty spot next to her where her date should have been.

"I'm flying solo tonight," she said, trying to sound breezy.

The man smiled thinly and motioned to someone in a headset, who opened the doors. A bare-chested bodybuilder in a turban and billowy pants gestured for Mira to join him. "Welcome to Savannah Ingram's Arabian Nights Sweet Sixteen," he said in a deep voice.

Mira had been to the Shore Harbor's ballroom before—almost all the five-star weddings in town were held at the boutique hotel—but she barely recognized it now. Multi-colored scarves draped across the ceiling gave the room the illusion of being in a giant tent. Persian rugs and hundreds of throw pillows were scattered on the floor, and the dance area was occupied by half a dozen belly dancers. If that wasn't enough of a spectacle, there were also fire breathers, jugglers, a henna tattoo booth, and a palm reader tent, which already had a long line.

Mira walked over to the welcome table and looked at the tiny flying carpets that had everyone's table numbers written on them. Hers said table three, which was odd because she could have sworn Savannah said they were sitting at table two. Most of the cards had already been taken, including Taylor's. Hayden had declined the invitation and gone to the movies with Izzie, but Mira wondered if Millie would be there. She'd overheard Izzie telling Hayden how Millie wouldn't show her face at swim practice. Izzie predicted she was going to quit the team over the necklace incident, which stunk because Millie was really good.

Mira placed a Tiffany box on the gift table, which was overflowing with gift bags and large boxes. Savannah always said the best presents came in small boxes, which is why Mira got her a sterling silver leaf pendant and chain. Mira hoped the gift would help smooth things over. Savannah had been out of school on Friday, probably to a spa, and Mira hadn't talked to her since their fight. She had sent Savannah a picture of her wearing the dress that afternoon with the text *Can't wait to party!* but didn't hear back.

"Ladies and gentlemen, I ask that you take your seats or move to the side of the room," said the DJ, who was dressed like an Arabian guard, "as we present to you your Arabian princess and sweet-sixteen hostess, Savannah Ingram!" The room erupted in applause as the ballroom doors opened and Savannah was carried in on what looked like a magic carpet by four hot Arabian guards. Savannah's belly-baring two-piece teal dress looked like it had been lifted from Disney's *Aladdin* and her blond hair was pulled back with a giant jewel-studded headband. She grinned and waved as her carpet was paraded by, but Mira didn't know if Savannah actually saw her. She decided to meet her at their table.

"There has to be some mistake," Mira said to herself when she found table three. It was occupied by Savannah's cousins, and they were all Connor's age. "I'm supposed to be seated with Savannah," she said to a passing waiter, who watched in disgust as the kids used their forks and knives as swords.

"The princess is over there," he told her. Savannah had just been handed off to Brayden. He was dressed the part of Aladdin in a ridiculous long white jacket with gold lapels, baggy white pants, and a big white turban with a purple feather. *He looks sort of miserable*, Mira thought. But they must have made up since the other night because seconds later, Brayden led Savannah to the dance floor for their first dance, which was to "A Whole New World."

Mira giggled, waving off a belly dancer who offered her a shot glass full of mac and cheese. *Izzie would hate this,* she thought as an Arabian guard walked by with a snake wrapped around his shoulders. Mira wouldn't turn sixteen till the spring. She made a vow right then not to do anything this excessive. Izzie might be right. Sometimes less was more.

As the chorus of "A Whole New World" finished up, Mira made her way to Savannah's table to straighten out the seating snafu. She stopped short when she caught sight of Lea and Lauren. "What are you wearing?"

Savannah had thought of every detail for her party, including what she wanted her best friends to wear. She'd picked out purple clingy gowns with sheer sleeves for Mira, Lea, and Lauren so they'd look like Savannah's harem girls. But now her friends had on different dresses. Slinky royal-blue dresses that were a lot prettier than the dress Mira was stuck wearing. The kicker: Millie was wearing the exact same dress as Lauren and Lea! Mira touched her beaded headpiece self-consciously. The girls didn't have that on, either. Something was wrong.

"Didn't you get my text? I changed my mind about the outfits," Savannah said, walking up behind Mira. She grabbed a stuffed grape leaf from a passing waiter and popped it in her mouth. "I was thinking about it yesterday and I decided I don't like purple anymore. It's kind of a traitorous color, don't you think?"

Mira was too taken aback to answer her.

"I picked these blue dresses for my best girls instead," Savannah said, gesturing to the others. "Doesn't Millie look cute?"

Millie was a bestie now? Just last week Savannah had tried to frame her! Mira shifted awkwardly in her stupid clear heels. She hated them, but Savannah had insisted Mira wear them. The other girls had on designer peep-toe heels, which were much cuter. It didn't take a genius to see what was going on. Savannah was getting back at her for what had happened at Corky's. As if Brayden's actions were Mira's fault! Savannah didn't seem to be frying him for it. "Vanna, can I talk to you?"

Savannah smiled at her apologetically as the DJ announced belly-dancing lessons on the dance floor. "I wish I could, but we've got belly-dancing lessons." She looked at the others. "Come on, girls! Brayden? I need a refill! A seltzer with lime, okay, sweetie?"

Brayden mumbled something under his breath as he grabbed Savannah's glass and then removed his giant turban. His brown hair was matted down and sweaty from the headdress.

As Lea filed past her, she glanced at the table card still

in Mira's hand. "How's your table?" she asked. "We had to move you to accommodate Millie. She's Taylor's date. She doesn't mind being a trophy wife."

Mira froze. Savannah had obviously told their friends what she had said about Taylor.

Lea nodded to where Taylor was standing a few feet away. "That would have been majorly awkward if we were all at the same table, wouldn't it?"

Mira was starting to feel a little queasy. This was crazy! She had to prove to Savannah that she didn't have anything to do with Brayden and Izzie hanging out. They'd been best friends too long to let a fight get this messy.

"Hey, Mira," Taylor said, walking over to her. He was wearing a black suit and a skinny reddish-pink tie. He looked ready for an espionage mission, or maybe a cologne ad. "You look...nice."

"I look ridiculous." She shrugged. She wasn't sure how to act in front of him. They'd only been broken up for forty-eight hours and already he had a date. She, on the other hand, had only missed him once, when she'd thought about coming alone tonight. "Blame it on the party girl."

He nodded. "Same goes for my date." They looked at the dance floor, where Millie was doing her best to impress Savannah with major arm movements. She waved to Taylor. "Savannah set us up," Taylor said sheepishly. "She thinks Millie's perfect for me."

Taylor performed best when he was with a crowd, Mira realized. That was what Mira had fallen for in the first place — the guy who was the life of the party. He wanted a girlfriend who looked pretty, was happy to cheer him on at games, and kept her mouth shut. For a while, Mira was happy to do that, but now she wanted more. She deserved a relationship that was more filling than candy. Maybe Millie was good for Taylor, but even if she was perfect, Mira's best friend shouldn't have hooked up her ex with a new girl so soon.

"Will you excuse me?" she said to Taylor. "I need to speak to Savannah." Mira walked into the middle of the girls' dance lesson and stood in front of Savannah. With their coordinated outfits, the girls looked like a pop group.

"Leaving so soon?" Savannah drawled, playing with her chunky gold necklace.

"No, I need to talk to you," Mira told her. She wouldn't take no for an answer.

"We can talk over here," Savannah told her, and led Mira to a corner full of oversize floor pillows. "We were just about to play your favorite game."

"Savannah, I need to tell you what happened," Mira said.

"Games first," Savannah scolded, plopping down and stretching out her long legs. "You can go first." Savannah's harem filled in around her.

Mira wasn't thrilled about an audience. "This is important. We should talk in private."

"No," Savannah said, getting comfortable and propping up some pillows. "Whatever you have to say, you can say in front of the girls. But first you have to play. Truth or dare?"

Mira was so frustrated she wanted to scream, but if Savannah insisted on games, Mira would play them. Dare was a terrible option. Savannah would probably make her streak Main Street or sing off-key at the party. That's what happened when they played this game in eighth grade. Everything about this night was turning out to be juvenile, and Mira just wanted it to end. Were Savannah and her friends really this quick to turn on her when they didn't know the whole story? "Truth," Mira decided.

Savannah smiled viciously. "True or false: You've been helping Izzie behind my back."

Mira gave her a look. "False. Did you really think she wouldn't find out that we had all the stores blacklist her?"

"How did she know about the DJ?" Savannah played with the pillow tassels and Mira froze. "I only told you about him on Thursday, and strangely enough he called me last night to say Izzie turned him down flat." Mira's face paled. "I guess you've made your choice. You picked Harborside over your own best friend. I hope your daddy's campaign doesn't suffer for that."

"Savannah, I…" Mira twisted her ring around and around.

"I can't believe you tried to hook Brayden up with Izzie,"

Savannah said, her eyes penetrating as a dart. "Did you really think Brayden would pick her over me?" She shook her head, her curls bouncing madly. "You can call her a Monroe, and teach her to walk like a Monroe, but that girl will never be anything like us." Lea and Lauren couldn't stop smirking while Millie stood by looking uncomfortable.

"You're wrong," Mira said. "Why don't you ask your boyfriend why he was hanging out with Izzie? I had nothing to do with it. If you would just listen—"

"Please return to your tables," the DJ announced. "The first course is being served."

"I'm bored," Savannah said, and put her hands out to Lea and Lauren to be helped up. She glared at Mira. "And I'm bored with you. Why don't you go back to the kiddie table, where you belong? Better yet, maybe you could be of use and provide some entertainment?" Mira didn't understand what Savannah meant, but she heard the girls laugh as they walked away.

The DJ's voice came over the mic again. "And now, Savannah's friend Mira Monroe would like to honor Savannah with a spotlight slow dance to her other favorite Disney song." Then he started to play "Beauty and the Beast."

Oh no. She had to get out of there quick, but before she even made it a few feet, a spotlight zoned in on her. She heard people laugh.

It was a low blow, even for Savannah. Mira could barely

see because of the glaring blue spotlight, but she knew all eyes were on her. Taylor was probably watching the whole thing with his arm around Millie, and Savannah was probably making Lea and Lauren video Mira's mortification to post on YouTube. She felt like a deer in headlights. She knew she couldn't stand there, but she didn't have the nerve to run across the room, either.

"Looks like you could use a dance partner."

This was an Arabian-themed party so she wouldn't be surprised if she were seeing a mirage.

"Kellen? What are you doing here?" Mira had never seen him in a suit before, but he could be her date at one of her dad's fund-raisers anytime.

"Filling up on churros," he deadpanned. "You look like you're having fun, too." He squinted in the bright blue light. "Guess I chose the right time to show up, huh?" He held his hands out to her. "Ready to waltz?"

"Well, look who had the nerve to show up." Taylor strode over as Millie hurried behind him anxiously. He bumped Kellen lightly, to Mira's surprise. "You're not welcome here."

"Funny, my invitation would seem to say otherwise," Kellen told him, shielding his eyes to actually see Taylor. "You really want to do this in front of an audience?"

Taylor looked around at the crowd waiting for Mira to dance. The song was half-over and they were still all standing there. The DJ thankfully sensed something was up and quickly invited the room to join Mira on the dance floor. As Savannah's aunts and uncles crowded around them, Taylor used the cover to lay into Mira. "So this is why you dumped me? For him?" he asked coldly as Kyle and Ryan appeared at his side. "Scholarship boy?"

"What are you talking about?" Mira snapped, sandwiching herself between them.

Taylor looked at his friends and then at Kellen. "You mean you didn't tell her?"

"Tell me what?" Mira asked, getting more upset by the second. What was going on tonight? She glanced at Kellen, whose face was tight.

"Did you know your precious art geek here is the Ingrams' scholarship student?" Taylor told Mira smugly.

Mira was at a loss for words. There were only fifty scholarship students at Emerald Prep and the majority of them went to school on one of the wealthier families' dimes. It was almost an unwritten contest to see which family funded the most students. EP got to say they opened their doors to the underprivileged, and the family got a tax write-off. It was a win-win situation. She looked at Kellen, feeling conflicted. "But…"

"But what?" Kellen asked. "I don't *look* like a scholarship student? Is that what you were going to say?"

"No!" But she *was* thinking it. Mira had assumed that she and Kellen were the same. They got along so well and liked the same things, and he knew so much about art history. Was she really that shallow to think a scholarship changed that? *Yes*, a small voice said, *because you judged Izzie the same way.*

"Way to continue your downward spiral, Mira," Taylor told her. "First you screw over Savannah and now me. Great company you chose to hang out with instead of your real friends."

"Friends? One fight with Savannah and no one will even talk to me!" Mira reminded him.

"Hey, man, let's go," Kyle said, putting a hand on Taylor's arm. "Savannah doesn't want you to get blood on the dance floor. You made your point. Just let it go."

"You're right." Taylor gave Mira a nasty look. "These two deserve each other. Come on, Millie."

Mira and Kellen stared at each other as people danced around them. "I'm going to get out of here," Kellen told her, but Mira grabbed his arm.

"Wait! I...Why didn't you tell me?" she asked quietly.

"Because it shouldn't make a difference," Kellen said, and he was right. Mira's heart began to pound to the beat as she watched him walk away. She saw Savannah laughing and started to feel enraged. She was not making the same mistake again. She ran up to the DJ booth. "Hey! I need a do-over. Can you put another slow song on for me?"

The DJ looked at her strangely. "Sure. You're on in forty-five seconds."

She nodded and then pushed her way through the crowded dance floor to find Kellen. He was saying goodnight to Savannah's parents. "Wait," she interrupted rudely. "You still owe me a dance."

"Mira," Kellen said with a sigh.

"You already offered," Mira reminded him, "and a gentleman never goes back on his word, does he, Mr. Ingram?"

"She's right, young man," Mr. Ingram said as Mrs. Ingram eyed her peculiarly. "Never deny a pretty girl a dance."

"And now Mira Monroe would like to take the dance floor again for a spotlight dance in honor of Savannah's sweet sixteen," the DJ said. Savannah's head whipped around as Mira led a reluctant Kellen back onto the dance floor.

"Why are you doing this?" he asked, sounding tired as she grabbed his hands and put them in the proper position to waltz. "Breaking up with the quarterback, hanging with the art geeks, dancing with me. They're only going to be harder on you, you know. I'd hate to see your EP royalty privileges revoked."

"I don't care," Mira told him. "You're a good guy, Kellen — too good for this crowd — and I want people to know we're friends." She looked down. "I'm sorry for the way I acted back there."

Kellen smiled just a little. "You choked. It happens," he said, and pulled her into a twirl.

"Where did you learn how to dance like this?" Mira asked.

"They teach all the scholarship students how to dance. It's an EP entrance requirement." His green eyes sparkled. "I'm kidding. My mom runs a dance studio."

"She taught you well," Mira said, watching their feet move quickly across the floor. "Think you can dance us out of here after this? I've had enough fun for one night."

"With pleasure," he said. The song was almost over, and Kellen slyly started steering them toward the ballroom doors.

Mira looked over his shoulder and watched Savannah's table spin by. There was a crowd near it and she could see people holding up camera phones. They were the same people she usually called her friends. What did it say about them that the minute Savannah told them to drop her, they did? Kellen held out his hand to spin her again. She twirled around, forgetting for a minute where she was and what this dance really stood for.

For the first time ever, she didn't care what Savannah, or anyone at EP for that matter, thought. As they spun closer to the ballroom door and the song ended, Mira made a quick pit stop. She searched the gift table till she spotted the blue Tiffany gift box she brought. She could think of a lot of people who deserved this gift more than Savannah did, including herself.

Twenty-Two

Mira walked into the Butterflies meeting and took a seat by the window, as far from everyone else as she could get.

Izzie couldn't help but think of the irony. Here she was, sitting with her new friends Violet and Nicole, and Mira, the Queen Bee's former number two, had been exiled. Everyone at EP was talking about Mira's fall from grace over the weekend. Taylor had dumped Mira (or she'd dumped him — that part was still murky), she had somehow betrayed Savannah, and Savannah had humiliated her at her sweet-sixteen party in retaliation. Now Mira sat alone and stared out the window morosely.

"Oh, how the mighty fall." Violet chewed on her pencil and stared at Mira. "I know she's your cousin and all, but I am so glad to see her get taken down a peg."

She looks nervous, Izzie thought, noticing how Mira tapped her fingers on her paisley notebook. It was almost as if she couldn't wait to leave the meeting, and being a Butterfly was one of Mira's favorite things. Or so Izzie had thought.

"Mira was getting as bad as Savannah," Nicole agreed. "It's nice to see at least one of them get what was coming to them." Nicole was pretty bitter about the situation, too. She had blisters from walking around EC in flip-flops yesterday while the three of them tried unsuccessfully to find party caterers.

Izzie couldn't blame her friends for how they were feeling, especially when she felt the same way. She should have known Savannah would try to sabotage the Butterflies' plans — it was stupid of her not to see it coming — but to find out that Mira had been in on it, too, was the final nail in the coffin for their relationship. What was Mira thinking? Her own father was making a campaign push at the Falling into You Fest. If the event went up in smoke, Lucas would have both their heads. *Let Mira sink herself,* Izzie thought. She was going to make this party work for Grams's sake, no matter what Savannah threw at her. And Savannah would arrive at the meeting with guns blazing.

"What are you going to tell Mrs. Fitz?" Violet asked as she examined one of her purple nails for a chip. "She's not going to be happy when she finds out we have nothing booked but dessert and a DJ."

"At least it's an awesome DJ," Nicole said a little too loudly as she checked messages on her phone.

Izzie saw Mira glance their way, and she shushed her. "Shock and awe, remember?" Nicole nodded. "We'll save that info for when Mrs. Fitz lays into me for accomplishing little else."

"We've got a location," Nicole reminded her, and dropped her phone into her bag.

"No one knows about that yet, either," Violet whispered. "But the new digs do kick the Monica Holbrook Arts Center's boring butt." Izzie shushed them again and looked at Mira out of the corner of her eye.

Mira was definitely listening to their conversation. How could she not? They were the only four in the room so far and Mrs. Fitz was nowhere to be seen. Izzie was surprised more people weren't late to things when they had to walk almost a quarter of a mile to get to some of the buildings. She was so busy quieting her friends that she didn't see Savannah, Lea, Lauren, and Millie glide in and go straight for Mira as if she had a bull's-eye on her forehead.

Savannah leaned on the desk and pressed her hands into Mira's notebook. "Hi, Mira. Have a good weekend?" Her minions stood behind her like a firing squad.

Violet, Nicole, and Izzie looked at one another. Izzie had

no idea what Mira could have done to face the wrath of Savannah, but it had to be huge if Mira had fallen that far from her good graces. Hayden said the two had been best friends for years.

"Why don't you talk to someone who cares?" Mira snapped, and turned toward the window. It was a nice view. The entire boys' soccer team was jogging by, and most of them were shirtless.

"Is that any way to talk to your best friend?" Savannah asked, and Mira looked at her strangely. "You do still want to be my best friend, don't you, Mira?"

"I thought I was being bumped up to best friend," Lauren mumbled.

Savannah must have felt Izzie and her friends staring because she turned and glared at them. "Do you mind? This is a private conversation."

"Then maybe you should have it in *private*." Violet flipped her dark brown hair à la Savannah.

Savannah motioned to the others, and Izzie tried not to laugh as they formed a circle around the desk to block Mira and Savannah from view. Izzie could still hear them.

"So?" Savannah said again. "Do you want to be my best friend or not?"

Mira sort of laughed. "After the way you treated me Saturday night? I don't think so."

"I'm sorry, but you had to be taught a lesson," Savannah

said simply. "You knew how I felt about helping *her*, and yet you gave *her* crucial information. What was I supposed to do?"

"She also knew about *her* and B, right?" Lea asked. Izzie heard a stomp, and then Lea yelped.

"I told you not to bring that up," Savannah said. "Brayden and I are fine. Mira and I aren't, but we could be."

Mira sighed. "What do you want, Savannah?"

"I want you to help me get what I want," she said matter-of-factly. "Follow my lead in the meeting. If you can do that, all will be forgiven, and neither of us has to get our daddies involved."

Izzie, Nicole, and Violet exchanged looks. *What was that supposed to mean?*

"Do you think you can manage that?" Savannah asked as Mrs. Fitz walked in and several girls slipped in the door behind her.

"Hello, Social Butterflies!" Mrs. Fitz practically sang, preventing Izzie from hearing Mira's answer. Savannah and the other girls sat down near Mira.

Mrs. Fitz opened her planner, and Izzie felt a knot form in her stomach. She had tossed and turned all night trying to come up with a solution to the party problems and around 3 AM, she finally came up with an idea. It was kind of crazy. Probably social suicide. But if she pulled it off, the party would be the talk of EC. She hadn't shared the idea with anyone yet, including Violet and Nicole. She wanted to make sure she could make it happen first. Izzie had made phone calls during lunch and had several things booked by gym class, but was still waiting on a few more replies. Her phone stayed in her lap all day as she waited for a final text that would seal the deal. Then she needed to suggest her idea in front of the group.

"Girls, we are in crunch mode," Mrs. Fitz told them. "Invitations have gone out, we already have two yeses, and flyers will go up this week to announce the Butterflies' first event of the season." She looked at Izzie, Mira, and Savannah. "Now, I just need the details. I can't wait to hear what you've got!"

Savannah motioned to Izzie with a sick smile on her face. "I'm sure Izzie wants to tell you everything. She *is* event chair."

Mrs. Fitz looked at Izzie expectantly, and Izzie's cheeks began to burn. All eyes were on her. Where should she start? Should she launch in with her proposed fix or explain what went wrong first?

"The truth is, Mrs. Fitz, Izzie has run into a huge problem," Savannah said before Izzie could answer. "I'm not sure how to say this, but the only thing she has booked is cupcakes, and the DJ she did have, I know for a fact Izzie canceled over the weekend. The town restaurants turned her down for catering. I called around to try to help, but no one else has an opening that night." Savannah lowered her eyes sadly. "I don't know why she didn't come to you sooner to tell you herself."

Mrs. Fitz glanced at Izzie worriedly. "I don't understand. We have a list of vendors we work with. Why would they all turn you down? You've had a week to work on this. I'm supposed to give Headmaster Heller a report this afternoon," she mumbled to herself, starting to sound crazy. "What am I going to say? Senator Monroe is coming and making a huge donation! And the press...the press!"

"Breathe, Mrs. Fitz!" Nicole told her. "It's okay. We have a location."

"Actually" — Savannah sounded apologetic — "the Monica Holbrook Arts Center has been double-booked. Izzie should have known that, too." Her face was so self-satisfied that Izzie could have punched her.

"Girls, how could you not come to me sooner and tell me you had a problem?" Mrs. Fitz reprimanded them, looking aghast.

"I'm sorry, Mrs. Fitz," Savannah said. "We tried to cover for Izzie, but we realize that was a huge mistake." She glanced at Izzie. "She knows nothing about how Emerald Cove works the way Mira and I do. That's why we think Izzie should be removed as chair immediately, and we should be put back in charge. Mira?" She stared at her former best friend. "Do you have anything to add?" Izzie noticed Mira was spinning her pearl bracelet around and around on her tiny wrist.

"Mrs. Fitz?" Izzie spoke up, and all eyes were on her. "I have something to say. I did run into problems, but I've worked them out. I haven't botched the whole party. I booked an alternate location last week. We have the barn on campus."

"A barn?" Savannah's heart-shaped face was skeptical.

"What better place to have a hoedown?" Izzie asked Mrs. Fitz, who looked curious. "We made a deal with the guy in charge, and he said we could have it for the whole weekend. It's big enough for a dance floor and seating, and it has a great vibe." Savannah squirmed in her seat, her plaid skirt getting more wrinkled by the second. "We are even working on getting horse-drawn carriages to take guests from the main campus to the barn for an extra donation."

"That's kind of cool," Izzie heard a girl whisper.

"What about catering?" Savannah asked. "Mira and I know for a fact that you don't have anything booked yet. Right, Mira?" Mira looked so conflicted, Izzie almost felt bad for her.

"Izzie booked a DJ," Violet said hastily.

"Oh really? Who?" Savannah asked.

Izzie pulled the contract out of her binder and held it up. She was starting to feel more confident. "I booked DJ Backslide. I think you've heard of him." The color drained from Savannah's face. "You tried to book him for your sweet sixteen, right? He told me he said no because he thought your theme was tacky."

Savannah looked momentarily flustered. "But you...*you*? You couldn't have booked DJ Backslide. He's booked for a year! Why would he work with you?"

"Didn't you hear?" Izzie said smugly. "DJ Backslide grew up in Harborside. We went to the same high school." It looked like steam was going to come out of Savannah's ears. Izzie noticed that Mira was trying not to laugh.

"But she still doesn't have any food," Lea said, trying to help out Savannah, who looked like she needed oxygen. "We can't have a party without food, and no one in town will work with her. Apparently, Izzie and her friends tried to bully them into donations."

"You skinny little liar," Violet snapped, starting to stand up. Lea's face paled. "The reason no one would work with us is because you and your friends told them not to!"

Mrs. Fitz wiped her brow as she looked anxiously from girl to girl. "I am so confused! What is the real story, girls? I've never seen you so divided before! Are you really telling me we've sold tickets to a party that has no food?"

"We're sorry, Mrs. Fitz, but it's the truth," Savannah said contritely. "We'd *never* humiliate another Butterfly, but Mira and I wanted you to know what was happening, even if Izzie is her cousin. If you'd just put Mira and me back in charge, I know we could wow you."

"Don't," Mira spoke up. "Izzie didn't screw up; we did. Violet's right. She couldn't book any of the food because the shops were blackmailed out of using her. Same goes for the DJ. He was purposely double-booked so he'd cancel on Izzie at the last minute." Mira looked at her cousin apologetically. Izzie was so stunned by Mira's confession, she just sat back and listened. "Izzie was set up to fail, and none of it is her fault. If you want to fire anyone, it should be me and Savannah."

"She's lying," Savannah said, her mouth agape. "Mira and Izzie must have been conspiring behind my back, Mrs. Fitz...."

"Enough!" Mrs. Fitz said, her breathing irregular. "I can't listen to any more of this fighting! I feel like I'm watching an episode of some crazy reality show! What has happened to my beautiful Butterflies? This party is a disaster! I mean, the barn is cute, and this DJ Blackjack—"

"Backslide," everyone in the room said.

"Backslide," Mrs. Fitz corrected herself. "He is a good get, but everything else..." She bit her lip, smudging her pink lipstick, and looked at Izzie. "We can't have a party without the rest."

Izzie heard a ping and looked at her phone. It was a text from Antonio, the owner of Harborside's supermarket. Antonio was a great guy. He had always been there for Izzie and Grams when they needed some extra help buying groceries. His wife always sent meals over, too.

ANTONIO'S CELL: The whole block is in! Call me to discuss details.

"Mrs. Fitz?" Izzie said, unable to hide her glee. "I have a solution."

"Good." Mrs. Fitz slumped in her chair. "Let me hear it."

"None of the caterers in town will work with me on the event — that's true," Izzie said, "And it doesn't matter why; it's just not happening. But I found other restaurants and stores that will work with us, and I think they make a lot more sense." Mira looked at her curiously. "Since we're raising funds for my old community center, I called some people from my neighborhood to see if they'd donate." Izzie's voice grew animated. "They're all in! I can guarantee Southern food that will make your mouth water — ribs, barbecue chicken, sweet-potato fries, chicken-fried steak..." Izzie listed half a dozen more options, all of which would come from restaurants in Harborside. Antonio had agreed to provide all the beverages from his supermarket and he had spoken to several restaurants Izzie knew and loved that signed on when they'd heard what the cause was for.

"You want EP to have a party catered by restaurants in Harborside?" Savannah said condescendingly.

"What's wrong with that?" Violet asked, her oval eyes like slits.

"I love the idea," Mira said boldly. Several girls, many of whom had never given Izzie a second glance, murmured their agreement. Everyone started talking about how different the idea was, as if using anything non-EC-related was so groundbreaking.

"So do I," said Mrs. Fitz, regaining some of her natural color. Savannah still looked like she might pass out. "I was getting tired of the same filet mignon and red roasted potatoes at every event. This is genius, Isabelle! I'm so relieved you came through for us! Headmaster Heller will love it! I can see the school press release now: 'Harborside gives back to their own with EP's help.' It's perfect."

When the meeting ended, Izzie was so busy taking congratulations from some of the girls that she barely noticed Savannah arguing with Mira. But once she did, she hovered nearby.

"What's wrong with you?" Savannah seethed. "I was offering you an olive branch back there, in case you didn't notice."

"I noticed," Mira said calmly. "I just didn't take it."

"Do you know what you're doing, Mira? If you side with her, we're done," Savannah hissed. "I will —"

"What will you do, Savannah?" Izzie strode across the

room, and Savannah sort of blanched when she realized Izzie was still there. "You're all talk. Mira is the one who has the real guts in your friendship."

"I'm not going to listen to this," Savannah said, her eyes darting from one girl to the other. "I was obviously wrong about you, Mira. You and your cousin deserve each other." She picked up her things. "I hope your dad finds a new cash cow for his campaign."

"What was that supposed to mean?" Izzie asked Mira, immediately thinking of Lucas.

"Nothing. It doesn't matter." Mira glared at the door shutting behind Savannah. "But thanks for sticking up for me just now. I don't deserve it."

"True, but you had my back in here today, too. That took real guts," she said, trying not to smile.

"Thanks," Mira said, looking sort of pleased. She pulled her notebook to her chest. "So you'll let me help you guys?"

Izzie looked her over skeptically. "For real this time?"

"Yes. And you should take the offer, too, because you need me," Mira pressed, causing Izzie's eyebrows to rise. Maybe telling Mira she had "guts" was a bad thing. "I'm good at parties," she added. "It's practically in my blood. I know EP inside, outside, and backwards, and whatever you've got planned, I can make it even better. You just have to give me a chance."

Izzie wanted to be stubborn and tell Mira to take a hike,

but she knew for this event to be a success she needed Mira's help.

"Okay," Izzie agreed finally. "When do we start?"

Mira smiled warmly at Izzie. Maybe for the first time ever. "Right now."

Twenty-Three

Two Saturdays later, Bessie the cow and her friends had temporarily moved out, and EP's barn had been transformed into fall fabulousness. Branches and paper leaves hung from the ceiling, and hay covered every corner of the floor, where bales doubled as seating. Everywhere you looked there was a pumpkin or gourd, many transformed into incredible centerpieces that Mira had the Butterflies carve from patterns she found on a website. There were pumpkins spray-painted with sparkly silver and black glitter on all thirty tables, which surrounded the stage that had been brought in for DJ Backslide. Outside, four horse-drawn carriages were at the ready, waiting along a road that would be lit by hand-carved pumpkins. In nearby white tents, members of the Harborside Community Center were getting ready to serve the meals that evening. Now that Izzie's whole hometown knew her plan, everyone she knew was pitching in.

Izzie stood in the hayloft overlooking the activity below. Butterflies were setting tables alongside her friends from home. Girls who'd never chipped a nail before were wheeling beverage carts alongside Kylie, Molly, and Pete. Along with her old town's shop workers, other EP students were helping DJ Backslide's people test the sound system. Emerald Cove and Harborside were working together, and they weren't killing each other. Amazement didn't cover what Izzie was feeling.

A few Butterflies looked up from the table they were setting and waved to her. "The place looks incredible, Izzie!" Piper Axon, a redheaded junior, yelled.

"Thanks!" Most of the Butterflies were friendlier to her now. She knew they were relieved that she didn't botch the event, but she also sensed that some had started to feel something else toward her: respect. *Maybe I could fit in here,* a tiny voice in the back of her head said, and for the first time, she didn't try to swat it away.

"The place looks incredible, doesn't it?" Mira climbed the ladder behind Izzie and stared at the large wooden rafters covered with leaves. She was dressed casually in jeans and riding boots, sort of in theme with the evening. Izzie had on sweats, and they were covered with paint from some last-minute pumpkin touch-ups. "It looks totally different than it did forty-eight hours ago," Mira added.

Izzie watched Kylie wheel in another box of soda with a handcart. "I still can't believe we pulled it off," Izzie said. It felt both weird and good to talk to Mira so easily after almost two months of smoldering anger and nasty looks. She didn't know where the relationship was headed after the night was over, but for now, it was surprisingly okay. "I can't believe almost three hundred people are coming tonight," Izzie said in wonderment. "Between raffles, carriage rides, and tickets, do you know how much money we're going to raise? The community center is going to have more money than they know what to do with it."

"About that," Mira said tentatively, "there is something you need to know…"

Izzie hushed her, apparently not hearing what she had said. "Do you hear yelling?" She didn't need any problems. Not when things were going so well. She looked around, but she didn't see anything out of the ordinary, so she peered out of the upstairs barn window.

Brayden and Savannah were near the side of the barn under a huge oak tree. It was a gorgeous early fall afternoon and the temperature was still in the eighties. The pair didn't seem to be enjoying the weather, though. They were having a heated debate, and Savannah was crying.

"What's going on — oh," Mira said, her eyes widening in disbelief.

Izzie felt guilty watching, but she couldn't tear herself away. Savannah kept trying to put her arms around Brayden, but he kept gently pushing her away. Savannah was saying something to him, but the sound system in the barn was being tested and it was hard to hear.

"It looks like they're breaking up," Mira said anxiously.

Brayden was talking to Savannah calmly, but she kept shaking her head and alternating between yelling and crying. Izzie had never seen Savannah so unhinged, and she went back and forth between feeling bad for her and being secretly glad to see her take a hit. Whatever Brayden was saying, he meant it. Izzie felt a sliver of hope as she watched the tragedy play out below. If Savannah and Brayden were breaking up, and she said *if*, did that mean Brayden was doing it to be with her?

How could she even think that? She had specifically told him *not* to break up with Savannah. Even if Brayden was unattached, that didn't mean anything could or would happen between them. Their lives were too different. It could never work. But…

"Maybe I better ask someone to check on Savannah before she causes a scene," Mira suggested. "If Mrs. Fitz sees them, she'll have a panic attack. She's already in overdrive with Dad coming tonight. He's actually presenting some huge check to the community center."

"He told me last night," Izzie said, remembering. It was the first time she had ever hugged him, but she really appreciated the gesture. He had looked mildly embarrassed. "That's incredible."

"Yeah," Mira said, hesitating slightly.

"*Fine!*" they heard Savannah yell.

"I better go," Mira said again.

Izzie continued to watch, unable to pull herself away. Savannah was almost pleading with Brayden now. Her makeup was smearing so badly she looked like a raccoon. Brayden tried to reason with her, but Savannah pushed him away and left. Izzie moved out of sight, but not before Savannah spotted her face in the barn window.

Izzie was a little unnerved, but she couldn't think about what had just happened when there was still so much to do. She threw herself back into the event, accepting deliveries, giving out assignments, and overseeing last-minute details. It wasn't until Mrs. Fitz firmly pushed her out of the barn at 5 PM to go home and get ready that she thought about Brayden again. It was hard not to when he was standing outside right in front of her.

"Need a lift?" he asked playfully, gesturing to one of the horse-drawn carriages. He wasn't ready for the hoedown yet, either. He was still wearing a ripped navy-blue tee with a pirate skull that said DEAD FREDDIE'S on it and paint-splattered jeans. "The driver's dying to time the run."

Izzie hesitated and touched one of the studs in her ear. How did you act around a boy you couldn't have but liked so much your heart hurt? "I would, but I have to go home quick to change and get back here." She started to walk away. Brayden blocked her path.

"This is the quickest way." He opened the carriage door. "Get in."

Izzie climbed in while he talked to the driver. Then Brayden jumped in next to her and the two sat awkwardly across from each other. Izzie did everything she could to avoid eye contact.

"So I guess you heard," Brayden said, breaking the silence after a few minutes. "Savannah and I officially broke up this afternoon."

"Oh," Izzie said, staring out the window to avoid giving anything away. "Are you okay?"

"Yeah, I am," Brayden said, sounding so sure of himself. "I was honest. I told her it's been over for a while and I have feelings for someone else — you." Izzie clutched her messenger bag tightly and refused to look at him. "Savannah must have known that. That's why she freaked out at Corky's that night. I tried to break it off, then," he explained, "but she wouldn't have it. She begged me to pretend we were still together till after tonight. She did not want to go to her sweet sixteen alone, which I get, but the Falling into You Fest...I just didn't see the point in pretending any longer. I want to spend tonight with you."

Izzie didn't look over at him, but she could feel his blue-green eyes on her.

"Iz, I know I should have been up front last summer about having a girlfriend, but I didn't know how to end things with Savannah when our parents were so close," Brayden felt the need to explain. "All I knew was that I hated who I was when I was with her."

The carriage gave a sudden lurch and Izzie grabbed the wooden seat for support. She was sure that if she didn't hold on, she would fall over and it wouldn't be the horse's fault.

Brayden crossed the carriage and sat next to her. "I know what you're going to say, Iz. We don't work. But you're wrong. When I'm with you, the whole world looks different." She could feel her heart beat loudly, and she wondered if Brayden could hear it, too. "I want someone who builds people up, not tears them down. I need someone who makes me laugh and isn't afraid to rib me when I'm being a royal jerk." She smiled a little. "You're that girl. I want to be with you, and I want everyone to know it."

Izzie felt like she was going to overheat. He wanted *her* and he didn't care who knew. Was she wrong to assume this couldn't work? But Savannah...It all came back to Savannah. Even if she and Brayden were broken up, Savannah would never leave them alone. She'd make Brayden's life hell, too, and that was unfair. At least she was used to the torture. "I..."

Brayden leaned in close, and Izzie could smell his after-shave. Her body went stiff as a board. She was almost afraid to look at him. "Say you'll think about it," he said softly.

"We've arrived at Emerald Prep's main gate!" the driver announced. "And it only took six minutes!"

Izzie turned her head quickly to make a joke and that's when it happened. Brayden kissed her softly on the lips. She was so caught by surprise that she felt like all the air had been sucked out of the carriage. She couldn't hear anything but swishing in her ears. Her hands started to tingle. The moment she had thought about so many times was even better than she'd imagined. Her eyes were still closed when she heard him leave the carriage.

But maybe Brayden leaving was a good thing. Now she had time to think about that kiss, and what her answer would be when she saw him again.

Twenty-Four

Mira stood at the back of the barn in a beautiful peach cocktail dress, her small silver clutch dangling from her arm. She couldn't help smiling with satisfaction. The twinkling lights were a great move. They illuminated the crowded dance floor, where DJ Backslide kept the hits coming. Her parents' friends kept stopping her to say how impressed they were with the food and the decor. "How imaginative," one alumni couple said. "Elegant and refined," said a local politician. "This must have cost a fortune!" marveled another. Mira stifled a laugh. This had been the cheapest party the Butterflies had ever thrown, and it was turning out to be the most successful. There was a line of people still clamoring for tickets (they were sold out), and parents, students, and alumni were mingling with the mayor, who couldn't get enough of the Harborside BBQ's ribs. People loved the party, and they owed it all to Izzie.

The more Mira thought about her cousin, the worse she felt for judging her before she ever got to know her. Izzie was more decent than half the people in that room, including herself. She knew her life needed a major reboot, and maybe she was finally doing just that. She stared at one of the large canvases she and Kellen had painted for the party. It was a picture of a scenic countryside, and in the middle, a girl was lying serenely in a lavender patch, studying the clouds. Mira wasn't as laid-back as the girl in the picture yet, but she would keep trying until she got there.

Mira heard Kellen's voice. "I wouldn't believe cattle lived here if I didn't hear them mooing out back." Mira grinned. "This barn smells like pumpkin pie and apples."

"You came," she said, and saw Kellen standing behind her near a huge cornucopia.

"You called it the party of the season. How could I miss that?" Kellen asked. "Especially when I got a free ticket for my superb artwork."

"*Our* superb artwork," Mira reminded him. She had the sudden urge to brush a string off his suit jacket. Instead she stood close and breathed in his cologne. "I'm glad you're here," she said softly. "It's nice to see a friendly face."

"You're in short supply of those these days, huh?" Kellen moved out of the way for the mayor. "I wouldn't worry.

Queen Bees never keep from the hive for that long." He thought for a moment. "Or is it they never leave the hive to begin with? Biology isn't my strong suit."

She laughed. "Well, in my case, I was never queen, and I don't think I'll ever be invited back to the hive." Mira heard DJ Backslide's next track. It was something soft, and the twinkling lights above them dimmed. "Do you want to repeat our dance moves from the other night?" she asked hopefully and touched his hand. "You're the best partner I've had in a long time."

He looked at the dance floor pensively. "I think I'm going to sit tonight out. I don't want everyone at EP to be jealous of my incredible dancing skills. Then they'll all want lessons," he said, and grinned. "Can I take a rain check?"

"Okay." Mira tried not to sound disappointed. Kellen had acted like her knight in shining armor the other evening and she had thought that meant he liked her. She played with the Butterfly costume ring she was wearing. She wore it for all the Butterfly events. "I'm going to hold you to that."

"I should probably say hi to the Ingrams," Kellen told her. "We'll catch up later, okay?"

Mira watched him disappear into the crowd, and she wondered what he was thinking. Taylor and Millie were in the middle of the dance floor, their arms intertwined as they danced slowly, looking like they'd been a couple forever. She wished it were her and Kellen out there. Maybe then the sting of falling so far from popular grace wouldn't be so bad.

No use standing there staring at them. Her parents would be arriving any minute. She headed to the front of the barn and passed the long line of people still trying to get in. Izzie was wearing a deep-blue cocktail dress that had several sheer layers, and her hair was pulled off her neck in a small updo. She rubbed her bare arms even though it was still seventy degrees. Mira thought she looked anxious.

"Hey." Mira walked up to her. "You should be really happy about now. You're the belle of the ball," she said, thinking of the irony. "Everyone is talking about how amazing the event is."

Mira's compliment didn't seem to faze her. "Your parents haven't arrived yet," Izzie said. "What if they don't like it or they think the affair is too casual for him to speak at?" She was freaking out. Mira had never seen her like this. "What if Lucas hates it?"

What did Lucas have to do with anything? Before she could ask, the carriage carrying her parents, brothers, and Lucas arrived. Connor was sitting up front with the driver, and he hopped down first.

"This is so cool," he gushed. "We rode half a mile in the dark by the light of pumpkins!"

"I know," Mira said wearily. "We were the ones who carved almost five dozen of them."

"No one said the Butterflies didn't have a strong work ethic." Hayden walked around the carriage. "I have to hand it to you guys. If the actual event is anywhere near as fun as getting to the party, you guys will have this thing nailed. Way to go, Izzie." He hugged her.

"Hey, Pea," Mira's dad said, and kissed Mira on the cheek. He was in a sports coat and tie, just like Hayden, while Lucas was in a dark suit. Lucas barely grunted hello before disappearing to talk to a local news crew. Reporters from the town paper and the *North Carolina Gazette* were there, too.

"Isabelle, I hear you had a lot to do with this party getting off the ground and everything to do with tonight's cause." Izzie looked at her strappy shoes. "Mrs. Fitz can't say enough about how inventive you are. Mira was lucky to have your help on this one."

"She ran the show, Dad," Mira insisted, gazing at Izzie proudly, but her cousin wasn't paying attention. She had her eyes on Lucas. What was that about?

"Well, we're very proud of you both," Mira's dad said, and squeezed Izzie's hand. "I only wish your grandmother were here to see how well you've settled in."

"Me, too," Izzie said quietly. They had thought about bringing Grams, but the home felt it would be too overwhelming for her. Mira knew Izzie was disappointed.

"Bill, will you look at that!" Mira's mom marveled, peeking over her head. She looked stunning in a cream floor-length dress. "They have real hay on the floor, and those pumpkin carvings are adorable. Girls, this is darling! I've been getting texts from friends who are here already and they all say the party is spectacular." She squeezed Izzie's shoulder. "I'm so glad you decided to join the Butterflies. Look at all you've accomplished already. I knew you could do it." Izzie blushed as her aunt smiled at them both. "You two are going to make a great team."

Izzie and Mira glanced at each other. They had been a great team the past two weeks or so, but she wasn't sure either was ready to commit to more than that.

Lucas interrupted the warm and fuzzy moment. "Bill, News 55 is here, and they want to do an interview about the check you're donating tonight."

"Absolutely," Mira's dad said, and adjusted his tie.

Lucas glanced at Mira and Izzie. In the flickering light of the pumpkins, Mira thought his face looked sinister. "Don't any of you go too far," he said. Mira noticed he looked specifically at Izzie. "We want to get that family photo done this evening while you all look your best."

"Don't we always look good?" Hayden asked, and winked at Izzie. Mira noticed Izzie squirm.

Lucas turned his attention back to Mira's dad. "Bill, remember your talking points. You're happy to give back to a community in need; this promotes strong family values; you're so impressed with your daughter and your niece, who is from Harborside, for putting together such a unique opportunity to remind others to give back. We want to rally this group to vote for you! Your nomination is coming any day now." He lowered his voice. "No mention of the coastal revitalization deal tonight, okay?"

"Bill?" Mrs. Ingram strode toward them with Mr. Ingram, arm in arm. If she knew Mira and her daughter weren't speaking, she didn't let on.

"Hello, all," Mr. Ingram said, and Mrs. Ingram smiled.

"Hello, Parker," Mira's mom said, giving him a kiss on the cheek.

"Could I have a word before you speak with the media?" Mr. Ingram asked Mira's dad. "I know you're making a donation. I just wanted to make sure that wouldn't jeopardize our *other* agreement."

Mira's dad looked at Lucas. "Absolutely. Let's discuss the matter in private." He steered Savannah's dad away. "Lucas, tell News 55 I'll be there in five minutes. The rest of you, I'll see you inside."

"I should probably make sure everything is going all right in the catering tent," Izzie told Mira, glancing back at Lucas to see what he was doing.

Izzie wasn't scared of anyone, but if Mira didn't know any better, she was nervous around Lucas. "I'll go with you," she suggested.

They took the path around the back of the barn. DJ

Backslide's jams vibrated through the walls, but the music was soft enough that they could still hear the crickets and cows. Bessie and her buddies had been moved to a fenced area outside for the weekend. Several troughs of water and hay lined the fence near their path, along with barn equipment that had been moved to accommodate all the tables inside.

"I thought I saw you two come back here." Savannah's voice caused both girls to turn around. "I couldn't have planned this better if I tried," she added as she walked toward them. Savannah's strapless pink sheath dress was illuminated in the moonlight.

"Are you sure you want to take digs at us right now?" Mira asked, looking around. "You don't exactly have an audience."

Savannah ignored her. "I wanted to congratulate you, Izzie. Look at you! You're wearing the dress, you've got the hair, and you have learned how to play the game. I guess you fit in at EP better than I thought."

"I don't play games. That's your territory," Izzie said, sidestepping Savannah. "If you'll excuse us, we have to check with catering and get back to my uncle. He's about to make a huge donation, and I don't want to miss it." Izzie grabbed Mira's arm and started to walk away.

"Yes, to your *community center*." Savannah emphasized the words. "Funny how Senator Monroe is willing to go onstage and tell everyone in EC how much he cares about his darling niece's home away from home when he just agreed to back my dad's bill to have it torn down." Mira felt her knuckles go white.

"Excuse me?" Izzie said.

"Oh, do you need me to repeat it?" Savannah asked. "My daddy is a huge commercial contractor, and he's about to start work on the coastal revitalization project that your uncle is backing. The bill allows rundown areas like your boardwalk and community center to be knocked down so big, shiny condos and businesses can be built in their place." She grinned slyly. "But that won't become public knowledge till next week. Tonight your uncle gets to look like a hero to your friends in Harborside. Next week, they'll probably want to roast him instead."

"*Moo,*" one of the cows said in agreement. It had moved to the trough directly behind them.

"You're lying," Izzie stuttered. "Why would he write a check if the center is being shut down?"

"Ask Mira." Savannah stared at her former friend. "She's known about it for weeks. Didn't she tell you?"

Izzie looked at her cousin. Mira's face was pained. "Is this true?"

"Yes…I mean, no, I…We can change his mind," Mira started to say.

"I can't believe I trusted you." Izzie's voice was quiet but angry.

"You can trust me." Mira tried to grab Izzie's hand, but Izzie pulled away and Mira stumbled.

"Aww, Mira, look what you've done! You've really hurt her feelings!" Savannah mocked. "Look how upset Izzie is to lose her precious hicksville hangout."

Izzie locked eyes on Savannah. "You want to see a hick?" Izzie moved toward her.

Savannah backed away, tripping over a garden hoe and losing one of her heels. "Don't touch me!" she said. She was so freaked out, she left her shoe right where it was in the mud. Izzie kept coming.

"You want to see a hick?" Izzie repeated. "I'll show you a hick." She shoved Savannah as hard as she could. A cow thankfully backed out of the way, so Savannah fell into the trough of cold water. Savannah screamed so loud Mira thought it would pop her eardrums.

Izzie didn't stick around for the postshow. Mira ran after her, but she couldn't keep up once they reached the crowded barn. By the time she got to her, Izzie was already approaching Mira's parents.

"Isabelle? What's wrong?" Mira's mom asked when she saw her face. They were standing by DJ Backslide's booth with Mrs. Fitz and Headmaster Heller. Hayden, Connor, and Lucas stopped talking when they saw her.

"What's with Iz?" Brayden appeared at Mira's side. "She just blew past me and she looked really upset."

"Is Izzie okay?" Violet and Nicole asked. For a moment, Mira forgot what had happened and thought about the people surrounding her. Izzie had made a great support system in a short amount of time.

"Is it true?" Izzie asked Mira's dad, ignoring everyone around them. "Are you backing a bill to knock down the center?"

"Isabelle." Lucas stepped forward. "This is not the time or the place to discuss this."

Izzie moved out of his way and looked at her uncle again. "Is it true?"

"It's complicated," Mira's dad admitted.

"How can it be complicated?" Izzie asked. "You're either doing it or you're not." Everyone looked confused, but Mira's dad's face couldn't hide the truth.

"We'll give you a moment," Mrs. Fitz said, staring anxiously at Izzie as she steered the headmaster and the incoming news crew away. Brayden, Violet, and Nicole, however, didn't budge.

"You're a liar," Izzie said to her uncle, her strong voice wavering. "Just like Mira." Mira's eyes welled with tears.

"Isabelle, I can explain," Mira's dad started to say.

Tears streamed down Izzie's face. "No! I don't want to hear it. I've tried so hard, but I hate it here! I'd rather be in foster care than stay in Emerald Cove! I'll figure out how to pay for Grams myself," she added, looking at Lucas.

"Isabelle, what are you talking about?" Mira's mom tried to console her, but Izzie kept backing away.

"I'm sorry, Aunt Maureen, you've been great, but I've got to get out of here."

"Isabelle, wait," Mira's dad said. "You can't go."

"And why is that?" Izzie asked, stopping momentarily to hear whatever big lie he was going to tell next.

"Bill," Lucas warned, "don't do this. Not here. The press is three feet away."

Mira's dad looked more pale and unsure than Mira had ever seen the potential U.S. senator. "Because you belong with me. You're not my niece, Isabelle. You're my daughter."

Mira felt like the rest of the world went radio silent. The room seemed to spin around her. She looked at her cousin's numb expression and wasn't surprised at what she did next.

Izzie ran, and she didn't look back.

Twenty-Five

"What did you just say?" Mira felt like she was going to hyperventilate.

Her father's face was pained. "Pea, I—"

Lucas grabbed Mira and her dad. "We can't do this here." He led them out of the barn, and Mira was too confused to protest. The rest of the family, along with Violet, Nicole, and Brayden, followed, and the group stood next to the cow holding area. It felt like days since Mira had been in the same exact spot, when in truth it had probably only been fifteen minutes ago. She slumped down on an overturned wheelbarrow, not giving a moment's thought to her dress.

Mira had to have heard her dad wrong. She was probably just losing her hearing after being in the barn all night, where the acoustics seemed to amplify the sound of DJ

Backslide by a hundred. But when she looked at her parents, they were staring at her the same way they did when they picked her up from school in third grade and told her that her beloved hamster, Porky, had bit the dust.

"Is Izzie my sister?" Mira asked. Saying the word *sister* out loud felt weird on her tongue.

Hayden put his hand firmly on her shoulder. He looked just as pale as she probably did. Mira wasn't sure who was supporting whom.

Her dad crouched down in front of her and took her hands in his. He looked up at Hayden and then at Connor, who'd walked to her side, too. "Yes. Isabelle is your sister."

"Did you have an affair?" She choked on her tears, glancing at her mom, who was holding her gold beaded clutch for dear life.

"I'm calling a car and getting us out of here," Lucas said, his voice shaky. He reached into his pocket for his cell phone, and Mira's mom snatched it away. "We can't risk anyone hearing this. It's not good for the campaign. Bill, if this gets out…"

"Let him tell them the truth, Lucas." Her mother's voice was sharp. "He should have been up front in the first place. Then we wouldn't be in this mess."

Hayden was aghast. "You knew?"

"We were advised not to tell you till the time was right," she said shakily. "Everyone was so worried about announcing your dad's bid for Senate. What would the polling numbers say? How would the press react?" She narrowed her eyes at Lucas. "We foolishly let you make us put a child's life second!"

"As I recall, Maureen, you were a little anxious about having a girl from Harborside come live with you yourself," Lucas snapped.

"Enough." Mira's dad ran a hand through his salt-and-pepper hair. "If you want to blame anyone, blame me," he told them. "I shouldn't have hid the fact that Isabelle is my daughter."

"Did you have an affair?" Mira repeated, refusing to let him get offtrack.

"No." His shoulders sank, making him look less senatorial. "It's complicated."

"Then uncomplicate it." Hayden sounded more angry than Mira had ever heard him.

"All right," Mira's dad agreed, his eyes locked on the trough like he was in a trance. "I was a rookie ballplayer in New York. I had only made it to the plate once that season with the Mets," he said, grimacing at the memory. "I spent all my off-hours at this restaurant in Brooklyn where Chloe — Isabelle's mom — was a waitress. We spent the summer together, and then I got traded. Naturally, we called things off," his voice cracked. "I had no idea when I left for the Braves that she was pregnant."

Mira had never seen her dad cry before—he said the only times he had ever shed real tears was when she and her brother were born and when the Braves lost the World Series to the Yankees. She didn't want to see him cry now. She felt like hitting him till he hurt as much as she did.

"When I came back to North Carolina, your mom and I started dating again." He smiled at her. "We were engaged within weeks, married within two months, and we had Mirabelle within the year." He leaned against the barn. "Hayden was two when I officially became his dad."

Mira knew her parents' love story by heart. They'd dated through high school and broke up when they went to college, and her mom had met Hayden's dad at Vanderbilt. After Hayden's dad was killed in the line of duty when she was pregnant, Mira's mom moved back in with her parents. That's when she ran into their dad again and they got back together.

"Izzie's mom never told you about her?" Hayden asked.

Mira's dad shook his head. "I didn't find out about Isabelle till this past winter. Her grandmother found Chloe's old journals and read that I was Isabelle's dad. I guess she knew her health was failing and Isabelle needed a home because she had Isabelle's social worker call me." He stared at the water trough Izzie had pushed Savannah in. "By the time we did a paternity test, her grandmother had slipped into a less lucid state. She couldn't even remember telling the social worker the story." Mira's dad looked at Lucas. "We agreed not to tell Isabelle who I was till the time was right."

"You mean till the election was over." Mira simplified it.

"It was a shock for all of us." Her mom's voice was raspy. "And yes, it's true, I hesitated to have Isabelle live with us at first. I stupidly worried that her upbringing would hurt our family, but then I got to know her and she's a great girl." Her voice trailed off. "How could we keep this from her? She's going to run away this time for sure. We have to call the police."

"Maureen, let's think this thing through," Lucas said. "If we get the press involved, this story could be misconstrued." He sounded like a political aide on the verge of a major scandal. Suddenly Mira didn't think he seemed so scary anymore. He was a twentysomething kid in way over his head.

"That's what you're worried about, Lucas?" Mira's mom asked incredulously.

"You're Lucas?" Violet stood behind them with Nicole and Brayden. Mira had forgotten they were there. She nudged Nicole. "This is the creep who has been blackmailing Izzie!"

Mira and Hayden looked at each other.

"I don't know what you're talking about," Lucas said, ushering Violet, Nicole, and Brayden away. "This is a private family matter, so we'd appreciate it if you'd leave and not repeat what you've heard here."

Violet wasn't afraid. "You threatened her! You said if she didn't clean up her act, you were going to have her grandmother pulled out of her nursing home!"

Mira's mom gasped. "What?"

Mira had never seen her father move so fast. He grabbed Lucas by the jacket. "Is this true?"

Lucas pushed him off and smoothed his jacket where her dad had just crumpled it. "Of course it's true!" he shot back. "I'm the only one who is thinking clearly around here. If she kept screwing things up for you, the press would be all over it. If you can't handle your own family, Bill, no one is going to trust you to help run the state. I was doing what was best for your career!"

"I want you to leave. Now." Mira's dad's voice rocketed off the barn, scaring her. His face was dangerously close to Lucas's. "And don't ever think of coming back. Because if you do, or you tell anyone about Isabelle before I do, I will make sure every campaigning politician in the country knows what a stunt you pulled."

Lucas straightened his tie and, without another word, disappeared around the corner of the barn. Mira's mom went over to her dad and hugged him.

"I should have done that a long time ago," Mira's dad said.

"What are we going to do about Izzie?" Violet said, focusing on the big picture.

"She jumped into a carriage before we could catch her,"

338

Nicole said. "She could be anywhere by now. She's not answering her cell phone, either."

Connor's voice sounded so tiny. "Are we ever going to see Izzie again?"

Mira tried to think. If she was Izzie and had gotten the shock of her life, where would she go? "Maybe she went home," Mira guessed, and everyone looked at her. "To Harborside, I mean."

"But where in Harborside?" Hayden asked. "It's not like the town is a block wide."

"The boardwalk, maybe?" Mira guessed. "There are probably dozens of stores or places she could be...." Her voice trailed off. Izzie really could be anywhere at the moment, and Mira didn't know her well enough to know where to look.

"If she's in Harborside, then she's probably at her old house," Brayden said. "I know where it is. I went there when I found out Iz had left Harborside, but her grandmother had already been moved out."

Mira tried to piece his story together. "You knew Izzie before she moved here?"

"Yeah," Brayden said, not giving much else away. "I know where she hung out, too."

"You should come with us, then," said Hayden, standing up. "Let's go."

"We'll go, too," Violet and Nicole agreed.

Mira shook her head. "No. I know you guys are her friends, but I think we have to do this on our own." She looked at Hayden. "We don't want to ambush her."

"We're coming with you," Mira's dad said, and pulled out his car keys.

"No," Mira pressed. "The last person she wants to see is you, Dad. I think Mom, Connor, and you should try her grandmother's nursing home. Maybe she went to see her."

"All right," he said, sounding anxious. "We'll split up, but if Izzie is not there and we don't hear from you within the hour, we're coming to Harborside, too. Understood?" Mira and Hayden nodded.

Her father's hazel eyes looked pained. Mira had the same eyes he did. So did Izzie, she realized.

"Pea," her dad said, his voice strangled, "I'm so sorry."

"I know," she said, even though she didn't want to. "I can sort of wrap my head around why you kept things from us, but how could you do this to Izzie?" His face crumbled, but there was no time to hear more apologies. Izzie needed her, wherever she was.

Twenty-Six

Izzie lay on the swing on Grams's darkened porch and stared at the cobwebs on the ceiling. She still had on her blue cocktail dress, but it had a huge gash from where it got caught on the porch steps. She knew her face had to be just as messy. The tears kept coming, and she didn't have the strength to brush them away. She still wasn't sure how she got to 22 Hancock Street. She remembered jumping in one of the horse-drawn carriages and then grabbing a cab at EP's main gate, but the ride to Harborside was still a big blur. Her uncle's words stuck in her mouth like taffy. *"You're not my niece, Isabelle. You're my daughter."*

Uncle Bill was her dad.

Mira was her sister.

Hayden was...what did that make Hayden, anyway? Her stepbrother?

Izzie wasn't sure, and she didn't care. She was never going to see anyone in Emerald Cove again.

She wanted to get as far away from the lifestyles of the rich and famous as possible. That's why she had gone to the only home she ever knew: Grams's. Technically she was trespassing. The *For Sale* sign on the lawn said *Under Contract*.

The house she had called home for fifteen years was no longer hers, and Grams was a shell of her former vibrant self. She had thought about going straight to Grams's nursing home from the event, but visiting hours ended at six. Even if she had shown up there, Grams wouldn't have had any answers for her. The two times she'd visited, Grams had spent the entire visit looking out the room window as Izzie told her stories. The one time Grams made eye contact with her, she had called her Chloe.

The tears spilled down Izzie's face, and for the first time she audibly sobbed. The sound was so surprising; she sat up, pulled her bare legs to her chest, and hugged her knees. What was she going to do?

Barbara wasn't going to help her. If Izzie's uncle was actually her dad, then Barbara would say that's where Izzie belonged. Kylie probably didn't even know Izzie had left the party. She was in one of the tents readying food, and even if she had reached her, she knew Kylie couldn't do much to help. Kylie's family barely had enough room in their apartment as it was. Pete slept under the boardwalk to avoid going home most nights, so that wouldn't have worked, either. What was she going to do about food? Clothes? School? Turned out coming back to Harborside wasn't a good idea, either. Even this town held nothing for her anymore. She covered her face with her hands and cried so hard she didn't hear the car screech to a stop at the curb.

"Izzie? Izzie! It's her! Guys, it's her!" Mira exclaimed. She jumped out of the car before Hayden had even turned off the engine. She could see Izzie crying on the porch, and she knew she had to get to her. She ran up the path and climbed the porch steps, hearing the tear in her dress immediately as it got caught on a rusty nail. She stopped feet from where Izzie was sitting. Izzie still didn't seem to realize Mira was there.

"Izzie?" Mira said again, her heart beating rapidly.

Izzie looked up. For a second Mira thought she was happy to see her, but then her face crumbled again. Hayden and Brayden walked up behind Mira. When Izzie saw Brayden, her lip began to quiver.

"What are you doing here?" she asked, and Mira knew the question was meant for Brayden.

"I came here for you," he said calmly, which was pretty good because in the car ride over he had been freaking out. They'd tried two boardwalk hangouts before they went to

Izzie's old house, and Brayden had started to get worried. Now he sat down on the swing next to her. "You can yell and protest all you want, but I'm not going anywhere unless you're coming with me."

Izzie didn't say anything, but she leaned her head on Brayden's shoulder as if it were too heavy to hold up. Mira thought she looked completely lost.

Mira sat down on the porch in front of her. "Are you...all right?" she asked, knowing the question was lame. Of course she wasn't all right.

Izzie's chignon had fallen out, and her makeup was streaky. She shook her head. "Are you?"

"No." Mira stared at the beat-up porch floor. "I can't believe my dad is your..."

"Dad," Izzie finished. "I know." She wiped her nose with the back of her hand before Mira could offer her a tissue.

"I'm sorry I didn't tell you about the community center," Mira said, her lip quivering. "I keep screwing up with you even though I don't mean to."

Izzie felt mixed up inside. She knew she should be mad at Mira, but yelling at her about the community center seemed ridiculous in light of everything else going on. She would find a way to save the center later, even if she had to fight Savannah's family herself. "I'm not mad at you," she said. "I'm mad at myself for believing all the lies *he* told me. All *he* cared about was keeping me quiet so it didn't ruin his chances in Washington." She knew she sounded bitter. She couldn't bring herself to say his name.

"What Dad did was crappy," Hayden agreed, "and I'm not defending him, but he told us everything, and he definitely knows how badly he screwed up. Apparently Lucas pushed him to keep the truth quiet till after the campaign."

Just hearing Lucas's name made Izzie have heart palpitations.

"When he found out Lucas was blackmailing you, he fired him on the spot," Hayden added.

Good riddance. "That doesn't change what your dad did," Izzie reminded them. "He was embarrassed of me."

She thought back to the few times she felt they had really connected. The night he tried to talk to her after she came home from the boardwalk, the corsage he gave her at her first event, how proud he was when she made the swim team. Maybe he *did* care, but it was too little, too late. Her eyes welled up with tears again. "He never wanted to be my dad. If he did, he would have shown up long before he had to by law."

"He only found out about you last winter," Mira said quietly. She hated that her dad had put her in the position of defending him. But she wasn't. She was trying to help Izzie cope. "Before your grandmother got sick, she found your mom's journal, and it said my dad was your father. Dad spent all summer waiting to hear about your paternity. When they knew for sure, he got Grams in the home and had you brought to us. He wanted you to have a better life."

So that's why the story of how we're related never added up, Izzie thought. Grams knew who Izzie's dad was. She knew, and she tried to bring him to her. Izzie wanted to be mad at Grams for keeping it from her, but that was pointless. Her grandmother was like a ghost now.

Izzie chose her next words carefully. "That does change things, but it still doesn't make what he did okay." She stared at the dining room window. The glow of the streetlight that had finally been fixed illuminated the darkened room. Seeing the house empty made Izzie feel very alone. She should have been embarrassed laying this all out in front of Brayden, but she had no fight left in her. "Your family took me in because they had to. He doesn't want me."

"*We* want you," Hayden insisted. "Mom adores you, Connor thinks you're the coolest thing to happen since LEGOs, and Dad, well, he's lousy at showing emotion. Call it a politician's curse."

"That's just it," Izzie said. "I don't know how to be a politician's daughter or work a social season. I don't understand your world at all. I tried, but I failed miserably. You saw it. I don't belong."

"You navigate it better than you think," Brayden said. "Look at what you put together tonight. You were a rock star! If I can survive in EC, so can you. You can do this. You have to," he stressed.

Izzie shook her head. "I can't go back there." She had swallowed so many tears her mouth tasted like salt. "You think my streets are rough? Emerald Cove is a trillion times harder. It's like a daytime soap opera! I'll get eaten alive if I stay." Her voice cracked.

For the first time, Mira became aware of her surroundings. Izzie's old home was in need of major repairs. The porch steps creaked, the railing was broken, and the fence had graffiti. Every house on the block was the same way. On the street corner, three guys lingered while they smoked cigarettes. They could have just been talking, but it creeped Mira out. "So where are you going to go?" Mira asked, folding her legs under her.

"I don't know." Izzie closed her eyes and let the motion of the swing take her away. The truth was, she didn't know how to survive on her own, either. She didn't want to tell them that, though.

"Who are you going to live with?" Hayden asked.

"I don't know," Izzie said, sounding stressed.

"What are you going to do about school? Money?" Brayden pointed out.

"I don't know!" Izzie was agitated. She needed sleep. Maybe when she woke up, she'd be back in her bed, Grams would be downstairs cooking, and her mom would be on her way home from work. That was the only way she could imagine her life being okay again.

"Do you know what I think?" Mira said, not waiting for a reply. "I think you have no guts."

"Mira," Hayden warned, but she ignored him.

"I'm mad at him, too," Mira said. "You're our sister and he didn't tell us." She looked down at the bracelet her dad had given her for her birthday last year. "If he had, maybe things would have gone differently between us."

"You mean you wouldn't have been so fake," Izzie said drily. It was the first time she had ever really stared at Mira's face. They had the same eyes. It wasn't just that they both had hazel ones; they had the same shape, too. Their eyes were just like their...dad's.

"Maybe," Mira admitted, "and maybe not. But I'm trying to be a different person. I'm not a doormat anymore. I'm doing the things I love and I want to to be friends with you. We're sisters."

Izzie closed her eyes, trying to forget that fact. It would be easier to disappear if she did.

"You've already lost one family," Mira said softly. "Don't give up on a second. I know this is scary, and it's not going to be easy for either of us, but we're not going away. You can run away from all the drama of Emerald Cove, but it's still going to be there. We're still going to be there waiting for you. No guts, no glory, remember?"

"You told her that story?" Brayden asked Izzie.

"What story?" Mira asked.

"It doesn't matter," Izzie said. "Your speech isn't working."

"Fine. Then do it for yourself! Prove EC wrong," Mira begged. "Prove Savannah wrong. Lucas, Emerald Prep — prove them all wrong. Show the world you can hack it as a Monroe."

"I'm a Scott," Izzie said. Her hazel eyes were brazen.

"You're both," Mira reminded her. Her eyes were just as determined. "Or at least you can be, if you have the *guts* to try."

Izzie gave her a look. "Enough with the *guts* talk. I get it, okay? I just…I don't know what to do." Izzie clutched the necklace her aunt had lent her for the event.

"We'll help you," Hayden said.

"We're not going to let you do this alone," Brayden agreed, and put his arm around her. His body was warm. "We just want you to give this a shot."

Izzie looked at their three open faces waiting so patiently for her to answer. *They care about me*, she thought, *and I care about them, too.* She looked around the bare porch. What did she really have to lose by giving EC another shot? "Okay," she said reluctantly. "I'll try."

Mira took Izzie's hand. "Text Dad," she told Hayden. "Tell him Izzie's coming home."

Izzie looked down at their intertwined fingers. "Can we

do something first?" she asked tentatively. "I want you to see Harborside. Maybe it will help you get to know me better."

Mira looked at Hayden. "To the boardwalk?" she said. Izzie nodded. "Okay," Mira said apprehensively, not wanting to let on about how nervous going there made her, "but we can't stay long. Mom and Dad won't stop calling till you're actually home."

It only took five minutes to get to the boardwalk. Brayden knew exactly where to park, as if he'd been there a hundred times before. Within minutes, Izzie was leading them up the ramp to the boardwalk, where a light wind hit Mira in the face and she could smell the salty air. She held Hayden's sports coat firmly around her shoulders, almost like a shield, wondering what she was in for. When she turned the corner and looked at the long stretch of well-lit arcades, pizza places, T-shirt and henna-tattoo shops, and candy joints, she inhaled sharply.

The place was packed. Even though it was close to eleven, the boardwalk was full of people, young and old, kids asleep in strollers, groups of teens huddled together laughing. No one looked like they were ready to start a fight or run off with her bag. She didn't see large packs of menacing guys brandishing knives. It was just a boardwalk, and it looked pretty cool.

Izzie was smiling again. She led the way, talking animatedly as if she was giving a tour. "The community center is down there," she said, pointing to an old two-story building. "It's closed tonight because of our event, but usually they have dances on Saturday nights, and you have to beat the senior citizens to the door to get a ticket. That's Boardwalk Pizza—they supplied the garlic knots tonight. And that's the arcade which is a five-and-dime store where we always bought hermit crabs that lasted about a week, and that's Scoops," she said, pointing out a brightly painted ice-cream shop that had a line out the door. "My friend Kylie has worked there forever." She glanced at Brayden. "I practically lived there."

Hayden whistled. "Look at that Ferris wheel!" He pointed to the amusement park on the pier. "Is that a log flume? And a wooden roller coaster?" He nudged Izzie. "I can't believe you've been keeping this place to yourself."

"I can see why you love it so much," Mira told her, watching a few kids skateboard by with cotton candy in their hands. She felt so foolish now. This is what she and everyone at EP had been making fun of Izzie for? This is what Harborside Boardwalk was really like? Izzie was right. "Maybe we can all come back one night," Mira suggested, still unsure about bringing her parents up by name. "Connor would love this."

"Maybe," Izzie said, mulling over the idea. It would be fun to take Connor to Scoops.

Hayden checked his phone. "Mom and Dad are texting

me like crazy." He looked at Izzie. "I think they're eager to see you safely back on their doorstep."

"Are you ready?" Brayden asked, and Izzie felt him slip his warm hand in hers and squeeze. She felt tingles all over, but she tried not to let on. She didn't want to think about what the gesture meant. She had still never given Brayden an answer. There were too many other things to think about.

Izzie took a deep breath. "I'm ready."

It wasn't going to be easy going back there, but she had to give it a shot. She took a final look around the boardwalk, taking in the lights and the sounds, and remembering some of her best memories there. Brayden was in nearly all of them. She could do this. She could be part of both worlds and make it work. She had to.

"Okay," Izzie said finally, gazing at Mira's smiling face the longest. "Let's go home."

Acknowledgments

Belles is truly a story about what it means to be a family, and I don't know where I'd be without my own.

Cindy Eagan and Kate Sullivan are not only amazing editors, but they're also excellent sounding boards, and this series could not have jumped from a jumbled mix of ideas scribbled on a pad to a published book without their excellent guidance and suggestions. Kate may have her own fancy office down the hall now, but she was never too busy to come back to *Belles* to offer the insight that only she can give. I'm forever grateful to her for that, as I am to my wonderful new editor, Pam Gruber, who is the genius who came up with the title to this very series and the girls' names. Everyone at Poppy and Little, Brown Books for Young Readers has taken *Belles* under its wings, and I owe so much to my übertalented longtime designer, Tracy Shaw, as well as Ames O'Neill, Andrew Smith, Lisa Ickowicz, Christine Ma, Jodie Lowe, and so many others.

I'm indebted to my agent, Laura Dail, who is always at the ready to talk me off the ledge and offer guidance, and to Tamar Rydzinski, who is on top of everything I do.

Christie Greff (aka the all-grown-up flower girl from my wedding) is the one who explained the differences between a heat and a medley and how competitive swimming works. Barbara Massina taught me what a social worker's role is and how a delicate situation like Izzie's would be handled.

Sometimes you can feel quite alone when you're sitting in your office, typing away, which is why I'm so grateful to be able to bounce ideas around (and, um, sometimes share a few moments of panic) with Mara Reinstein, Sara Shepard, tour buddy extraordinaire Elizabeth Eulberg, Sarah Mylnowski, Kieran Scott, and the girls in the amazing Beach Bag Book Club, including Larissa Simonovski, Jess Tymecki, Kelly Rechsteiner, and Pat Gleiberman.

And, of course, to my mom and dad, who always go over and beyond to help me make my deadlines, and my family, Mike, Tyler, and Dylan, for giving me everything I need from home and more.

The secret is out, but the drama is far from over.

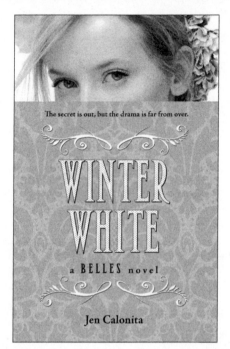

Isabelle Scott and Mirabelle Monroe are still reeling from the knowledge that they're not cousins after all—they're sisters. But with cotillion season right around the corner, the girls barely have time to process the news. Mira has been dreaming of making her debut in a gorgeous white gown forever—if only she could find an escort. Izzie, meanwhile, is still struggling to fit into Emerald Cove society, and when troublemaking former debutante Dylan rolls into town, Izzie thinks she's finally found someone she can relate to. As cotillion preparations heat up, though, there are dance steps to learn, manners to perfect . . . and secret initiations to complete? As if sophomore year wasn't hard enough!

Turn the page for a sneak peek at *Winter White*,
the second book in Jen Calonita's Belles series,
coming in October 2012.

100% CASHMERE. Mira stared at the sweater tag in her hand and smiled. Just the words *100% cashmere* were enough to put her in a good mood.

The pale pink sweater with a ballet-scoop neckline was so soft that she could have slept on it. Prepsters, Emerald Cove's popular high-end clothing boutique (so named for girls like her who went to Emerald Prep and could afford three-hundred-dollar riding boots) must have just gotten a shipment because the cashmere sweater was available in every size and color. The only decision Mira had to make now was pink or taupe. She was going to try on both along with a pair of those new jeans she saw on the table at the front of the store. While she was here, she might as well look for some casual dresses, too, to wear to a few of her dad's fund-raisers she was dreading. There was so much to choose from at Prepsters, she wished she could stay all day.

Shopping really was retail therapy. Maybe that was why Mira had been doing so much of it in the last few weeks. When her dad apologized to the family for the first time, Mira ran out afterward and bought expensive white flip-flops with interchangeable bands. When her mom cried over a blog that said she was crazy for standing by her dad, Mira bought luxurious lavender 900-thread-count sheets for her bed. And when Savannah, her friends, and pretty much the whole tenth grade blacklisted her, Mira bought her and Izzie matching sterling-silver evil eye rings so she would have something to look at in class when her former friends were talking about her.

Today's TV interview with Waa-Waa Wendy had shot Mira's nerves so badly that she headed to Prepsters in search of new sweaters. It was getting colder — well, cold for North Carolina — and she needed something to warm her up, especially now that she was single and didn't have a boyfriend's arms to wrap around her.

Not that she was that upset about the boyfriend part. Taylor Covington, EP's own version of the Ken doll, had been nice to look at, but he wasn't really boyfriend material. Mira knew she was better off without him; she just wished she had a few more shoulders to cry on. But Savannah had taken those away, too. Losing friends had definitely turned out to be worse than losing a boyfriend.

Mira piled a few pairs of jeans on top of the cashmere sweaters she was carrying and headed to the fitting room. She made it only a few feet when she spotted a wine-colored sweater dress with a turtleneck collar that would look adorable with her new riding boots. She stopped to check it out, and that's when she heard talking.

"Sarah Collins, daughter of Myra and Peter Collins, was escorted by Todd Selzner, at the White Ball in Birmingham, Alabama...."

Hearing the voice made Mira freeze with her hand on the dress tag.

"Miss Collins is a proud cotillion participant who hopes to someday study special education at her mother's alma mater, Ole Miss."

"What does she look like? Stop hogging the magazine, Lea!"

"Would you two stop? Give it to me. I paid for it. Which one is she? Oh, *her.* Talk about bad lighting. She looks like she should play a vamp on *The Vampire Diaries.*" The others laughed. "What a waste of a gorgeous gown. See what I mean, girls? My mother is right. One bad photographer can ruin your whole cotillion."

Cotillion! How could Mira have forgotten about her favorite tradition in Emerald Cove? Making her formal debut into society was something she had dreamed about since she was in pre-K. She'd spent the last three years preparing for the sophomore girl tradition — taking etiquette classes, going to Saturday morning dance lessons, and doing approved Junior League charity work — and somehow she had let all this drama with her dad make her completely forget the most important event of the year!

"It says here Sarah Collins made her debut with forty-five girls. That's not a debut; that's a cattle call. Maybe that explains why half these girls look like cows." The girls' laughter increased, and so did the snorting.

Mira prayed they couldn't see her behind the rack of sweater dresses. When she peeked through the rack, she saw exactly what she'd suspected. Savannah, her former best friend, and her two — make that three — sidekicks, Lea Price, Lauren Salbrook, and their protégé, Millie Lennon, were huddled around the latest issue of *Town & Country*, reading the magazine's debutante announcements. It's something Mira had done with Savannah many times before. She used to love picking up the latest issue, getting iced coffee, going for pedicures, and then ripping apart each girl's announcement sentence by sentence. It wasn't till Izzie showed up that Mira realized words, however nicely said, could still cut so deep that they made people bleed.

"Miss, can I help you find something?"

Mira looked up. *Dang.* A saleswoman had spotted her. She could only imagine how this looked. She was crouched down, her right hand clutching a dress like a towel and her left arm holding the cashmere sweaters and now-crumpled jeans. The saleswoman did not look pleased.

Mira shook her head, hoping that would be enough to send the woman away. If she opened her mouth, Savannah might realize she was there.

"Should I put that dress in a fitting room for you?" The woman attempted to pry the wrinkled dress from Mira's hands, but she wouldn't let go. "Or wrap it up?"

That would work. "Yes," Mira whispered, and reached into her bag for her credit card. "Wrap it. Please. Quickly. I, uh, have a doctor's appointment to get to."

The woman glanced at the name on the credit card, and her expression changed. "Are you Senator Monroe's daughter?" she asked, her voice going up an octave. "You look just like your father!"

This was Mira's cue to get out of there. She left the dress on the counter and snatched her credit card back before the saleswoman had the chance to react. "I'll come back for this later," she said, and headed for the exit. She'd made it to the accessories table when Savannah and the other girls stepped into the aisle and blocked her path. They looked like the fashion mafia in their color-coordinated designer outfits.

"Hi, Mira," Savannah said pleasantly, looking like she had just come from a modeling shoot. Her long pale blond hair was as glossy as ever, held back in a plaid headband, and she had on the same fitted navy sweater as the mannequin behind her that always modeled Prepsters' latest must-have outfit. Savannah gave Mira a brief once-over. "What are you doing here?" she asked with a thick drawl. "I hear you were on TV. *The Wendy Wallington Show* is so" — she hesitated, trying to find the right word to make Mira flinch — "quaint. I don't think anyone outside the state even sees that show."

"Probably not." Mira glanced helplessly at the door feet away.

Savannah smiled. "I haven't seen the show because I was at school, but my mom said you managed okay."

Savannah was like a python. Mira had learned to watch her closely because she was never quite sure when she would strike. Even her compliments were venomous. Mira ignored the comment and looked at the others. "Hi, guys." The girls responded by glancing at their shoes or the items on the accessories table. Millie seemed particularly interested in a thick headband that was clearly last season.

"You're not here alone, are you?" Savannah's eyes widened innocently. She knew the answer without Mira even saying it. Who would Mira hang out with? Savannah had claimed all their mutual friends after their nasty friendship breakup, and she'd probably destroy any girl stupid enough to befriend Mira now.

"I was just leaving," Mira said.

Savannah and the others didn't move out of her way. "I never understood how anyone could go clothes shopping alone," Savannah said, leaning on Lea. "I could not make a single decision on dresses for cotillion events without backup. You *are* still going to do cotillion, aren't you?"

"Of course," Mira said, feeling drained. "Why wouldn't I?"

"Oh, I...never mind." Savannah broke into another one of her patented plastic smiles. "I'm glad you're still going. We'll see you at cotillion rush events, then."

"When does that start?" Lea asked, her voice anxious.

"I don't know for *sure*," Savannah stressed as if she had a clue. She always acted in the know even when she wasn't. "I heard Mary Beth Pearson might be running it."

"Your cousin?" Lauren asked. "Lucky you! She'll give you the easiest tasks."

Cotillion pledging. Rush. Debutante initiation. Whatever you wanted to call it, Mira had forgotten about this secret tradition, too. While the Junior League didn't approve of it, or even acknowledge its existence, over the years it had become customary for former debs to put the current cotillion class through a series of sometimes funny, sometimes mortifying games to prove their worthiness like they were a college sorority pledge class. No one knew who ran the rush till the games ended, but participating was pretty much mandatory. Those who didn't do it were socially blacklisted for the rest of the year, and no one at Emerald Prep wanted that.

"You guys have nothing to worry about." Savannah pushed her bangs out of her eyes. "If it's Mary Beth, and I bet it is, she'll take care of you guys." She glanced at Mira. "She knows who my friends are."

If Mira needed proof that she was no longer in Savannah's inner circle, that was it. Savannah made her feel worse about herself. Weren't friends supposed to do the opposite? The school's reigning queen was never going to forgive her. Mira had chosen Izzie over Savannah, and Izzie had won Brayden, which left Savannah out in the cold. And she did not do the deep freeze well. She liked to cause hell rather than be in it.

"But enough about cotillion," Savannah said, stepping closer to Mira with an expression of deep concern. "How are *you* doing? I would be mortified if I had to go on TV and talk about my dad having a kid he never told us about. Not that my dad would ever do such a thing," she added just as quickly. Lauren tried to hold in a snicker.

"I'm fine." Mira tried not to sound testy. She was glad she had changed out of the outfit she wore on Wendy's show and into her fitted green tunic and capri leggings. She felt like her go-to outfit gave her superstrength, which she needed right then.

"Are you sure?" Savannah frowned, and the wrinkles that formed around her mouth almost screamed in protest. "You look pale, and you have bags under your eyes, but that's nothing that a little under-eye cream can't fix." Savannah rooted around in her enormous designer bag and pulled out an equally expensive eye cream. "This is my mom's. She has horrible bags, too, so this should help." Lea smirked, while Millie looked mildly mortified. She was new to Savannah's group, so she was still learning how cutting Savannah could be.

Mira noticed the saleswoman watching the girls' exchange with interest. The pile of clothes Mira had left were still in the woman's arms. Mira took the clothes from her. "I changed my mind," she said, and dumped the sweaters, jeans, and dress on the counter. "I'm going to take everything." She deserved some new clothes for putting up with Savannah. "I am in a rush, though, so if you could ring me up, that would be great."

"Where are you off to? Another tabloid interview?" Lauren asked with an evil glint in her eye.

"God, no." Mira tried to smile. "*Teen Vogue* called this morning and offered Izzie and me a fashion layout in the magazine." Savannah's eyes widened, so she kept going. "They want to know the real story, not the silly rumors people are spreading."

"*Teen Vogue?*" Savannah repeated slowly, almost tripping over her own words.

Mira nodded. Was it her imagination or did Savannah look jealous? "I am meeting our publicist to discuss whether we're going to take it." She looked at Lea's surprised expression and laughed to herself. "I mean, who knew *Justine* and *Teen Vogue* would be fighting over us? We might do *People*, too." She made a mental note to call Callista later and persuade her to get them in a magazine. Any magazine!

"Wow, you do sound busy," Savannah said, pushing the cheer back into her voice. "So busy that you probably don't even miss having a boyfriend like Taylor. Did you hear Taylor officially asked Millie out?"

"He gave me this." Millie thrust her arm at Mira, showing off a thin silver bracelet with a dangling starfish. Taylor had given her one just like it when they started dating. "Savannah helped him pick it out." Savannah's smug smile returned.

Mira had to hand it to Savannah. She knew how to twist the knife. For a moment, Mira thought the boyfriend talk and the bracelet would make her crumble. Instead, she quickly recovered. "Cute, Millie! I'm surprised Savannah helped him pick that one, though." She frowned. "The one Taylor got me tarnished quickly." Millie paled, making Mira feel slightly bad, but she couldn't back down now.

The saleswoman handed Mira the credit-card slip, and Mira turned away from the girls to sign. "Speaking of jewelry, I've been meaning to buy myself something nice to wear for all these magazine interviews. I just have to find the time. My publicist said *Teen Vogue* needs days for an interview and photo shoot. They even want me to paint a picture for them to put in the story. Can you believe it?"

"No, I can't," Savannah said without thinking. When Mira turned around again, she noticed Savannah's posture was stiff as a board.

Mira collected her bags and walked past her. "See you at school!"

Savannah looked jealous! Mira thought with glee as she hurried down Main Street toward Corky's before Savannah could retaliate. She couldn't stop replaying their conversation in her head. The look on Savannah's face when she mentioned *Teen Vogue*, Millie's reaction to what she said about Taylor's bracelet... those moments were priceless! Her friends had made her feel as worthless as a cockroach the past few weeks, but now she felt like she could take on the world. *Who needs those girls, anyway?*

You do, a small voice inside her head said. *Maybe you don't need Savannah, but you do need some friends,* the voice reminded her. Mira's run slowed to a crawl. Since their big fight, she hadn't had anyone to talk to or hang out with. She shopped alone, avoided parties, and spent most of her nonschool hours in her room. That wouldn't do.

She and Izzie had made strides in the friendship department, but Izzie still wasn't someone who would go for manicures or sit with her and gush over a picture of Taylor Lautner's abs in *Us Weekly*. She missed doing that stuff. *How are you going to survive cotillion without friends or a date?* the voice taunted. *Your debut is going to be ruined.*

More juicy novels by
Jen Calonita

Secrets of My Hollywood Life

The fabulous (and not-so-fabulous) sides of being a hot teen star in Hollywood.

Sleepaway Girls

Turns out you can't hide from high school drama—even in the wilderness!

Reality Check

A TV exec picks four normal girls as THE next big thing in reality TV. Can their friendship withstand the spotlight?

Belles

A brand-new series about two very different girls sharing one roof . . . and a secret that will change their lives forever.

"Will capture readers with its **honesty** and **heart**."

—Publishers Weekly

Fourteen-year-old Kentucky girl Ricki Jo Winstead,
who would prefer to be called Ericka, *thank you very much*,
is eager to shed her farmer's daughter roots and become part of
the popular crowd at her small-town high school. But her best friend
and the boy next door, Luke, says he misses "plain old Ricki Jo."

Where does Ricki Jo belong, and
what will it take for her to find out?

poppy
www.pickapoppy.com

Where stories bloom.

poppy

Visit us online at
www.pickapoppy.com